"EMPYREAN LAWS FORBID PROCREATION WITH ANYONE NOT FROM OUR WORLD."

Elizabeth's gaze found McCoy's again. "Anna's father was not Empyrean."

The doctor's eyebrows rose in surprise. "Does she know?"

Elizabeth shook her head. "No one does. But it's about to be revealed, and I won't be able to stop it. I'm sure to be dismissed as President. . . . Anna and I could both be banished from Empyrea"—her voice wavered—"even executed."

"Can't you get in touch with her father? I'm sure he'd help if he could."

"That's what I'm hoping," she said, clenching and unclenching her jaw, trying to control her fears. "That's why you're here, Leonard. That's why I asked for you to come."

"Me? What can I do?" He really had no clue at all.

She shrugged helplessly. "I don't know. But . . ." Her voice shrank to a whisper. "You see . . . *you* are Anna's father."

Look for STAR TREK Fiction from Pocket Books

Star Trek: The Original Series

Star Trek: The Next Generation

Star Trek: Deep Space Nine

STAR TREK®

THE BETTER MAN

HOWARD WEINSTEIN

POCKET BOOKS

New York   London   Toronto   Sydney   Tokyo   Singapore

An *Original* Publication of POCKET BOOKS

POCKET BOOKS, a division of Simon & Schuster Inc.
1230 Avenue of the Americas, New York, NY 10020

This book is published by Pocket Books, a division of Simon & Schuster Inc., under exclusive license from Paramount Pictures.

ISBN: 0-671-86912-4

First Pocket Books printing December 1994

10 9 8 7 6 5 4 3 2 1

POCKET and colophon are registered trademarks of Simon & Schuster Inc.

Printed in the U.S.A.

For Cindi,
who works in outer space
(sort of)
while I just write about it . . .

And Kenny,
my first friend

Author's Note

September 7, 1974 . . . a day that will live in infamy?

No. Just the day *half my life ago* that I became a publicly known, officially *professional* STAR TREK writer. It was nine days before my twentieth birthday when the episode I'd written ("The Pirates of Orion") opened the animated STAR TREK's second season on NBC's Saturday morning schedule.

Twenty years ago! I can't believe it.

Times flies . . . whether you're having fun or not. Those of you over twenty-five have probably already realized this temporal truth. (If you're under twenty-five, you'll find out soon enough. Take my word for it.) As Mel Brooks's classic comedy character, the Two-Thousand-Year-Old Man, might say, "I don't know where the millennium went. Hoo-boy! It was only yesterday Murray was packing for the Crusades, and here it is almost the year 2000."

And soon to be STAR TREK's thirtieth anniversary. It seems like only yesterday—okay, maybe last week—that NBC canceled the original STAR TREK for the second and final time. And then the reruns started. And the conventions. And then the first space shuttle was christened *Enterprise.*

More conventions. And then the first movie. And then the second and the third and the fourth. And then STAR TREK: THE NEXT GENERATION. And two *more* movies.

Then STAR TREK: DEEP SPACE NINE.

Now, Paramount is about to launch yet another new series, STAR TREK: VOYAGER. And the first *Next Generation* big-screen movie is on its way.

What an incredible ride Gene Roddenberry started for us three decades ago. When I jumped aboard with that animated episode, I had *no idea* I'd still be writing STAR TREK twenty years later.

But here I am with my sixth STAR TREK novel for Pocket Books, and I'm finishing up my fourth year writing scripts for the monthly "classic" STAR TREK comic book for DC Comics. What's next? Who knows.

It's appropriate that this book should be about a character for whom my affinity grows with each passing year—that loveable curmudgeon, Dr. Leonard McCoy. Like McCoy, the older I get, the crankier I get.

In fact, I hoped to write a hardcover McCoy story. But my DC Comics stablemate Michael Jan Friedman beat me to the punch with his fine novel *Shadows on the Sun.* (Is that any way to treat a fellow Yankees fan, Mike?) However, STAR TREK editor Kevin Ryan was nice enough to buy my story anyway.

I've always admired McCoy, who has uttered many of STAR TREK's most memorable lines over the years. Part of his appeal is that he's less the obvious hero than Kirk or Spock. Not that he's any less courageous, just that ostentatiously heroic deeds don't come quite as naturally to him.

But McCoy has always risen to the occasion, and when he does, it's a conscious choice. As McCoy himself might scoff, "*Hero?* I'm a doctor, not a sandwich."

No homage to the character created on paper by Gene Roddenberry would be complete without a few words of appreciation for the actor who has brought him to life. For me and so many other fans, DeForest Kelley's portrayal has been one of STAR TREK's most consistent pleasures all these years. His way with a line, that skeptical twitch of an eyebrow, his voice and gestures, all help to make writing about Bones McCoy a hell of a lot of fun.

Before I let you get on with your reading, a special word of thanks to Michael Okuda and Rick Sternbach. Their *Star Trek: The Next Generation Techical Manual* proved invaluable in the creation of what has affectionately become known as "technobabble," which this story needed and I could not have invented without Mike and Rick's clever and imaginative guide to the inner workings of STAR TREK's many doohickeys and gizmos.

Enjoy the voyage!

Howard Weinstein
September, 1994

THE BETTER MAN

Chapter One

"BONES?" Jim Kirk stood in Dr. McCoy's doorway, peering cautiously into his chief surgeon's dimly lit cabin. "You're not going to throw a bowl of *plomeek* soup at me, are you?"

Kirk knew his friend to be a man of wide-ranging, fast-changing moods, but he was not normally given to seeking refuge in a dark room. At the moment, Kirk couldn't even see him and wouldn't have known McCoy was there had he not heard an exasperated "Come *in* already" a moment before.

Even that not-so-encouraging invitation had come only after Kirk had pressed the door chime a half-dozen times. Following the third, he had fleetingly considered giving up and walking away. It was possible that McCoy, in fact, did *not* want to be disturbed. But if you can't barge in uninvited on a troubled friend, Kirk reasoned, who *can* you barge in on?

The captain entered, and the door obligingly slid shut behind him. "Where the hell are you?"

Dr. McCoy's favorite lounge chair sat a few feet away, its back toward him as he squinted into the gloom. The room's ambient lighting was so low, a half-dozen fireflies would have made it look sunny by comparison. As Kirk's eyes adjusted, he saw a hand rise slowly over the chair's high back, give a feeble wave, then sink from sight. He rounded the chair and found McCoy slouched deeply into the cushions, his bare feet pressed against a hassock, a glass of iced amber drink cradled on his chest.

"So," McCoy drawled, "it's come to this: 'How shall I compare thee to a hormone-crazed Vulcan?'"

"Let me count the ways," said Kirk, finishing the fractured paraphrase.

"Have I been that abominable?"

"As a matter of fact, you have. So what's wrong?"

"You do get right to the point," McCoy said, then proceeded to ignore Kirk's direct inquiry. "Y'know, the day Spock threw that bowl of soup at Christine Chapel will always be one of the highlights of my life."

Kirk's eyebrows twitched. "I suppose that says something about your life."

"Just when I think I've seen it all, there's something waiting just around the bend."

"Are you sure you haven't gone around the bend yourself?"

McCoy held his glass up, giving it a measuring glance. "This is my first. Scout's honor." He sat up a little straighter, forcing the memory into focus. "I can still see that bowl flying out through his cabin door, smashing into the wall. Poor Christine. She poured her heart and soul into that vile liquid—"

"Figuratively speaking, of course."

"Of course. Though with Christine, you never knew. Remember how she used to look at Spock when she thought nobody was watching?"

Poor Christine, indeed, Kirk thought. She'd always made such an obvious effort to appear businesslike

2

around Spock when on duty. But she couldn't keep secrets from McCoy, with whom she'd worked so closely, first as head nurse and now as a fellow doctor. Kirk, too, had been aware of her unrequited affection for the Vulcan first officer, despite the fact that Spock was utterly incapable, by constitution and custom, of returning her feelings. Yet, as McCoy had observed, she never gave up hoping—a persistance that made that one afternoon of excruciatingly public embarrassment virtually inevitable.

Spock had been uncharacteristically irritable and snappish for days. Then came his threat to break McCoy's neck—a rather inappropriate response to the doctor's well-meaning suggestion that Spock might benefit from a physical exam.

Even before that, Kirk had observed instances of Spock's increasingly odd behavior. But he was as entitled to privacy as the next man, and Kirk had tried to overlook those moments when Spock resembled nothing so much as a pressure cooker threatening to blow its seal. However, the infamous soup incident, recalled so fondly by McCoy years later, was impossible to overlook.

Innocently hoping that the way to a Vulcan's heart was indeed through his stomach (even though, as McCoy had observed on more than one occasion, Spock's heart was where his liver should be), Nurse Chapel had discovered a Vulcan delicacy she thought Spock would find irresistable: *plomeek* soup.

Disdaining the food synthesizers, Christine had actually *cooked* the soup herself—boiling, chopping, seasoning—only to have her offering hurled by a roaring Vulcan. The bowl barely missed her head as she fled his cabin, then smashed into the corridor wall opposite his door. And it was all witnessed firsthand by Kirk, McCoy, and assorted other passersby.

In Spock's case, there'd been an explanation for his behavior: an instinctual Vulcan mating drive had

3

made him quite unaccountable for his own actions.
But Kirk hadn't a clue to the cause of McCoy's current
sulk. "Spock was going through *pon farr* when he
tossed that soup bowl, McCoy. What's your excuse?"

"If you mean, have I got an urge to mate with a
Vulcan, forget it."

"Then, what *is* the problem?" Kirk spaced his
words evenly for emphasis and to indicate that his
patience was *not* infinite.

"Problem?" McCoy repeated with an innocent bat-
ting of his blue eyes.

"Yes—*problem.*"

"No problem."

"The hell there isn't. If it's the new uniforms—"

"I'm a doctor, not a damned fashion consultant,"
McCoy growled. "Besides, I kinda like the new uniforms. I just wish Starfleet would make up its mind so
I don't have to worry about getting court-martialed
for wearing the wrong thing one morning."

Kirk knew deliberate obtuseness when he saw it. He
also knew a friend under extreme stress. "Okay. No
problem. Then how do you explain the incident in the
lab?"

McCoy turned a bland eye toward Kirk. "The
incident in the lab?"

The incident in the lab . . .
In the examining room, Dr. Chapel had just finished a routine check of sterile-field generators when
she heard the first crash from the adjacent laboratory
—the unmistakable sound of unbreakable glassware
bouncing off a wall. For a moment, she attributed the
crystalline impact to someone's clumsy lapse of attention. A moment later came a muttered string of
curses, punctuated with one final loud oath, then the
clatter of more falling glass.

She rushed through the doorway just in time to see

McCoy clearing a jumble of beakers, tubes, and bottles off a lab table with an angry swipe of his left arm. "Dr. McCoy!"

He jumped at the sudden sound of her voice intruding on his private tantrum, then whirled and glared at her. "Good God! Doesn't anybody *knock* anymore?!"

Chapel stared at him, quite astonished.

"I didn't know you knew about that," McCoy said mildly to Kirk.

"Well, I do, including the fact that you refused to explain your wrecking-ball routine to Christine. And then you stood me and Scotty up for dinner the last two nights—when I planned to cleverly and subtly interrogate you about the lab incident—*and* you pretended you weren't here when we came to check on you. Should I go on?"

"So that gives you the right to bust in here and pry into my personal miseries?"

"You're the one who opened the door."

"Yeah, well, I'm starting to regret *that*," McCoy said tartly as he got to his feet and padded over to the small cabinet he used as his bar. "You want a drink?"

"No," Kirk said, following him across the cabin. "I want an explanation."

"I'm fine. I'm a grump. I've been a grump ever since you've known me. What's more, I was a grump long before *that*. Now go 'way and let me stew in peace."

Kirk reached over and grabbed the bottle of amber whiskey before McCoy could. Then he poured generous drinks for both of them and ushered the doctor back to his chair. Kirk pulled up a second chair and set it face-to-face. "Talk to me, Bones. I'm not leaving until you do."

"Bull. You've got a ship to run."

"Bull. I left Spock in charge, and you know what an

iron pants he can be. He could stay in that command
chair for *days* without my relieving him . . . so I've
got nothing pressing to pull me away."

McCoy rolled his eyes. "There's never a damn bowl
of soup around when you need it." With a rueful
shake of his head, he puffed out a defeated breath.
"All right, dammit. If there's no other way to get rid of
you—"

"There isn't. Talk."

"Is that an order?"

If McCoy was hoping Kirk would get tired of his
verbal dodging, give up, and go away, he was bound
for disappointment. Instead, Kirk pointedly ignored
the sarcastic question and pressed on as if conducting
an evidentiary investigation. "As near as I can recall,
this started right after we got our orders to divert to
Starbase 86. Is it something about Starbase 86?"

"Don't be ridiculous," McCoy said with a dismissive wave of one hand. "Even I'm not *that* eccentric."

"Is it Mark Rousseau?" His tone of voice made it
clear Kirk considered the question a rhetorical toss.

But when McCoy greeted the name of the Federation ambassador they were to pick up at Starbase 86
with stony silence, Kirk knew he'd uncovered the burr
under McCoy's saddle.

"It is, isn't it?" Kirk prodded with a slight arch of
his eyebrows. "What do you have against Mark Rousseau?"

McCoy responded with a lengthy silence. "Do you
really want to know?" he finally said. At Kirk's nod,
he added, "Don't say I didn't warn you."

"As someone once said, 'Scout's honor.'"

"All right, Jim. What do you know about Mark
Rousseau?"

"Not much. He's about your age, used to be a
starship captain. I met him once years ago. He was on
the fast track to his admiral's braid when he quit
Starfleet and went into the Federation diplomatic

corps. As far as I know, he's considered to be a gifted
mediator—"

"A *natural*," McCoy said.

Kirk looked hard at his friend, trying to read
McCoy's expression and the way he'd said that one
word: *natural*. A jumble of sarcasm, irony, deference
. . . even envy? If Kirk was right, McCoy had a serious
case of mixed feelings about this man. "I assume I'm
safe in saying you know each other?"

"Since I was nine and he was eleven. Met him on
the first day of school . . ."

. . . *We'd just moved to this small town, so I was the
new kid. Hardly had time to learn anybody's name,
much less make any friends. Hadn't had my growth
spurt yet either, so I was this skinny little kid whose
jeans were a little too baggy and hair a little too short,
thanks to one of Mom's famous kitchen haircuts—a
nice ripe target for gettin' picked on . . .*

"Nice haircut, kid," hooted the beefy boy with the
blemished face. He and his three friends orbited
around nine-year-old Leonard McCoy, keeping pace
with him as he trudged along the tree-shaded sidewalk. They didn't impede his progress, but they did
form a threatening ring from which they drawled their
taunts.

They were not particularly clever or creative. Their
teasing was rather mundane, aimed at the
underwhelming physical attributes of the scrawny boy
with the uneven thatch of hair. The bathroom mirror
had told him the unavoidable truth that morning: He
was not the fairest of them all, not in Georgia or any
other land. Why did his mother have to cut his hair so
short on the sides and back and leave the front long
enough to keep falling limply in front of his eyes?

"Whose pants you got on? Your daddy's?"

Leonard tried to ignore them. It was only seven-
thirty in the morning, but he already felt a trickle of

sweat down his back. Southern summers didn't care that the calendar said September. They lingered, as damp and persistent as the morning mist hugging the grass and hanging over the stream gurgling alongside the road to the old-fashioned clay-brick schoolhouse.

Had they been placed in an old-fashioned police lineup, Leonard would not have been able to identify the bullies. All he knew was that two were skinny, two were stocky. They were all older boys, maybe eleven, and all a head taller than him. He'd have had to look up to see their faces, and he was too busy watching his feet, making certain that he didn't trip over the sidewalk squares pushed up by the roots of the old trees stooping like drowsy old men watching the world pass by.

Without thinking, Leonard hugged his lunch box tight under one arm. A moment later, he regretted the action.

"Hey, kid, must be *some* special lunch you got!"

Though it was only a momentary distraction, it was enough to make Leonard trip and sprawl on the rough walk. The lunch box skittered free of his hands, coming to rest just out of reach. The lead bully snatched it up. For the first time, Leonard looked up at the bigger boy's face. It wasn't what he'd expected. No scars, no cruel eyes, no sneering mouth.

No fangs.

Just a bland round face with freckles and sun-bleached hair. The bully took a quick glance at the lunch box now in his hands. It was as unremarkable as he was, except for the corner labeled with Leonard's name. "What do they call you, kid—*Leeeon?* Or maybe Leonardo."

"Leonard," said the smaller boy as he tried to get up. One of the skinny junior bullies used his foot to shove Leonard back onto his rump.

"Well, you're Leonardo to me," said the leader as

8

he shook the lunch box next to his ear. "What'd yo' mama give ya for lunch, *Leonardo?*"

"Hey! Don't shake it!" Leonard desperately wanted his voice to come out as a snarl, but all he got was a quavering plea.

The bully turned his attention to the lunch box latch. "Must be somethin' special—like *baby food.*" He basked in his friends' derisive laughter.

The latch snapped open. Leonard's eyes widened with fear, which turned out to be a surprisingly strong motivation. *"Don't open that!"* he shouted, scrambling to his feet and springing toward the bully, reaching for the elusive lunch box.

But Leonard's headlong leap was aborted by several hands that held him in place while the leader laughed. "Why not?" he teased, lifting the lid partway. "Well, lookit! *Leonardo*'s got a *live frog* for lunch!"

Leonard felt his face flush hot and red with anger and embarrassment as his four tormentors exploded in loud laughter.

"He's not lunch, you jerk! He's a pet!" He tried to wriggle free, but hostile hands held him tight. God, he'd never wanted to punch anybody as much as he did right now! But all he could do was watch in horror as the bully opened the lid all the way, and the frog literally leapt at the opportunity for freedom.

It landed awkwardly on the grass, then bounced straight for the stream.

"Let go of me!" Leonard wailed.

But the bullies ignored him, as if they'd forgotten they were holding him. They were fascinated by the frog. "Lookit 'im jump!"

From a well of fury Leonard McCoy didn't even know he had, he summoned up a genuine snarl. *"Let me goooo!"*

"Hey, *Leonardo,* that's no way—"

"Calvin, you *might* want to let him go," said a

deeper voice from behind McCoy. It was calm, but the tone left no doubt the speaker wasn't merely making a suggestion.

Leonard turned to see his would-be savior. He was a black boy with a patient expression instead of the avenging fire McCoy had hoped to see in his eyes. He didn't look any older than the bullies, and he was no taller than they were. But he was broader than even the beefy leader, and the contours under his knit shirt made it obvious he had already developed real muscle where the bully had baby fat.

Calvin's wide smirk shrank down to a wan smile. "Hey now, Mark. Don't want no trouble."

"Never said you did," said the savior, Mark. "So let's get to school before we're late—unless you all're headed for the pond for a little extra summer vacation."

The bullies were still holding McCoy, but their grip had relaxed as their attention turned toward Mark and making a face-saving retreat. Leonard finally pulled free and watched for a moment, even though he really wanted to search for his runaway frog.

"What if we were?" said Calvin. "You weren't plannin' on tellin' on us, were ya?"

Mark shrugged. "I don't care what you do."

Calvin and his junior thugs backed away. "Okay then, Mark, we'll see y'all in school"—he laughed, doing his best to sound superior—"in a coupla weeks or so."

The bullies left the scene of their crime, sauntering with a studied casualness, trying to make their exit look as voluntary as possible. Watching them go, Leonard tensed as he felt a hand on his shoulder.

It was just Mark. "You okay?"

McCoy shrugged. "I guess. Thanks."

"My name's Mark Rousseau."

"Leonard McCoy."

"Not Leonardo." The boys shook hands. "You want some help looking for your frog, Leonard?"

"Yeah. Thanks."

We never did find that frog. But I found a friend . . . my first friend there—

"—and my best friend for years after that."

Kirk frowned as McCoy paused to drain his glass. "And then what?"

"What do you mean?"

"That's obviously not the end of the story. The guy saves you from bullies, you become best friends, and forty years later the very mention of his name makes you want to throw crockery against the wall."

"You're the one who thinks I want to throw crockery—"

"Do you *love* the guy or do you *hate* him?"

"Yes." McCoy sighed in reaction to an exasperated roll of Kirk's eyes. "It's not that simple, Jim. Mark was one of those kids who was good at *everything*— sports, music, school, you name it. He had umpteen girlfriends and every one of 'em ended up being best friends with him even after they broke up. *Everybody* liked him. It was hard *not* to like him . . ."

McCoy's voice trailed off but not before betraying his conflicting emotions toward Mark Rousseau, the man who wasn't there—but who *would* be in another day or so. Before Rousseau set foot on the *Enterprise,* Kirk wanted to understand this complex relationship between his chief surgeon—*Kirk's* best friend—and the special ambassador coming aboard to execute some vital mission still to be revealed to Kirk and his crew by Rousseau himself.

"It was hard *not* to like him," Kirk repeated, *"but—?"*

The pained flinch in McCoy's jaw made his resistance obvious. It was almost as if he felt he'd be committing sacrilege by saying something negative about Mark Rousseau. But he knew Kirk wouldn't let him get away with any sidesteps at this point. His shoulders sagged. "Have you ever known anybody who was just too damned perfect sometimes?"

"Other than you?"

"Very funny. Sometimes, as hard as it was to *not* like Mark, it was *just* as hard to be his friend. You know how competitive kids can be. With him, it's like there was this natural law: I'd *never* be better than him at *any*thing. And God knows I felt inadequate enough without knowing *that*. I'm not proud of this, but sometimes I just wanted him to fall flat on his face in front of the whole town." McCoy paused in his difficult confession. When he finished, it was a whisper. "Sometimes I prayed for it."

"Did it ever happen?"

"Of course not."

"And you survived your childhood envy?"

"I survived. And we grew up." McCoy poured himself a refill, then went on without any further prodding from the captain. "And even though we moved again, Mark and I stayed friends. We hadn't seen each other for a while when I got invited to his going-away party . . ."

. . . It seemed like only yesterday we were wading into that stream, looking for my damned frog. And now he was heading off to Starfleet Academy . . .

The four cars of the bullet-shaped trolley slid silently to a stop at the Savannah station platform. As McCoy stepped out, his overnight bag slung over one shoulder, he caught sight of an onrushing bulk coming from his right. He barely had time to brace himself when he felt Mark Rousseau's strong arms wrap him in a bear hug.

"Leonard! It is so great to see you. Your being here means a lot to me."

"How could I miss it—now that you *finally* decided what to do with all that talent." With an exaggerated gasp, McCoy slapped his hands to his cheeks in a sarcastic imitation of distraught youth wrestling with life's choices. "Symphony pianist—or starship captain? Oh *whatever* will I do?"

"Very funny, McCoy." Mark looked his friend up and down. "So you're finally as tall as me, even though you'd still get blown away by a stiff wind."

It was true. At seventeen and nineteen, the two young men were eye to eye, but McCoy still felt small compared to his muscular friend.

"So how about you, Leonard?" Mark asked as they followed the shady walk away from the station. "You made any decisions yet?"

"Well . . . medical school, probably."

"Mmm. The family business," Mark said with a knowing nod. Then he looked directly at McCoy, eyes bright with possibilities. "Hey, you should join Starfleet, too! We could serve on the same ship."

McCoy gave his friend a slow, dubious glance. "I suppose *you're* gonna be the captain?"

"Naturally," Mark said with a grin. "You'll be my chief surgeon."

"You'll never get me into a transporter, I can tell you *that.*"

"Then I'll just have to court-martial you."

They both laughed, then walked quietly for a while. McCoy really *wasn't* sure what he wanted to do. All the nights he'd lain awake, hours after going to bed, listening to the sounds outside his bedroom window, the clicks and chirps and croaks he'd always found so soothing . . . And now they were like so many voices peppering him with choices about what to do with his life and who to do it with and where they'd go and who they'd be.

Choices that had to be made, sooner or later. Choices that no one could make for him. McCoy had

13

read enough psychology to know that struggling with seemingly momentous decisions was an inescapable part of coming of age. But preparation didn't make it any easier. Even Mark, who'd always seemed so sure of himself, had taken a year off before setting course for Starfleet. But now that the decision had been made, McCoy had no doubts that his friend would sail smoothly toward inevitable success.

"You met somebody," Mark said flatly, interrupting McCoy's tangential thoughts. It wasn't a question, but a statement of certain fact.

It caught McCoy off guard. "Huh?"

"You met somebody."

"What makes you so sure?"

Mark shrugged and smiled. "You look even more confused than usual, that's what. I'm right, aren't I." Again, a statement, not a question.

"Of *course* you're right," McCoy said with a rueful shake of his head, glaring at Mark as he bit off each word. "You're *always* right. Don't you get *tired* of being so damn *right* all the time?" Then he turned away, wondering if Mark had noticed the angry edge that had crept into his voice. He hadn't meant for that to happen . . . or *had* he? In any case, Mark either hadn't picked up on it or he'd opted to ignore it.

"And how does this special lady feel about beaming around the galaxy?"

"I don't know. We haven't gotten that far yet."

There was that all-knowing Rousseau nod again. "You will," he said cryptically.

The comment and tone might have been infuriatingly smug from someone else. But so many times in the decade they'd been friends, Mark really *did* seem to know, so McCoy could neither get very mad at him nor stay mad for long. "So, how about *you?*" McCoy asked in fair turnabout.

"I—I guess I'm seeing somebody," Mark said with uncharacteristic hesitation.

"You *guess?*" McCoy teased.

"I'm seeing somebody," he said with more certainty, grinning sheepishly at his own equivocation. "Erica."

"Is Erica as perfect as you?"

"Actually, she really *is* perfect," Mark beamed. "She'll be there tonight. You'll like her, Leonard."

McCoy's brows lowered like stormclouds into a mock threatening frown. "Oh-*ho, that's* why you wanted to know if I was seein' somebody. You wanted to be sure I wouldn't steal perfect Erica away from you."

With a laugh, Mark threw his arm over McCoy's shoulders and pulled him close. "That's it. Thanks to your lady-friend, I can relax and enjoy myself . . ."

"Nobody ever stole a girl from Mark Rousseau," McCoy said, peering into his glass as he swirled the brandy around.

"So he went off to Starfleet—" Kirk prompted.

"—and I lost my best friend."

"Didn't you keep in touch?"

"Yeah. But it wasn't the same. Didn't get to see each other much . . . I got married, and then I started med school. He had Erica, two perfect kids in perfect domestic bliss, and his Starfleet career. And then, well, it's a big galaxy. You know how that goes."

Kirk scratched the back of his neck, looking perplexed. "Then I don't get it. If you and Rousseau were such great long-lost pals, why aren't you thrilled at the prospect of seeing him again?"

"Let's just say we had . . . a falling out."

Kirk blinked in disbelief. "After all that, a 'falling out' hardly begins to—"

"Jim, leave it *alone.*" McCoy's tone made it clear he considered the subject closed.

Kirk raised both hands in a gesture of surrender.

"Fine. If you feel like telling me the rest, you know where to find me. Otherwise, consider it left alone—"

"Good."

"—except for one thing."

McCoy groaned, but Kirk continued without comment. "Mark Rousseau's coming aboard for this mission whether you like it or not. Is that going to be a problem for you?"

"I'll manage."

Kirk left, but he found himself wishing McCoy had sounded more convincing—both to Kirk and to himself.

Chapter Two

Captain's personal log, Stardate 7591.4.

We'll be reaching Starbase 86 within the hour. Starfleet has provided no details of our mission other than the fact that Ambassador Mark Rousseau will be in charge. And now I find out that McCoy and Rousseau go way back—once the best of friends, and now? I don't know . . . but I *do* know there's a lot more to it than McCoy has told me.

"COMPUTER," SAID KIRK, easing back into the lounge chair in the corner of his cabin, underneath the small collection of vintage firearms displayed on the wall.

"Working," came the instantaneous response.

"Access Starfleet service record of Mark Rousseau, retired."

"Accessed," the computer replied in its soothing female voice.

"List his commands."

"First command: science–exploration–survey vessel *U.S.S. Richard Feynman* in 2254. Second command: experimental vessel *U.S.S. Manhattan* in 2255. Third command: starship *U.S.S. Hood* in 2256. Fourth and final command: starship *U.S.S. Lexington* in 2261. Retired from active Starfleet service in 2264."

Few officers achieved any command as rapidly as Rousseau had, and even fewer skip so quickly from smaller vessels to heavy-cruiser-class starships. "What was Captain Rousseau's exact age when posted to the *Hood?*"

"Thirty years, seven months, twelve days."

So that's how much I beat him by, Kirk thought with a hint of a smile. He'd always wondered but had never bothered to check. Before Kirk came along, Mark Rousseau had been the youngest starship captain in Starfleet history. Kirk had wrested that honor away from him, assuming command of the *Enterprise* just after his thirtieth birthday. Sooner or later, of course, somebody would come along and beat Kirk's benchmark, just as he had bested Rousseau's.

But until then, Kirk could forgive himself for privately indulging his justifiable pride in that particular achievement. It was one of the few personal vanities he allowed himself, and it meant even more now that he'd learned something about the kind of man Mark Rousseau was.

"Computer, access Dr. Leonard McCoy's service record."

"McCoy, Leonard H., M.D. . . . first deep-space assignment as Starfleet junior medical officer in 2253, aboard *U.S.S. Republic*—"

"Uhh, skip that," Kirk said with a wave of his hand. "Cross-reference service records of McCoy and Rousseau, reporting coincident assignments."

"Acknowledged. Concurrent service of Dr. McCoy and Captain Rousseau aboard Starfleet science–

exploration–survey vessel *U.S.S. Richard Feynman* in 2254."

Kirk's eyebrows went up. "Oh? That's interesting. What was McCoy's rank and posting?"

"Rank: lieutenant. Posting: chief medical officer."

"How long was McCoy aboard the *Feynman?*"

"Seven months, nine days."

Hmm . . . not very long, Kirk thought. What's more, this was the first he'd ever heard of that assignment. McCoy had never mentioned it. "Where did McCoy transfer when he left the *Feynman?*"

"Transferred to the med-evac emergency vessel *U.S.S. Koop.*"

"As?"

"Junior medical officer."

Kirk frowned as he digested what he'd just learned from the computer. It would have been unusual— almost unheard of—for a doctor with as little deep-space experience as McCoy had when he joined the *Feynman*'s crew to be appointed chief surgeon on *any* Starfleet ship on merit alone. No matter how good a doctor he may have been, such an assignment would have taken a miracle—or strenuous string pulling by the ship's commanding officer. In this case, that commander had been Mark Rousseau.

Still, such interventions did happen. Starfleet was hardly immune. So McCoy would have been reunited with his boyhood pal, just as they'd dreamed years earlier.

You'd think he would have been happy about that, Kirk mused. But the facts pointed to an opposite outcome: a precipitous transfer off the *Feynman* along with a demotion in stature, if not rank, and the subsequent twenty-year estrangement of old friends. It didn't take a great detective to conclude that something serious must have gone wrong.

But *what?* Kirk had no idea, but he was determined to find out, preferably *before* Rousseau came aboard.

The singsong whistle of the intercom interrupted the captain's inquiry, followed a moment later by a familiar voice. "Spock to Captain Kirk."

"Kirk here."

"We are on final approach to Starbase 86, sir."

"Thank you, Mr. Spock. On my way. Kirk out."

Kirk reached for his uniform jacket and headed for the bridge. Unfortunately, his quest for answers to lately revealed mysteries of McCoy's past would have to wait.

The sleek form of the *Starship Enterprise* slipped into orbit around Starbase 86, an unremarkable space station positioned in the Alpha Kratonii planetary system, known primarily for a string of productive mining colonies.

Commander Scott was already behind the console when Kirk and Spock walked into transporter room 3 to greet their incoming guest.

"Coordinates already set, sir," Scott said.

Kirk looked from his engineer to his first officer. McCoy was notably absent. "Well, are we ready to meet the legend?"

"We're kind o' legendary ourselves, sir," Scott said with a sly smile.

"That we are, Scotty. Energize."

Scott engaged the unit. The familiar hum modulated up, then down, as a tall, burly man materialized in the chamber. Before Kirk could move toward him, the man was already down the steps in one stride, his right arm outstretched. He grasped Kirk's hand with a firmness that was virile without being intimidating.

A perfect handshake, Kirk found himself thinking. He wondered if he'd come to regret having McCoy tell as much as he had about Rousseau. It would be hard to avoid measuring the flesh-and-blood man against the myth of McCoy's memories. "Welcome to the *Enterprise*, Ambassador Rousseau."

"Thank you, Captain." Rousseau's voice carried a resonance altogether fitting for a man of his imposing physical stature. His precise diction suggested an amalgam of all the accents to which he'd been exposed as both starship commander and diplomat, yet without a trace of the Southern drawl McCoy had retained despite all his years away from Georgia's red-clay soil. "It's good to see you again."

"I didn't think you'd remember our having met," Kirk said with a touch of honest surprise. "It was quite some time ago and rather brief, as I recall."

Rousseau smiled broadly. "Almost ten years ago— at that Starfleet conference on that Klingon mischief near Donatu 5. You'd just taken command of the *Enterprise,* and I was just about to retire from the *Lexington.*"

"You've got a good memory, Mr. Ambassador."

"How could I *not* remember the fellow who snatched away my record as the youngest captain in Starfleet," Rousseau said with a hearty laugh and a friendly squeeze on Kirk's shoulder.

Kirk gestured toward his officers, who acknowledged their introductions with respectful nods. "This is my first officer, Commander Spock, and Commander Montgomery Scott, chief engineer."

"Gentlemen, your reputations precede you. I don't mind telling you all I was quite jealous of Chris Pike having Mr. Spock as his first officer those last few years he had the *Enterprise.* And I harbored some ill will toward *you,* Captain, when you inherited him. I tried my damndest to steal him away. And, Mr. Scott, I must say the *Enterprise* is as impressive as I thought she'd be from reading your tech reports on her refit."

"You read those, sir?" Scott said, genuinely amazed. It had always been one of Scotty's private peeves that Captain Kirk never seemed all that interested in the technical minutiae of the ship for which they had such mutual affection.

Rousseau leaned toward Scotty, who looked quite pleased at the compliment. "An old habit from my Starfleet days. I almost became an engineer myself. You should be proud of the work you did on this old girl."

"I am, sir."

Rousseau scanned the room, then sighed. "And where's my old friend, Dr. McCoy?"

Kirk's eyes shifted, trying to cover any visible discomfort. "Uhh, he had some business to take care of. He'll be meeting us at the briefing room."

"Well, then, I guess we should get right to it so you'll know where I'm dragging you off to and why."

McCoy sat alone at the briefing room table, looking up as the door slid open. Mark Rousseau seemed to fill the doorway with his grinning face. "Leonard!" he boomed.

McCoy stood slowly and had barely risen from his seat by the time Rousseau rounded the table and wrapped him in a hug. In return, McCoy patted Rousseau's back with noticeable diffidence— noticeable to everyone but the ambassador, it seemed. He looked nothing short of pleased to see his old friend, McCoy's lack of enthusiasm notwithstanding.

"You look *great*—for an old guy," Rousseau said with a chuckle.

"You, too," McCoy said as he disengaged from the hug, "though you have put on a few pounds."

Rousseau shrugged and patted his ample midsection. "The perils of home cooking." Then he turned to the others who had spread out around the long table. "We're old chums, haven't seen each other in years. But we'll have time to catch up after we're under way. So, let's get down to business."

As everyone took their seats, Rousseau sat at the main terminal and popped a data cassette into its slot.

Then he leaned forward, resting his big clasped hands on the table. "We've got a crisis to deal with—at Nova Empyrea."

The only *Enterprise* officer to react was McCoy. His eyebrows shot up at the name of the planet. Kirk noticed.

"I've never heard of Nova Empyrea," the captain said, "but apparently *you* have, Doctor."

"There's no reason for any of you to know about Nova Empyrea, Captain," Rousseau said. "No reason for anybody here—other than Dr. McCoy and me. It was a colony we stumbled across when I was captain of the *Feynman,* and Dr. McCoy was my chief surgeon. We were exploring the Campana Sector, the first survey ship out there." He touched the computer keypad and the sector star chart lit the viewscreen.

"What kind of colony?" Kirk asked.

"A *human* colony," McCoy said, his tone flat. "The founders left Earth back in the early days of warp drive, about a hundred and fifty years before we bumped into them."

"They weren't exactly happy to be found by us," Rousseau continued. "But their star system was an unusual binary configuration—an older, established system had captured a younger star with planets just forming. We'd never come across one quite like it. We couldn't pass it by."

Rousseau touched the keypad again, and images from the *Feynman*'s original visit were displayed on the viewer, showing how the combined solar systems looked from the distant perspective of an approaching starship.

"Fascinating," Spock said softly. "Quite rare, and certainly worthy of study."

"That's what Starfleet Cosmology and Astrophysics and the Federation Science Academy thought. So we were ordered to negotiate for permission to set up a

Federation science outpost at Nova Empyrea. Our talks went on for almost four months, which gave us time to not only start our own astrophysical studies, but also to learn more about this colony, which was almost as interesting as their stars."

"How so?" Kirk asked. "You said they weren't exactly happy to be found."

"They weren't just another lost colony," Rousseau said. "From the day their founders set out, they *meant* to sever all ties with Earth. Their goal was to establish an isolated society, sealed off from outsiders."

"Intentionally isolated? For what purpose?" asked Spock.

McCoy spoke up. "They wanted to use the most advanced genetic management techniques to help the human organism reach its highest possible level of physical and intellectual quality."

"Which is where Bones came in," Rousseau said. "He led our investigation into the biomedical side of the colony. Well, to make a long story short, we managed to convince the Empyreans to allow our outpost. It's quite extensive, actually, with a ground base, an orbital platform, and a network of satellites. It's been operating for the past eighteen years, though under conditions of strict separation from Empyrean society."

Kirk suppressed a shudder. It had only been a half-dozen years since the *Enterprise* had found the *S.S. Botany Bay,* the centuries-old sleeper ship adrift near the Mutara Sector. Their confrontation with its commander, Khan Noonien Singh, and his cadre of genetic supermen had nearly cost the lives of Kirk and his crew. So, here and now, none of them were predisposed to welcome with anything but wary misgivings the notion of a genetically perfected enclave.

"We've had our own experiences with the products of genetic engineering," Kirk said coldly.

Rousseau nodded. "I read about your run-in with Khan. But this was different. These were not people bent on conquest."

"Most madmen swear to benign intentions."

"The original Empyreans knew that, Captain, and they didn't want to leave anything to chance. They set up a code of laws as rigorous and well thought out as any I've ever seen."

"Jim," McCoy said, "God knows I'm the last person to defend Khan or the whole damned concept of *un*natural selection. But the Empyreans knew all about the Nazis and the Eugenics Wars. They'd *studied* them. They believed that good science coupled with staunch morality and benign motivation might actually accomplish something."

Scotty didn't bother to disguise his skepticism. "And what might that be, Doctor?"

"Good as we are," McCoy said, "we humans are far from perfect. From a scientific standpoint, you've got to admit there's room for improvement."

Kirk gave him a measuring look. "You sound like a convert."

"Not on God's green earth," McCoy said with an emphatic shake of his head. "But I've got to tell you that colony was pretty damned impressive in a lot of ways."

"What we found was an enlightened, peaceful society of outstanding cultural, scientific, and physical achievement," the ambassador said as he keyed the data cassette again, this time displaying a series of images of himself, McCoy, and other *Feynman* crew members on Nova Empyrea eighteen years ago.

From what Kirk could see of their clothing, architecture, and artifacts of daily life, the Empyreans favored a style best described as clean classicism. The people themselves were strikingly handsome but not abnormally so. Including all human races as well as

25

racial mixtures, they seemed a notch better on all physical scales than garden-variety randomly bred humans.

"As you can see," Rousseau narrated, "they were bigger, stronger, and more physically perfect than the human norm but not homogenized in any way. In addition, compared to random populations of similar size, we found them to be more intelligent, intellectually gifted, and talented in areas running the whole gamut of human endeavors, from athletics to the sciences to the arts."

The ambassador scanned the faces of McCoy's crewmates around the table. They were clearly skeptical. "Well, I can see I'm not going to convince you with this little presentation. You'll see for yourselves what Dr. McCoy and I saw."

"Maybe," Kirk said, his one word giving voice to the resistance he shared with the rest of the senior officers present. "You mentioned a crisis. Specifics?"

"The Empyreans want the astronomy outpost removed."

Kirk's eyebrows rose. "After eighteen years? Why?"

"No reason given. The Federation Science Academy believes there's still great value in keeping it there. So we've asked for one last chance to negotiate a renewal of our treaty. The Empyrean Council was not encouraging about the possibilities, but they've grudgingly agreed to let us send a delegation. Because of our past dealings, they specifically requested me—and Dr. McCoy."

Kirk glanced reflexively toward McCoy, who looked more than a little startled.

"If the Empyreans don't change their minds," Rousseau continued, "the *Enterprise* is to dismantle the outpost and remove Federation equipment and personnel."

McCoy blinked in confusion. "I can see why they asked for you, Mark. I mean, you led the negotiations.

But why me? I'm a doctor, not a diplomat. I had nothing to do with that treaty."

"To be honest," Rousseau said with a shrug, "I have no idea why they wanted you along, Bones. But they did. So when we get there, you'll be joining me in meeting with Council President Elizabeth March."

At the mention of the name Elizabeth March, Kirk glimpsed a shadow of jumbled emotion in McCoy's eyes. It wasn't enough to determine what was flashing through the doctor's mind at that moment, but more than enough to evoke additional concern on Kirk's part. His friend had already found Rousseau's arrival unsettling for reasons Kirk still didn't quite understand. *What else isn't McCoy telling me, and how far should I push him to find out?*

Kirk leaned toward the doctor. "Is this council president someone you knew?"

"Not really. The name just rang a bell, that's all," McCoy said, seeming just a little too insistent as he avoided Kirk's gaze. "She was some midlevel science attaché. Just somebody I worked with. Competent."

McCoy's blue eyes flickered toward Kirk for a moment, then looked away again, fanning Kirk's suspicions further. "That's it?"

"That's it," McCoy repeated.

"You've got a better memory than I do, Bones," Rousseau said. "I don't think I remember her at all." Then he looked around the table. "That's all I have. Does anybody have any questions?"

No one did. Kirk swiveled his chair and stood. "All right, then—"

McCoy was already on his way out the door without a word or a look back. Kirk watched him disappear from view as he continued. "Thank you, Mr. Ambassador. The *Enterprise* is at your service."

Rousseau smiled. "Much appreciated, Captain. I'd love to see the bridge, if you don't mind some kibbitzing from an old hand."

"Not at all. Consider yourself welcome anywhere on the ship. Mr. Spock, why don't you escort Ambassador Rousseau to the bridge. I'd like you to take the conn for a while. Best speed to Nova Empyrea."

Spock nodded. "May I ask where you will be, Captain?"

"Uhh, tending to some unfinished research."

Chapter Three

"JIM, YOU ARE one nosy sonofabitch," Dr. McCoy growled, glaring up at Kirk from his cabin lounge chair.

"Thanks. I try."

"That was *not* a compliment!"

"I don't care," Kirk said pleasantly, helping himself to a drink and sitting in a facing chair. "What I *do* care about is you. If you're going to hide things from me, how the devil am I going to help you deal with this?"

"I didn't notice I was *asking* for help."

"Well, fortunately, I did."

McCoy rubbed his eyes wearily, losing the bite in his voice. "Lord protect us from starship captains who think they're psychotherapists," he moaned. Then he lowered his hands, peeking out as if hoping Kirk would no longer be sitting there, looking at him. But the captain hadn't budged an inch.

"Now, tell me what *really* happened between you and Mark Rousseau aboard the *Feynman.*"

"All right," McCoy sighed. "It wasn't long after I shipped out. I was still getting used to Starfleet life, getting used to the idea that being a space doc was as different from my dad's practice in Georgia as night and day. There I was, as green as grass, and Starfleet's sending me from one emergency to the next . . ."

. . . Those first few months away from Earth, I saw more blood and butchery than I ever thought I'd see in ten lifetimes. I still wasn't sure who I was or what I was doing. I still wasn't sure I shouldn't go back home and try to make some sense of everything I'd run away from.

When I'd go to sleep, I'd see the faces I left behind. My wife . . . I still didn't know why our marriage didn't work. And Joanna . . . how she looked the last time I saw her. My little girl . . . and I wasn't going to be there to see her grow up.

And then, out of the blue, I get transfer orders. Nobody told me why, and I was too chicken to ask questions. So there I am, hopping a Starfleet supply ship on its way to a starbase rendezvous . . .

Every time McCoy stepped into a transporter, the little wise-ass voice in the back of his head would laugh maniacally: *Your atoms are about to get scattered to the four winds. Say bye-bye, sucker . . .*

So far, though, the little voice had been wrong. And once more, McCoy gratefully found himself wholly reconstituted in the transporter chamber of the *U.S.S. Feynman*. Seeing the hesitation in his step, the transporter chief waved him off the platform.

"You've got to move your feet, son," said the gray-haired woman. "Nobody's going to do it for you."

His duffel bag slung over his shoulder, McCoy nodded dumbly and shuffled down the steps, hoping someone would eventually tell him why he was here. When the doors to the corridor suddenly slid open, he looked up with a start as Mark Rousseau strode through.

"Welcome aboard, Leonard!" he said, clapping McCoy on the shoulder.

Caught thoroughly off guard, McCoy could only blink. Then he realized his friend was wearing a captain's uniform. "Mark, is this your ship?" he finally managed to ask.

"Damn right," Rousseau said, grinning. "And you're my new chief surgeon."

McCoy's eyes bugged wide and his Adam's apple bobbed. "Ch—chief surgeon?"

Now, keep in mind I had about as much right being a chief surgeon at that point in my career as you do, Jim. It didn't take long for me to find out how I got there: Mark happily admitted he'd greased the right wheels and whistled the right tune. Hell, he was Starfleet's pride and joy, so they couldn't begrudge him a little favor, like having his completely underqualified friend assigned as his chief medical officer . . .

"What makes you think I want to *be* your chief medical officer or *anybody's* for that matter?!"

McCoy had been aboard long enough to find his cabin and his righteous indignation. Right now, he found himself in a private corner of the *Feynman*'s cramped rec lounge, waving his arms angrily at his old friend and new commanding officer.

"Cool your rockets, Leonard."

"Is that an order—*sir?*" McCoy said sarcastically.

"What are you so upset about? Didn't we talk about serving together? Well, I was in a position to make it happen."

"So I'm supposed to spend the rest of my life thanking you?"

"Once would be enough, if you ever stop snarling at me."

McCoy shook his head. "What the hell am I thanking you for?"

"Well, for one thing, most doctors have to wait years to make chief surgeon, even on a little science ship like this one. Or aren't you interested in career advancement?"

"Geez, Mark," McCoy said, getting up and pacing to the observation window, "I don't know *what* I'm interested in. I don't even know if I'm gonna stay in Starfleet." He felt a supportive hand touch his shoulder, but he refused to turn away from the window that overlooked the starbase asteroid sparkling in the starlight.

"Leonard, you can't keep looking back. You've got to get on with your life."

"Shouldn't that be *my* choice?" Bitterness colored McCoy's voice, but he didn't care. He was tired of wrestling with the grief and the self-pity and just as tired of keeping it to himself. Hell, lots of marriages flop. His wife wasn't the first to find comfort in the arms of a man other than her husband, and McCoy knew he was to blame for pushing her toward that fateful step with his own unintentional indifference.

And Mark's right, damn him. I should be moving on. But McCoy frankly had no idea if he'd ever be strong enough to do that, decisively and finally. And until he was, he knew he'd resent and resist anybody— however well-meaning—who tried to help him. He knew how stupid it was to feel that way, how much energy it wasted, but he couldn't help how he felt.

At last, he turned toward Rousseau. He spoke softly. "I'm not a goddam chess piece."

Mark frowned at his friend for a long moment, then nodded slowly. "You're right. I probably should've asked if you wanted to transfer here."

"Probably?" said McCoy with a jiggle of his eyebrows.

Mark shrugged in surrender. "Okay. I should have. If you want to go back to whatever godforsaken place I saved you from, just say the word. I'll look like an idiot—"

"Not that uncommon, apparently."

"—but I'll do it for you. We're not leaving starbase for two days. Why don't you think it over for that long?"

"Fair enough."

"You stayed?"

McCoy nodded at Kirk, taking a sip of brandy. "Entropy. I was there already. It's not like I had anyplace better to go. But I never got over how I felt, not completely."

"The resentment?"

"Yeah. I kept thinking the Mark Rousseau I knew before would never've done anything so high-handed and presumptuous."

"Maybe he really thought he was doing you a favor."

"He probably did," McCoy said with a shrug. "But that's not how I saw it. We hadn't seen much of each other since we were kids, almost ten years. People can do an awful lot of changing from nineteen to twenty-nine. And I couldn't decide if he'd changed or if I'd never really known him at all. After seven months of that, I finally decided Mark was right. I *did* need to get on with my life, without all the baggage I'd left behind on Earth—and without him. So I transferred off the *Feynman*."

Kirk sat quietly for a moment. "That's it?"

"That's it. Sorry there weren't any more fireworks."

"If you say so."

"I say so."

"Good." Kirk stood up. "I'm glad you feel better."

"Who said I feel better," McCoy grumbled.

"No need to thank me," Kirk said as he left the cabin with a wave over his shoulder.

The door slid shut, leaving McCoy back in his preferred solitude. Should he have told the rest of the story, what had really happened on Nova Empyrea? Was it dishonest to tell only the partial truth? He'd answered the questions Kirk had thought to ask. Probably best to leave the *unasked* ones buried as long as possible.

After all, he had no idea what would happen once they got to the Empyrean colony. Maybe what happened all those years ago would remain in the past. Maybe he had nothing to worry about. *Maybe pigs'll fly,* he thought ruefully.

He got up and padded barefoot to the computer terminal at his desk. "Computer," he said as he sat down, "access records of the *U.S.S. Feynman*'s mission to Nova Empyrea."

"Accessed."

McCoy rubbed his eyes and took a deep breath. He couldn't believe this—going back there after almost twenty years. He tried to recall the person he'd been back then. Could he trust his own memories? It seemed like more than a lifetime ago, yet as close as yesterday. Despite his knowledge of the human psyche, it still amazed and puzzled him the way the mind could encompass concurrent perceptions of time that were utterly and mutually exclusive.

"Does this file have Empyrean personnel records?"

"Affirmative."

McCoy swallowed like a diver taking a gulp of air right before a deep plunge into unknown and murky waters. "Okay. Let me see the file for Elizabeth March."

In barely a heartbeat, she was there on his viewscreen. He knew it was a romantic cliché of the worst kind, but the dark-haired, dark-skinned beauty of her image took his breath away today just as it had when he first saw her eighteen years ago.

"Bet you never took a bad picture either," he

muttered to the image displayed on his monitor. Even in this two-dimensional representation, her pale eyes sparkled with a knowing intelligence. He could almost see her full lips curling into a smile, almost taste them against his.

He remembered everything, every feeling, every sensation. *Like yesterday* . . .

But none of it happened yesterday. Almost two decades had passed. She was the president of the Empyrean Council now, and he didn't have the slightest idea why he'd been summoned. Or what *she* remembered. One thing was certain: He hoped to God she *didn't* remember the first time they'd met . . .

"I said, what's your name?"

Unable to find his voice, young Dr. McCoy stared at the woman who had just asked him a fairly simple question. Twice.

Her dark hair softly framed her face, just brushing her shoulders. Her flawless skin was the shade of medium coffee. She was as tall as he was, and he couldn't keep himself from looking into her sky-blue eyes. Which was just as well. Had he looked away from those eyes, his gaze would have wandered up and down her faultlessly proportioned body, taut and firm beneath the clinging knit of her clothing. Compared to the effortless physical perfection of the Empyreans he'd seen, he felt like a scarecrow, his uniform hanging on his rawboned frame.

He knew he was making a complete fool of himself, but he couldn't help it. It was that simple. He just couldn't help it.

It wasn't her looks alone. She wasn't classically pretty, if there was such a thing. Individually, some of her features could be called imperfect. Nose a bit too long, with a noticeable bump at the bridge. Mouth a bit too wide. In combination, though, they were as striking as a golden-fire sunset.

But it was more than that. Though she'd barely said more than hello, he knew without a doubt that she had a soul, a spirit, an intellect, like no one he'd ever met. He didn't know *how* he knew. He just *knew*. No woman before had ever bewitched him so completely or so instantly.

The pathetic truth was, he'd barely looked at a woman since he'd joined Starfleet. And it wasn't that no one had stirred him. No, no, not at all. In fact, there'd been quite a few ladies who might have caught his eye, both at the Academy and in his first few assignments away from Earth, had he been willing to permit himself the pleasures of their company.

But after crawling away from the self-wrought wreckage of his marriage, he didn't think he could be trusted with companionship, much less romance. What's more, he didn't think he deserved that kind of happiness. Not after winning his one great love, and then losing her.

Could it be that, deep down inside, McCoy had always felt like a fraud with his wife? Taking a good, hard objective look at himself, he had no idea what she could possibly have seen in him. With what sleight of hand had he convinced her to marry him? And if he had no clue to what that magic had been in the first place, how in hell could he possibly conjure it up again and again, through all the days and weeks and years that were to follow?

Could that have been why he'd allowed his career to take over his life, knowing damn well it was exactly the *wrong thing* to do? Maybe the hours spent away from home, studying and working, were the least painful way he could convince his wife he wasn't the man she'd thought he was, giving her the chance to conclude on her own that she deserved better and that she should end their marriage sooner rather than later. Why wait for years of bitterness to build walls that simultaneously trapped and separated them?

Maybe he had never quite been able to shake his belief in a self-fulfilling prophesy based on the old joke about not wanting to belong to any club that would have him as a member.

I'm a great one for self-analysis. Too bad I can't reach any useful conclusions.

In any case, in the couple of years since his marriage had ended and he'd joined Starfleet, he'd been following the road upon which fate and his own flaws had set him. He'd devoted himself completely to medicine. Women were colleagues and casual friends. He had allowed no sparks to strike and would not unless he could be certain he would not repeat the mistakes he'd made with his ex-wife, not until he was ready to believe he deserved to love and to be loved. Not until he set eyes on Elizabeth March, the young Empyrean science attaché (he guessed her to be about twenty-five) who had just asked him that simple question.

"Your name?" she prompted one more time, slightly amused by his dumbstruck reaction. "Come on, you can do it."

He blinked to clear the hormonal haze around his brain. "Uhh, McCoy, ma'am. Leonard McCoy, M.D."

A hint of a smile played at the corners of her mouth. "Well, it seems we're going to be working together, Leonard McCoy, M.D. That is, if you're up to it."

He managed a lopsided smile and a charming tip of his head. "I'm up to it, Dr. March."

"Good."

And I was up to it, too, McCoy thought, permitting himself a smile as he allowed Elizabeth March's face to fade from his monitor screen. Now the question was, would he be up to it again?

37

Chapter Four

THE PRESIDENT OF THE Empyrean Council sat curled in the corner of her office sofa, the loose cushions carefully arranged in her favorite position of relaxation, supporting her back, neck, and legs as she balanced a small computer on her lap.

With a few fine lines etched at the corners of her eyes and mouth, she looked only slightly older than she had when she was the young scientist in the picture viewed by McCoy on the *Enterprise*. Her form-fitting jumpsuit showed that she'd hardly gained a pound.

The intercom on her desk across the room chirped softly.

"Yes?" she said distractedly, still frowning at the mathematic equations cramming her laptop computer screen.

"Tamiya here. Just wanted to let you know we've picked up the *Enterprise* on long-range scanners. They'll be here within the hour."

"Thanks, Ibrahim."

A knock on her open door startled her and she looked up to see a tall man standing in her doorway. He had flowing silver hair gathered into a ponytail that gave him a roguish appearance, and he held a black guitar case in one hand. As with March, time had left few marks of passage on his face, and his actual age was difficult to pinpoint. Just now, his mouth was set in a taut line of disapproval. "Elizabeth, it's not too late."

"For what?" she asked rhetorically. On the one hand, she knew exactly what he was harping about; on the other, she hoped her moment of feigned ignorance might convince him to drop the subject.

He dashed those hopes and stepped inside the office. "To tell the Federation once and for all to go away and leave us alone."

"Clements," she said, with a reservoir of patience she didn't think she had, "the Council voted to let them make their case—"

"—after *you* twisted a few arms. The vote *would* have gone the other way, and it *should* have."

"But it didn't. And I'm not about to change my mind or anybody else's."

Clements shook his head. "Letting them come here was a mistake twenty years ago, and it's a mistake now. You'll see."

"Your glass is always half empty."

"Skepticism is good for the breed."

"So is music. Go give my daughter her guitar lesson."

He turned and left her alone. March leaned back, closed her eyes, and massaged her thick hair with both hands. Maybe Clements was right, but she didn't care.

Not that she needed any reminder, but she kept telling herself that she had her own unspoken reasons for wanting the *Enterprise* to intrude on Empyrean solitude one more time. For Elizabeth March, those reasons, which would have to remain private, transcended everything else.

Kirk leaned on the railing near Spock's science station. "I don't know, Spock. I read McCoy's data from twenty years ago. Objectively, dispassionately, I suppose these Empyreans *are* an improvement on us old-fashioned humans. But it still seems . . . *unnatural* to me."

"An understandable reaction, considering past experiences with genetically engineered variations on random human reproduction."

Kirk shook his head. "Listen to me. I sound like a small-minded Luddite resisting progress. Humans have been using genetic management on plants since Gregor Mendel in the eighteen hundreds. And nobody seemed to mind much when we started using the same techniques on farm animals and endangered species back in the twentieth century."

"That is not entirely true, Captain. Though it was eventually overcome, there was some measure of popular resistance. A few critics—some well-meaning, others merely self-indulgent—fanned public fears."

Kirk looked surprised. "Fears? Of what? Mutant cows taking over the planet?"

"Those who did not understand the benign nature of the work were concerned about the possible release of dangerous genetic agents into the environment at large."

"Seems kind of silly now," Kirk said with a smile. "But that was about cows and corn. Somehow, when it comes to applying the same scientific principles to humans, I can't seem to get around that word—it's *unnatural.*"

"Perhaps. But contemporary biomedical sciences do include procedures that might have been deemed 'unnatural' in the past. And many techniques once considered state of the art are now viewed as quaint at best and barbaric at worst. For instance, Dr. McCoy only rarely uses his leeches, beads, and rattles."

Kirk couldn't help smiling again. Who said Vulcans don't have a sense of humor.

"Keptin," Chekov said, "ve are entering standard orbit, per Empyrean coordinates."

"Thank you, Mr. Chekov," Kirk said, returning to his seat.

As the *Enterprise* completed its approach, it passed over a metallic object glinting in the sunlight as it circled Nova Empyrea. It was too far away to discern details. Kirk glanced back at Spock. "Is that the Federation observatory platform?"

"Affirmative, Captain."

"Let's have a closer look."

Spock called up an image from the aft scanners, enlarged it, and displayed it on the main viewer. The orbital facility was an ungainly structure, with three modules mounted on a central boom and five transceiver arrays attached at various points.

At Kirk's nod, Spock keyed his computer. The image of the space platform was replaced by the standard view of the planet below. It looked quite similar to Earth in coloration and land-to-water ratio, though the arrangements of the land masses were unique. Kirk knew from the *U.S.S. Feynman*'s mission records that the colony occupied a medium-sized island continent in the northern temperate zone.

The turbolift door behind Kirk's right shoulder slid open and Mark Rousseau came out onto the bridge. "Ready when you are, Captain Kirk."

"Uhura, hail the colony."

"Aye, sir."

A moment after the communications officer signaled the planet, March's image appeared on the main viewscreen. As Kirk stood for his formal greeting, he noted that she looked very much the same as her twenty-year-old file photo, and there was something undeniably magnetic about her presence, even on the viewscreen.

"President March, I'm Captain James Kirk, of the *U.S.S. Enterprise.*"

"Welcome to Nova Empyrea, Captain." Then she paused and directed a warm smile at Rousseau as he stepped down from the outer bridge ring to take up a position at Kirk's side. "And welcome back, Mr. Ambassador. It's good to see you after all these years."

Kirk glanced back at Rousseau, who beamed at March's viewscreen image.

"All *what* years, Madam President? You've hardly aged a day."

"Why so surprised?" she vamped. "You *knew* we had good genes."

What's all this familiarity? Kirk wondered. He was almost certain Rousseau had claimed in his mission briefing that he didn't recall Elizabeth March at all. Kirk made a mental note to find out about that contradiction later.

"President March," Kirk said, "the Federation would like you to know how much we appreciate your invitation to at least talk about renewing our treaty."

"Well, Captain, if I were you, I'd make that appreciation conditional. The Council approved this meeting by the slimmest of margins, and I would be less than candid if I encouraged your hopes for a continuation of the old agreement. Our feelings about contacts with Outsiders have been made quite clear, I believe."

"They have." Kirk weighed her neutral tone against her bluntly negative assessment of the situation. Was she just trying to lower expectations, or were the prospects really as bleak as her choice of words made them sound? He would know soon enough. "If you're ready to receive us, our delegation can transport down at any time."

"And who will be in this delegation, Captain?"

"Ambassador Rousseau and Dr. McCoy, as you requested, and my first officer and myself."

March shook her head. "I'm sorry, Captain. The council resolution approved a maximum of two Federation representatives for these talks, plus a technical team of two—and *only* two—to get started on the preliminary work of dismantling the science outpost. That way, there'll be a minimum of time wasted once a final decision is made to remove your people and equipment."

Kirk couldn't help frowning. Obviously, the Empyreans' xenophobic policies were unchanged. On top of that, President March made it sound like the Empyreans had already made up their minds to boot the Federation off their world. *Fine and dandy,* Kirk thought. *Their planet, their choice. But then why bother with the charade of "negotiations"?*

Rousseau spoke up. "Madam President, surely there's no harm in—"

"I'm sorry, gentlemen," March said, politely but firmly cutting off his mild protest, "these conditions are nonnegotiable."

"In that case," Kirk said, "Ambassador Rousseau and Dr. McCoy will beam down alone, say, in thirty minutes?"

"That would be fine, Captain Kirk. Sorry we won't get to meet in person."

He had a feeling she didn't mean it. "Another time, perhaps," Kirk said with a diplomatic smile.

"Perhaps but, under the circumstances, not likely. March out."

She disappeared from the viewscreen, replaced by the standard orbital view of the planet below. Kirk swiveled toward Spock and Rousseau standing behind him. "Unfriendly and cordial all at once. A consummate diplomat."

"It's not that the Empyreans are unfriendly, Captain," Rousseau said. "Not consciously anyway. But after a century and a half, their policies on contacts with outsiders are more like an article of faith. It's the foundation of their whole society, not something easily changed."

"Yet, they made exceptions when your ship originally encountered them," Spock said.

Rousseau nodded. "Serendipity. We just happened to find them at a time when they were considering opening up their society. During the four months we were here, there was talk of not just tolerating the presence of outsiders, but actively welcoming them."

"An attitude that was apparently short-lived," said Spock.

"Conservatism won out, I'm afraid. That's how the personnel at the science outpost wound up completely segregated from the Empyreans."

"So what's your evaluation, Mr. Ambassador?" Kirk asked, sounding less than hopeful himself. "Is there any real chance they'll renew this agreement?"

Rousseau grinned broadly. "You know the first thing I learned when I switched careers? Diplomats *always* think there's a chance. Only a cockeyed optimist could walk into a room, stand between sworn enemies who would love nothing more than leaping over the table to slit their opponents' throats—and see common ground."

Chapter Five

"Y'RE SENDIN' ME *where* t' do *what?*"

"You heard me, Mr. Scott," Kirk said as his chief engineer stared at him. Scotty looked genuinely offended. "The Empyreans have made it clear they want us to be ready to remove the science outpost at a moment's notice. But they're only letting us send two people down to size up the job. The logical choices— you should pardon the expression—are Mr. Spock and you."

Scott continued staring without saying a word. The low, rhythmic *thrummm* of the engine room sounded like a heartbeat, filling the uncomfortable verbal silence. Finally, the Scotsman shook his head with a grimace of distaste.

"I s'pose we're goin' to have t' deal with some o' their genetically perfected technical types," he said, not bothering to disguise the sarcasm in his voice. He turned and walked toward his office, with Kirk following.

45

"Some interaction will be necessary, I assume. But based on what we've seen so far, I wouldn't think you'd be working hand in hand with hoards of Empyreans. They seem to want minimal direct contact with us."

Scott muttered a Gaelic oath. "Well, isn't that just like 'em, avoidin' us like we've got the plague. Of all the ill-mannered, rude—"

"I thought you *wanted* to have as little to do with them as possible."

"I *do,* sir," Scott said indignantly. "I just want it to be *my* idea—not *theirs!*"

"You still love the transporter as much as you used to?"

McCoy gave Ambassador Rousseau a sidelong glance. "Does an alligator chomp in the swamp?"

Rousseau chuckled as the two men entered the *Enterprise* transporter room. "Bones, if ever there was a fellow *not* cut out for a life in space, it's you. I thought you'd retire years ago and set up a little country practice in Georgia like your daddy."

"What, and waste all my natural charm on one planet?"

They took their places on the transporter pads. Rousseau nodded to the ensign handling the console. "Energize."

They materialized in the middle of a series of formal gardens that covered the hillside leading up to the presidential mansion. Lush geometric beds of flowers surrounded diamond-patterned walkways of perfect brick and slate, with immaculately trimmed hedges guarding the garden's perimeter. Sweet floral fragrances hung in the soft summer air. The branches of four towering oaks met in the center of the gardens, forming a cool canopy over benches and a fountain.

McCoy looked up at the wispy clouds decorating

the blue sky and took a deep breath. "Smells a lot like home, Mark."

"This place is as beautiful as I remember it."

So was Elizabeth, McCoy thought.

As they moved through the gardens and up the gently sloping path, they caught the faint sounds of music drifting on the current of the breeze, barely discernable from the music of the wind itself as it whispered through the trees. As they got closer to the house, the music grew more distinct: elegant arpeggios tumbling down the hill.

McCoy and Rousseau paused in their approach, waiting on the white gravel path just outside a domed solarium with its doors open to the gardens. From there, they could see inside where, among an array of colorful plants and small potted trees, a dark-haired young woman sat playing classical guitar. A tall man with long silver hair stood over her, watching and listening critically. Though his stance made it clear he was her teacher, not her audience, it was just as obvious that he was enraptured by her playing.

Bent forward, she cradled the instrument like a lover, her fingers caressing the six strings, magically drawing forth a melodic cascade worthy of an orchestra. The curves of her back and arms and legs blended with the contours of the guitar's shimmering amber body. Her concentration was complete.

McCoy and Rousseau listened at the open doorway, spellbound by her performance. Her fingers flew and danced over the strings as her tempo quickened. Her head bobbed in matching rhythm, and the emotions in the melody shaped her face as she and her music flowed toward crescendo and climax. Then, with a flourish of fingers, she was done.

After a moment of silence, both she and her teacher snapped their heads around, startled by the sound of applause from the garden doors. The teacher looked annoyed by the intrusion, but the young woman recovered her poise and bowed her head in gracious acknowledgment as McCoy and Rousseau entered the sunroom.

"I see you've met my daughter," said a familiar voice from another doorway that led to a corridor and the rest of the mansion. They all looked up to see Elizabeth March coming in.

"Not formally, President March," Rousseau said.

Elizabeth approached and stood beside her daughter. The resemblance was unmistakable—the same lustrous, dark hair and shade of skin, the same strong features and glittering intelligence in their eyes. "Anna, this is Ambassador Mark Rousseau and Dr. Leonard McCoy."

"My stealthy but appreciative audience," Anna said with a sly smile.

Clements scowled. "The music apparently compelled them to sneak up on us."

"We didn't sneak up on anybody," McCoy said, scowling right back. "We were listening, and we didn't want to disturb the performance."

"Your presence on our planet is a disturbance all by itself," Clements retorted.

"And *your* presence is our pleasure, Anna," Rousseau said, deftly turning the conversation away from political confrontation. He took hold of her hand and gave it a courtly kiss.

"Even *he* never played that well," McCoy said.

"I admit it, Doctor," Rousseau said. "You do play magnificently, Anna. Was that a Mozart piece transposed for guitar?"

"Actually, Anna wrote it," the silver-haired man huffed.

"This is Anna's music teacher, Clements," Elizabeth said. "He's also our leading forensic investigator."

"And about as much of a diplomat as I am," McCoy

quipped. Then he looked at Clements with an inquiring tilt of his head. "Forensic investigation? As in criminal forensics?"

"Some—and unexplained medical cases," Clements said.

McCoy glanced from Clements to Elizabeth. "Genetically perfected and you've still got crimes to investigate?"

"We don't claim to be perfect, Doctor—just better," Clements said in a tight voice. He picked up his guitar case and nodded curtly toward the visitors. "I hope your stay is pleasant—and brief." With that, he turned and left through the garden doors.

"You're a talented composer, Anna," Rousseau said as the girl wiped her strings with a cloth and laid the guitar in its case like a mother putting her baby in its cradle.

"Thank you, Ambassador Rousseau, but I'm not so accomplished as you might think. I wrote this piece for a recital competition last month."

"You must've won," McCoy said.

Anna's mouth curled into a self-mocking smile. "I finished ninety-third out of a hundred and twenty entrants."

Elizabeth hugged her daughter. "She may be remarkable by Earth standards, but here on Nova Empyrea, she's just average." Elizabeth's remark was neither boastful nor deprecating, just matter-of-fact.

"Ah, yes," Rousseau said. "A better breed of human."

Elizabeth released her daughter and propelled her toward the door with a gentle push. "Now, you have studying to do and we have a treaty to discuss, so if you'll excuse us . . ."

Anna looked like she'd rather stay, but she grudgingly picked up her guitar case and turned toward McCoy and Rousseau. In that moment, she seemed less like a perfected product of genetic management and more like any teenager longing to be part of the adult world, told instead to go to her room and do her homework.

"Well, the president has spoken," she said with a tinge of adolescent sarcasm. "Perhaps I'll see you later, before you leave Empyrea."

"We'd like that," McCoy said. "That is, if it's okay with 'the president.'"

"If we get a chance, I'd love to play a duet," Rousseau said.

"Show-off," McCoy muttered.

Anna smiled. "I'd like that."

"Stop flirting, Anna," Elizabeth scolded.

"Yes, Mother," Anna said with a world-weary roll of her eyes.

She left, and Elizabeth ushered both men toward wicker furniture clustered in a corner of the solarium. "In case you couldn't tell, she's my pride and joy."

"No surprise there," McCoy said. "How old is she?"

"She's just turning eighteen."

McCoy did a veiled double take, thinking he saw the vaguest flicker of apprehension in President March's eyes. Was it something to do with her daughter? Or just the strain of having to deal with this science outpost business?

He couldn't be certain, but her heart didn't seem to be in these Empyrean efforts to terminate the colony's limited flirtation with the Federation. He wondered what planetary politics were behind the Council's decision. Should he ask? Elizabeth and Mark were making small talk, the diplomat's way of sidling toward touchy subjects.

Who am I to interrupt? Then again, I'm obviously not here for my statesmanship . . .

"Are you in favor of getting rid of this outpost?" he blurted.

The question caught Elizabeth off balance. "Uhh, the Council has—"

McCoy shook his head. "I'm not talking about the Council. I mean you, personally."

Rousseau shot him a warning look. "Leonard—"

"No, I want to know. Is there anything wrong with asking straight out?"

"No," she said, "there isn't."

McCoy grinned. "Good. I hate gettin' tangled up in all the diplomatic niceties—"

"No chance of that," Rousseau mumbled darkly.

"The Council and I speak with one voice on this, Doctor."

That didn't sound very convincing, McCoy thought with a frown. *So much for my experiment with the direct approach.*

Chapter Six

THE FEDERATION's ground-based observatory complex perched on the flat top of Mount Placidus, a round-shouldered peak overlooking the colony's main city. The observatory consisted of a trio of domed structures, along with a microwave transceiver array on a thirty-meter-high tower.

Per Kirk's agreement with the Empyrean leader, Spock and Scott beamed down to begin their survey work, materializing in the outpost's small lobby.

With its gray-slab walls, indirect lighting, and absence of sound, the observatory felt cool and tomblike. There weren't even any plants to brighten up the place. It scarcely seemed that anyone had ever occupied the complex, much less operated and inhabited it for the past eighteen years.

For the sake of the outpost's personnel, Scott hoped their living quarters were more homey than this section. "It looks deserted," he said as he slipped his equipment bag off his shoulder and set it down on the hard, cold floor. "Didn't they know we were comin'?"

"That is *why* it's deserted," said a frosty voice from behind them.

They turned to see a typically tall Empyrean man walking toward them. He was in his early thirties, as gracefully muscled as a racehorse, and his features seemed to be a felicitous mix of racial characteristics.

"I don't understand," Scott said, sizing up the man. "Where's the observatory staff? We were told there're a dozen scientists assigned here."

"I'm Dr. Ramon Ortega," the man said. "I'm your outpost liaison. The Federation staff has been sent to the Isolation Center. It's standard procedure when an Empyrean visits the observatory—part of the antifraternization statutes that have been in effect ever since the outpost became operational."

"Now *there's* a lovely thought," Scott said, not even trying to conceal his sarcasm.

With vague contempt showing in his narrowed eyes and pursed lips, Ortega looked from one officer to the other, as if measuring their obvious defects. He dismissed Scott with a glance and then turned his attention toward Spock.

"You're the first Vulcan we've ever encountered, Commander Spock. I understand your physical and intellectual evolution places you on a level above the average Terran—perhaps even equal to us in many ways."

Spock met Ortega's interest with a neutral gaze. "I am unaware of any such empirical comparison between Vulcans and contemporary *Homo sapiens*. In any event, it would be academically irrelevant. Terrans and Vulcans possess variant characteristics— some inherent, some adaptive—but neither species is demonstrably superior. In fact, I am half human and half Vulcan."

"Oh?" Ortega's eyebrows rose. The revelation seemed to further pique his interest. "Composite lineage. Planned and supervised, of course, considering Vulcans' reputed devotion to science and logic."

"Actually, Dr. Ortega, my combined heredity was neither planned nor supervised. Although my father must have deemed his marital union to have logical value, my human mother was guided by feelings of affection and admiration for my father. Her choice was predicated upon emotion, not logic."

Ortega's fascination abruptly diminished. "So it's merely a case of *impure* lineage. Random genetic combination?"

"So I would conclude."

If Scott hadn't known better, he'd have sworn that Spock was baiting the Empyrean scientist. But Ortega didn't seem to notice.

"How unfortunate," Ortega said disdainfully. "Well, then, if you'll follow me, we can get started."

Scott and Spock lagged back a couple of strides and the engineer leaned close to one pointed Vulcan ear. "Looks like so-called genetic perfection hasn't done away with the occasional horse's ass."

"A cogent observation, Mr. Scott, if I understand the reference."

"That y' do, sir."

Kirk was not at all pleased to learn that the members of the Federation observatory staff were being detained off-site. In fact, he was damned annoyed. Though it was his job to be sympathetic to what he might consider to be assorted cultural oddities of other worlds—and he'd run across some pretty outlandish alien customs in his travels—he found the Empyreans' obsessive separatism increasingly irritating.

There was something downright infuriating about humans, genetically perfected or otherwise, having such institutionalized prohibitions against so much as laying eyes upon other humans (or allied aliens) just because they came from other planets. For a culture constructed upon such elaborate scientific foundations, he couldn't find a shred of rationality underlying their rabid segregation.

However, Kirk's feelings were irrelevant, and he knew it. It wasn't his place to tell the Empyreans what he thought of them or how to conduct their affairs. But the least he could do—and probably the most, as well—would be to liberate the Federation group from their confinement. Immediately after Spock's check-in report, Kirk had Uhura establish contact with President March, interrupting her session with Ambassador Rousseau and Dr. McCoy.

"It's not like they've been thrown in a dungeon, Captain," President March said once she knew why he'd called. "The Isolation Center is as comfortable as their regular quarters, and they've been following this procedure for years."

"Well, I'd like to offer them alternate accommodations aboard my ship until this treaty renewal is settled one way or the other, if that's all right with you."

"I certainly have no objection. As I said, they're not prisoners—"

"They're just not at liberty to move about freely," Kirk said, his disapproval quite clear.

"That's right, Captain," March countered. "That's the way things are. Feel free to contact the Isolation Center directly and make your offer. If Dr. Skloff and any of his staff would rather spend their downtime on the *Enterprise,* that's fine with us. Is that all, Captain?"

"Yes. Thank you, President March. Kirk out."

Kirk's face had barely faded from the viewscreen on the president's desk when Mark Rousseau's passionate rumble of a voice filled the silence in March's office.

"There's got to be something I can say to change your mind about this treaty," he implored.

"I doubt it," President March said from across her desk. By now, they'd moved their talks to her private office in the mansion, where McCoy and Rousseau sat in a pair of highbacked chairs. Gossamer abstract sculptures of crystal and metallic filament stood on the credenza behind her. A rainbow of plants abloom with flowers filled a large bay window looking out over other gardens.

"I can't accept that, President March. Think of the promise we saw blossoming eighteen years ago. Isn't it worth another effort to nurture that hope by renewing this treaty?"

Elizabeth sighed. "The Council apparently doesn't think so. The Empyrean way is a separate way. You already know that."

McCoy shook his head, waving one hand up toward the sky. "Isolation from all that variety of life out there? How can that possibly benefit Empyrea? Lord knows I don't always understand the Vulcans and their infernal logic, but they've got this belief: infinite diversity in infinite combinations. And I've been roaming the galaxy long enough to know there's a lot of good in that idea."

But President March was clearly unmoved. "Someday, maybe we'll subscribe to that belief, too. But before we do, we want to give ourselves every opportunity to perfect what we are, to develop every attainable advantage before we interact with all that diverse life."

"Then I'm afraid you've got a long road ahead of you, President March," McCoy said. "Life forms are inherently imperfect."

"We don't agree. But even if that's true, there are degrees of near perfection. We believe the highest degree is worth pursuit, without the genetic and cultural distractions that come along with intrusions from the outside."

"So it's up to your Council, then," Rousseau said.

Elizabeth nodded. "If you want to pursue this to the bitter end, feel free to write up a formal proposal, Ambassador. I'll present it for a vote."

Rousseau nodded. "I never give up till the last dog dies. You'll have our proposal by the end of the day tomorrow. Is that soon enough?"

She nodded and stood. "That'll be fine. But, as I said, don't be surprised at the outcome."

"Well . . . I guess that's that," McCoy said, taking his communicator out. "We'll be in touch as soon as Ambassador Rousseau's ready. McCoy to *Enterprise*, two to beam up."

"Uhh, Doctor," Elizabeth said hastily, "would you mind staying behind for a few minutes? I don't want to keep the ambassador from starting on his proposal, but there's another matter—a medical matter—I'd like to discuss with you."

McCoy shrugged. "No, I don't mind. *Enterprise*, make that one to beam up; Ambassador Rousseau. I'll be up in a little while."

The transporter officer acknowledged McCoy's request, then beamed Rousseau back to the ship. Elizabeth waited until the last sparkle of molecular disintegration had faded. Then her businesslike expression softened, and she approached McCoy as a woman instead of as an official.

He watched, more than a little confused as she moved closer. He had no idea what she was about to do.

"I didn't know how it would feel to see you again, Leonard."

"And?"

She smiled. "It feels good." She touched his cheek with one slender finger.

He swallowed, trying not to respond. "Beth, what's this all about?"

"Can't I just be happy to see you?"

Despite his best efforts to retain some professional reserve, he gave a boyish shrug. "I guess."

Impulsively, she put her arms around him and rested her chin on his shoulder, as if putting down a longtime burden. With conscious ambivalence, he returned the embrace.

What the hell is going on here?

"I really never thought we'd see each other again. But I'm glad you're here, Leonard."

"And exactly why *am* I here, Beth?"

"Beth," she repeated softly. "No one's called me that since you left."

As she looked directly into his eyes, he found a mixture of worry and relief in hers. He also found her gaze to be just as hypnotic and unsettling as it had been eighteen years before. He struggled to maintain a semblance of equilibrium as he felt her warm breath against his neck.

"Why am I here?" he asked again.

She responded by brushing her lips against his. Then she kissed him, and he returned the passion. When they parted, his voice came out as a husky whisper.

"Not that I should be lookin' gift horses in the mouth at my age," he said, clearing his throat, "but nobody needed me on this trip for my negotiating skills. And, much as I'd like to believe it, I don't think you brought me all the way here for an illicit kiss. So . . . why am I here?"

"Because I need you." She looked away, as if flinching from a painful truth. When she looked back at him again, there was urgency in her eyes. "I need your help. Thanks to my poor judgment, Anna's freedom is in danger . . . maybe even her life."

"Why? What's wrong? Is she sick?"

58

She took a step back and a deep breath, then squared her shoulders. "Empyrean laws absolutely forbid . . . procreation . . . with anyone who's not from our world."

"I know they used to—"

"We never changed those laws."

"Anna's father—?"

Elizabeth's eyes flickered closed for a moment of what seemed like shame. Then her gaze found his again. "He was not Empyrean."

McCoy's eyebrows rose in surprise. For all their enlightenment in other areas, he was well aware of how completely the Empyreans believed in their chosen path. But he didn't know the specifics of the colony's legal code and could only imagine what the consequences might be. "Does she know?"

Elizabeth shook her head. "No one does. I've kept this dirty little secret all her life. But it's about to be revealed, and I won't be able to stop it. I'm sure to be dismissed as president. Anna and I could both be banished from Empyrea"—her voice wavered— "even executed."

"Can't you get in touch with her father? Is he one of the Federation scientists? I'm sure he'd help if he could."

"That's what I'm hoping," she said, clenching and unclenching her jaw, trying to keep control of her fears. "That's why you're here, Leonard. That's why I asked for you to come."

"Me? What can I do?" He really had no clue at all.

She shrugged helplessly. "I don't know. But . . ." Her voice shrank to a whisper. "You see . . . *you* are Anna's father."

Chapter Seven

THROUGH GLASSY EYES, McCoy stared at nothing for what seemed like several of the longest, most excruciating hours of his life. In truth, it wasn't more than a few seconds before he managed to croak his first response: *"Me?"*

"You," she said, nodding somewhat sadly.

Was that sadness for him? For her? Or for Anna? As he wondered, it dawned on him that he was part of a dilemma the scope of which he had only just begun to comprehend.

He groped for the seat he knew to be somewhere behind him. Relying on more than a little blind faith, he sat without looking and actually managed to hit the chair. *OhmygodOhmygodOhmygod* . . . He squeezed his eyes shut as reflexive denial flooded his brain. *This is impossible—it couldn't be—there must be some mistake! What if it is true? What am I supposed to do? What've I gotten myself into?*

"Beth, how could this have happened?"

"You're a doctor," she said dryly. "Don't they teach you that in medical school?"

"Very funny." It wasn't at all funny. "It was a long time ago, but I'd *swear* you said you were using birth control."

"*I* never swore," she said, mildly insulted.

"Maybe not, but you obviously did *lie*." *Lie* was a loaded word, and McCoy used it deliberately. He wanted to see just how defensive she might be.

"Well . . . yes," she admitted with a sheepish shrug. "I did."

"Good God, Beth," he moaned. "If I'd known, I never would've—"

"I knew that. That's why I lied."

He blinked in confusion.

She knelt in front of him. "What are you thinking?"

He took several deep breaths, trying to collect some semblance of comprehensible cognition. "How I've just gone from having one daughter I *knew about* but hardly *knew* to having a second one I never knew about at *all*." He couldn't help thinking that probably made more sense before he said it out loud.

"I didn't know you had a child."

"I did, before I met you—from a marriage that crashed and burned before I went into Starfleet."

"Is that *why* you joined Starfleet?"

"The modern equivalent of running off to join the French Foreign Legion, I guess. Joanna was just a toddler when I left. After that, I pretty much stayed out of her life for a long time."

"By choice?"

He nodded.

"Why?"

"I figured she'd be better off without me." Without a father who not only wasn't going to be around to see her grow up—*Hell, I wasn't even gonna be anywhere*

61

near the planet—but who additionally and firmly believed he had no idea whatsoever about how to *be* a parent.

"How did your ex-wife feel about that decision?"

"She never tried all that hard to change my mind," he said with a short laugh, hollowed by bitterness. "To say I bungled my one intentional pass at fatherhood would be one of the great understatements of the twenty-third century—maybe the millenium." For the moment, at least, he knew the sadness in Beth's eyes was for him.

"Did you ever get back in touch with her?"

"My wife? Or my daughter?"

"Your daughter."

"Funny thing about that. I bounced around Starfleet for quite a while—ship to ship, one assignment to another, par for the course. I'd send Joanna birthday cards and small gifts every year, but I never let her know where I was. I didn't want her to even have the option of getting in touch with me. It would've been too hard—"

Elizabeth gave him a dubious look. "On her or you?"

He shrugged. "Probably me. Then, a few years ago—it was toward the end of my first five-year tour of duty on the *Enterprise*—I got a letter from her."

"She tracked you down?"

"Yeah, through Starfleet. It was her eighteenth birthday, and she'd just graduated from high school. She was on her way to college . . ."

. . . And that seemed like enough of a milestone for her to try and break the silence . . .

Dr. McCoy sat in his quarters, watching the self-assured young woman talking to him on his desktop viewscreen. He knew he couldn't talk back to the prerecorded message, but he wanted to. It was the first image he'd seen of Joanna since her tenth birthday.

His ex-wife had offered to send photos on a regular basis, but he'd asked her not to. Knowing his daughter was navigating life without him was painful enough, even if he was certain that was best for her. But seeing pictures of her changing and growing—that would have been more than he could bear.

Yet, now that this unexpected letter had arrived, he found himself filled with more pride than regret as he saw the woman she was becoming. She looked very much like her mother had at the same age, but there was a balanced serenity neither of Joanna's parents had ever possessed. *Now where the devil did that come from?*

". . . I'm not sure what I want to be yet, Dad," Joanna said with a thoughtful expression. "I thought that would scare me, that I'd be in big trouble if I didn't have my mind made up by college. Instead, it's only a few weeks away and I'm excited about it. I think it'll be fun to dabble a little bit before I make any decisions."

On the viewscreen, Joanna scrunched her face up as if something forgotten had just popped into her head. It was the same expression she'd made as a little girl, and McCoy blinked back the dampness he felt welling up in his eyes.

"Oh, yeah," Joanna continued, trapping the errant afterthought. "I just wanted you to know I thought about sending you a graduation invitation. But I knew you wouldn't have been able to make it, since the *Enterprise* was nowhere near home. So I figured, why make you feel bad?"

"How *did* you feel?" Elizabeth March asked as she handed McCoy a drink of fruit juice.

"Well, at first I was a little hurt. But she was right—there was no way I could've been there. And it's not like I deserved to be included. So I realized she'd made the right decision, not telling me about it till it was too late for me to feel lousy about missing it. And that was how I discovered that Joanna had more diplomatic common sense than both of her parents combined."

"Did you see her after that?"

"Matter of fact, I did. Near the end of her letter, she asked me to visit her at school when I came back to Earth. She told me she'd long since come to terms with our fractured family, and she said she forgave me for all the times she'd wished her father had been there to hug her . . . or scold her . . . or laugh with her . . . or cry with her."

He felt the sting of remembrance in his nose, and he struggled to keep the tears from starting up again as they'd done when he'd first watched Joanna's letter. "Last thing she said was how she wanted her own children to know their grandfather."

With a wisdom McCoy doubted he had now, much less at the tender age of eighteen, Joanna had offered him a second chance.

Elizabeth's eyes were glistening too. "So, what happened?"

"Well, not too long after that, the *Enterprise* went back to Earth for a stem-to-stern refit. I got reassigned to shore duty, and I got up the nerve to take her up on that invitation. It was kind of strange at first, really getting to know each other for the first time, but she made it easier than I ever could have.

"Then I left Starfleet for a couple of years, and we got to make up for some of that lost time—at least as much as that's possible. And I do plan for those theoretical grandkids to know their granddaddy. I mean, she's my only daughter"—he stopped and swallowed—"at least she *was,* until now."

He shook his head to clear it, averting his eyes. If he had new responsibilities to face, here on Nova Empyrea, he had no intention of running from them. But there were so many questions careening around his mind, and he had to ask them, no matter how painful or uncomfortable they might make Elizabeth.

If he was going to be a father—whatever that might mean in this situation—he had a right to know. He looked right at her. "Beth, you were a deputy health minister. You knew as well as anyone the sanctions you'd face, having a child who wasn't pure Empyrean."

She nodded. "You're right. I did."

The more she said, the more bewildered he became. "I don't understand. Is my genetically nonperfected brain missing something here?"

It was Elizabeth's turn to take a deep breath and gather her thoughts. "When your ship first found us, we were probably just another lost colony to you. Am I right?"

"It's not like we bumped into lost colonies every other day."

"But finding us it didn't completely alter your view of the universe, did it?"

"No, I suppose not." McCoy grinned. "Although that first night with you came pretty close."

She gave him a look of weary tolerance, like a mother with a frisky child. "That's not what I meant."

"I know."

"Do you? I'm not sure that's possible. You and your crewmates from the *Feynman* were the first living Outsiders I'd ever laid eyes on. It's one thing to be part of a civilization that's too primitive to know about intelligent life on other worlds. We *knew* other societies were out there—we just couldn't have anything to do with them . . ."

. . . until you came along. Those were strange times for us, Leonard. A lot of young people had doubts about Empyrea's policy of self-imposed isolation. When our leaders let you transport down and actually work with us . . . well, that was pretty close to a miracle.

Dr. McCoy looked up from his microscope when Elizabeth March burst into the lab. They'd been working together for the better part of two weeks now—enough time for him to master the nervous fluttering in his stomach and the clammy palms that developed every time he saw her. *Well, almost enough time.*

In truth, they'd been too busy when they were together for him to give much thought to romantic feelings. *Never mind the fact that I've got no idea why in heaven's name she'd be interested in me anyway* . . .

At this point, he didn't know how long the *U.S.S. Feynman* might be staying around Nova Empyrea, and the scientific data on the colony's genetic management history were as copious as they were fascinating, so he'd made a conscious decision to focus on work. To get the most scientific knowledge out of this encounter, distractions had to be kept to a minimum.

Lord knows Elizabeth March would be one hell of a distraction . . .

Instead, he channeled his feelings into establishing a cordial, respectful, and thoroughly professional relationship with her. However she may have felt, that seemed to meet with her approval. And they'd been working well together, sharing their passion for science and nothing more.

But now, here she was, rushing toward him like a romping puppy, nearly bowling him over as she threw her arms around his neck, her words tumbling out. "There's going to be a treaty!"

He inched his face back for a better look at her glowing smile and luminous eyes. This was a face he didn't mind having in close proximity to his own. "What're you talking about?"

"Your Federation wants to set up an astronomical observatory here, and our government's agreed to negotiate!" As if suddenly struck by the impropriety of what she'd done, she blushed and released her hold on McCoy. Then she stepped back, smoothed her clothing, and averted her eyes. "I—I'm sorry, Doctor. I didn't mean to—I mean, I just heard, and I—"

He smiled, trying to be more reassuring than awkward and probably failing miserably. "No harm done. Glad to hear the good news. I just hope it doesn't fall through."

Her expression clouded. "Why would you say something like that? Have you heard something?"

"No, no, not at all. It's just that it would mean quite a change in the Empyrean way of doing things."

"That's not impossible, you know," she huffed. Then she cleared her throat and slipped demurely into the seat next to his at the multiterminal computer console where he'd been studying data on genetic variations within the Empyrean population. "Well, I guess we should get back to work."

"I guess so," he nodded, easing back into his chair, trying to cover his nervousness. Her reaction to the news of a potential treaty surprised him. And now, he could kick himself for deflating her enthusiasm. There was a palpable chill at their console as they reached simultaneously for a data disk and accidentally brushed hands.

"Sorry," he mumbled.

"Excuse me."

"My fault."

"No problem."

Then, silence. They worked wordlessly for several minutes, both making a conscious effort to keep their eyes on their individual work stations, without so much as a stolen glance at each other.

Elizabeth relented first, her gaze flickering at him from beneath her long, dark eyelashes. "Once the treaty is signed, do you think you might stay?"

"Hadn't really thought about it," he said, without looking back at her.

Then, more silence. He turned slightly to get out of

his chair at the same moment as she turned toward him. They both flinched to avoid a collision.

"Sorry," he said. This time, though, he looked at her.

As if summoned by silent signal, he leaned closer. This time, she didn't flinch. Their lips touched in a brief, tentative kiss.

"Should we be doing this?" she asked a moment later.

"I don't know. Only if we want to, I guess."

"Do we?"

They kissed again with slightly more pressure and longer duration. "Apparently, we do," he said.

The third kiss lasted much longer.

"I'd never met anyone like you, Leonard," Elizabeth said.

"I'm hardly anybody's idea of exotic."

"But that's *exactly* what you were—you and everybody from your ship. You were the answer to the prayers of a little girl who desperately wanted her world to change, who grew up dreaming about embracing all the infinite possibilities *out there,* beyond our 'Great Wall of China.'"

"Did you really think our relationship could last? I never said I was going to stay here."

"I know you didn't. But that didn't matter to me. Lots of us believed things were about to change for the first time since our society began here. We saw new freedoms just around the corner, and they *were* intoxicating. I thought a child born of those changes and freedoms would be a symbol."

"But your leaders apparently didn't share that intoxication."

She sighed, remembering the crushing disappointment when the hopeful flame lighting the way toward a different kind of future got snuffed out. "The conservatives won. I couldn't believe they'd let an

opportunity like that slip away. Such a limited treaty
. . . nothing had changed. You were gone. And I was
pregnant."

"But you decided to go ahead and have the child."

Elizabeth nodded. "It took a lot of soul-searching. I
knew I'd have to keep her origin a secret. Maybe it
would've been easier to stop the pregnancy. I had the
time. It wasn't a child yet, just an idea, what might
have been. One night, I was lying awake, thinking, and
that's when I knew."

"Knew what?"

"Even if no one else could ever share what I felt,
Anna would still be a symbol to me, a reminder every
day of our lives that there was always hope for
change."

McCoy's eyes narrowed. "I don't get it. You did
what you did back then, but here you are, leading a
government that's dead set against the kind of change
you say you always wanted."

"And you're wondering what happened to that
young dreamer." She looked into his eyes and sighed.
When she spoke, her voice came out soft and sad.
"She became president . . . and found out that
dreams get lost along the way."

"Lost for good?"

She shook her head. "I don't know."

"How did you keep anybody else from finding out
the truth about Anna?"

"It wasn't that hard. I had access to all the files, so I
just falsified the important records. I listed the Genetic Bank as Anna's paternal source. That didn't raise
any questions, since lots of women use the bank for
artificial insemination." She gave a shrug of resignation, her shoulders sagging under the weight of eighteen years of deception. "After that, it was easy
enough. All I had to do was commit Empyrea's most
serious crime: genetic fraud."

Chapter Eight

KIRK MADE A POINT to be present in the transporter room, along with Chekov, when the Federation scientists beamed up in two groups of six. The outpost's director, Dr. Linden Skloff, was a burly man of about sixty, with an avuncular grin and shoulders stooped from years hunched over lab consoles. At the head of the first group, he loped down the steps of the transporter chamber and greeted Kirk with a robust handshake. His five colleagues followed, arrayed respectfully behind him.

"Welcome aboard," Kirk said as the remaining six scientists materialized.

"Thanks for having us, Captain," Skloff said. "Wondered if I'd still have my space legs after fifteen years."

"You haven't been off Empyrea in fifteen years?"

"That's right. Not this high up anyway. Never any further than our little space platform. Yep, I've done hard time," Skloff said with a twinkle. "Not every-

70

body in our little group's been here as long. But I haven't minded."

"Well, we want you to consider the *Enterprise* your R-and-R stop for the next couple of days, until you either go back to Empyrea or go home if that treaty isn't renewed. Mr. Chekov will show you to your guest quarters and fill you in on shipboard facilities. Make yourselves at home. If, however, at any time, you'd prefer to return to the Isolation Center, just let us know and we'll be happy to beam you down."

Chekov gestured toward the opening door. "Right this way."

"Dr. Skloff," Kirk said quietly.

He stopped and turned. "Captain?"

"Would you mind staying for a minute?"

"Something on your mind?"

"As a matter of fact, I've got a few questions."

"Fire away."

Kirk squinted at the older man. "Fifteen years?"

"You seem quite amazed by that, Captain Kirk," Skloff chuckled. "Sometimes I'm amazed by it myself."

"Haven't you found it—I don't know—*frustrating* to be kept apart from Empyrean society?"

Skloff mulled the question for a few moments, giving his choice of words careful consideration. "Not frustrating so much. More like disappointing. I knew the setup when I came here. Kept hoping things would ease up. Never did. The Empyreans are a stiff-necked bunch."

"I think I'd feel like a prisoner."

"There's some of that," Skloff admitted. "But there's a big difference. The Federation team's all here voluntarily. Confined to that compound, but free to leave the planet any time a supply ship comes."

"Sounds limited, at best," Kirk said.

"The compound's got most of the comforts of home. Don't get me wrong. I think the Empyreans have a lot to offer the galaxy, and I know we have a lot to offer them."

"But they don't see it that way."

"Nope, they don't. But I'm just an ol' astrophysicist. Never claimed to be a diplomat. Not a social sciences fella. But this is such an unusual stellar binary. Well, the work's been enough to keep me happy. Still got a lot to learn." He paused for a moment. "Anything else you wanted to know, Captain?"

"Just one thing—this Dr. Ortega. You've worked with him?"

Skloff made a sour face. "Yes, indeedy. He's a bit of a—well, not to be too diplomatic about about it—"

"You just said you never claimed to be a diplomat" Kirk said helpfully.

"That's right. And Ortega never claimed to be a horse's ass, but sometimes he is."

A rueful smile crossed Kirk's lips. "So I've heard."

Without looking away from his computer screen, Dr. Ortega waved his hand dismissively over his shoulder. "You, Engineer, go get the—"

"The tricorder's right here," Scott said, reaching over from the adjacent console to hand the device to Ortega.

Without lifting a hand to take it, the Empyrean turned slowly, giving Scott a frosty glare. "That's not what I wanted, Engineer. I wanted you to bring me my cup of tea. I left it over on the diagnostic console."

Scott withdrew the proffered tricorder, clenching his teeth. "Why can't y'get your own tea, laddie?"

"A—You are closer, and B—you are not contributing anything significant to this phase of our analysis."

"Not contributing anything!" Scott exploded as he jumped to his feet. "Of all the—"

"Here is your tea, Dr. Ortega," Spock said, smoothly sliding the half-filled fine China cup onto the

Empyrean's console. Then he hooked a hand under Scott's arm. "Mr. Scott, may I confer with you?"

"I'll give you a conference," Scott sputtered. But he couldn't shake free of Spock's iron grip, and he gave up after a momentary tug. He knew he had no choice but to follow Spock across the room, where the Vulcan sat and pretended to enter some data into a terminal.

"Mr. Scott," Spock said quietly, "your reaction to Dr. Ortega's provocations is not constructive."

"Not constructive!" Scott hissed through clenched teeth, barely able to contain his anger. "Ever since we got here, he's been treatin' me like I'm some sort o' menial servant and you like an inferior freak o' nature—*sir!*"

"Your pique is quite understandable, and I too find his attitude objectionable. However, we are here to accomplish certain tasks—"

"So we're just supposed t' grin and bear all his insults?"

"In a word, Mr. Scott, yes . . . unpleasant as that may be. We are unlikely to reverse Dr. Ortega's fundamental prejudices in our encounters with him. At best, we can devote our efforts to making the duration of those encounters as mercifully brief as possible."

Scott noticed the brittle tone in Spock's voice. Controlled as they were, even Vulcans were not completely immune to irritation. "He's gettin' t' you, too."

"I do not know what you mean, Mr. Scott," Spock said with deliberate neutrality.

"Aye, sir," Scott said. "Enough said. I'll try to keep my temper until I can get back t' the ship and put Dr. Ortega's face up on a shootin' gallery target."

"A worthwhile suggestion."

Scott couldn't help grinning. Ever since Spock's mind-blowing journey through the vast penetralia of the machine-being V'ger a couple of years earlier, he had seemingly become much more at ease with himself and with the concept of humor. Scott doubted he'd ever live to see Spock belly-laughing or even cracking an obvious smile, but the Vulcan first officer no longer viewed the occasional dry comment as an inappropriate sign of weakness or betrayal of dreaded emotion. On the whole, it made Spock considerably more pleasant to be around.

"I've found a problem requiring your attention," Ortega announced from across the room.

Scott sighed, reminding himself of the promise he'd just made to Spock and swallowing unspoken a comment that could at best be called discourteous. "What's that, Doctor?"

"There are fluctuations in the plasma flow. Sensors are detecting it here and here." He pointed to a couple of conduits on the system diagram glowing on his computer screen. "That means excess strain on the power-transfer couplings."

"I know what it means," Scott snapped, his patience thinning.

Spock was already calling up the pertinent data on his computer monitor with a speed that Scott proudly noted exceeded Ortega's genetically enhanced abilities. "Curious," Spock murmured. "And potentially troublesome."

"It had better *not* be," said Ortega. "No delays in the dismantling of this outpost will be tolerated."

"The rejection of the treaty renewal is not a foregone conclusion," Spock said.

Scott leaned over Spock's shoulder, then pecked at the keypad. "This complex has a self-contained power source."

"Of course it does," Ortega said.

"Of *course,*" Scott echoed sarcastically, drawing a cautionary glance from Spock. "No integration with anything Empyrean, no threat o' cross-cultural contamination."

The chief engineer ran through a series of technical schematics, then let out a derisive snort. "How quaint. This whole power generation system's built around a Sternn fusion core."

"So? That's state of the art for a system of this generating capacity. We've refined it over and over."

"State o' the art? Maybe seventy-five years ago it was. They musta stopped usin' these beasties altogether in the Federation when I was just a wee bairn."

"Stopped using them? Why?"

"Because we found somethin' better. Apparently . . . you haven't."

"Well, maybe your Federation gave up on the Sternn core more quickly than it should have."

"I doubt that, Doctor."

"This technology has served our needs quite well."

"Aye. I'm sure it has," Scott said, his sarcasm undisguised. So much for the conversational truce Spock had requested.

"It's proven technology—reliable, efficient, expandable—*perfectible*. It isn't always necessary to reinvent the wheel."

As he opened his mouth to launch another technical taunt, Scott noticed Spock's severe look—a nonverbal rebuke if ever there was one. Solely out of respect for his senior officer, Scotty backed down, but he couldn't resist muttering, "Aye, stick with the square wheel y've got."

Ortega glanced up over at him. "What was that, Mr. Scott?"

"Nothin', Doctor. Nothin' at all. Whatever's wrong with this old girl, I'm sure we'll have it taken care of in two shakes."

Ortega pushed back from his console and stood. "You'd better. The treaty's fate may not be a foregone conclusion, but I wouldn't bet a wooden nickel on renewal. All Federation equipment is to be removed as soon that official decision is made."

"We'd better take care o' this? What about you an' y'r staff?" Scott said, glancing toward Spock, then glaring at the Empyrean scientist.

"This *is* a Federation outpost. It's *your* responsibility, not ours. Diagnose the problem, and correct it."

That eliminated what little was left of Scott's peaceable resolve. *"Correct* it?! Look, *Doctor,* you've been treatin' us like servants since we walked in that door—"

"Have I?" Ortega interrupted with a mildness so disarming that it made Scott stutter to a stop in midtirade. "I meant no disrespect. It's just that we Empyreans are accustomed to perfection. And while you may be an exceedingly competent engineer, Mr. Scott, you are clearly not up to our genetic standards through no fault of your own. And as for you, Mr. Spock, well, genetic hybridization *is* what it *is.* I can hardly be expected to ignore the obvious, now can I?"

All Scott could do was stare, balling his fists as his face reddened with slow-burning rage, repeating to himself: *I will not clean his chronometer. I will not clean his chronometer* . . .

By nature or design, Ortega seemed oblivious to Scott's change of complexion. He approached the two Starfleet officers and patted Scott on the shoulder. "Good. I'm glad you understand it's nothing personal. Now, do get on with this diagnostic work, there's a good fellow." And he left the lab.

Scott took a deep breath, then let it out very slowly through gritted teeth. "Y'know I'm not one for ribbons, medals, and parades, sir—"

Spock nodded. "But you do deserve a commendation for admirable restraint."

McCoy looked up at the darkening sky splashed with scarlet, purple, and gold. "That's not a genetically perfected sunset, is it?" he asked dryly as he walked with Elizabeth March through the gardens outside her presidential mansion.

"No. We don't take any credit for that." Then, after a droll pause: "But we *are* genetically better able to *appreciate* it."

He knew she was kidding, but he had to wonder how much of good taste *might* in fact be genetically based. He'd been to few places that were more beautiful than the Empyrean colony, with its mix of architecture and landscaping that always managed to be harmonious without also being bland.

This section of the gardens overflowed with flowers of all sizes, shapes, and colors, not at all orderly in the style of a formal garden, yet far less random than a field of wildflowers.

"So, this is your retreat?"

"I guess you could say that. It's my other pride and joy—"

"After Anna."

She nodded with a wry chuckle. "You know how life has a way of getting away from us."

"I've had the feeling once or twice."

Elizabeth bent over to pluck a multicolor blossom with broad petals. She slipped the stem through her hair and set the flower just over one ear. "I come here, and I feel like there's someplace I have at least *some* control. I've developed fifty-seven new hybrids."

"Genetics isn't an exact science, though."

"That's true. Sometimes, I'm not at all sure what I'm going to wind up with. Raising a child isn't an exact science either, even without some self-created sword of Damocles hanging over us. But seeing Anna grow up . . . that made up for all the anxiety. There were days I almost stopped dreading her eighteenth birthday."

They stopped and sat on a gracefully curved park bench. "What happens at eighteen?"

"When Empyrean children are born, they're given a routine screening to register their genome and certify genetic perfection."

"Even under the most controlled reproductive circumstances, mutations pop up. What if they're *not* born genetically perfect?"

"Those with imperfections are sterilized."

McCoy's mouth tightened with disapproval. "Lovely."

"You make it sound cruel. It's not, and it's not like that happens very often," she said defensively. "The rest are given a genetic brand that identifies them at the cellular level as being the offspring of an Empyrean mother—and it also blocks reproductive activity."

"Hmm . . . birth control at birth. Till what age?"

"Eighteen. Empyreans aren't permitted to have children until then. When they reach eighteen, they have another scan to make sure no new genetic defects have cropped up. If they pass, the reproductive inhibitor is overridden."

"I don't get it," McCoy said with a thoughtful frown. "If Anna's not genetically pure, how did she pass the postbirth scan?"

"She didn't. I falsified those results, too. But there wasn't any way to encode her cells with my genetic brand—"

"And now she's turning eighteen and she's facing her reproductive certification scan?"

"Which I can't fake, and she can't pass. And that's when she'll be revealed as a genetic illegal." Anna closed her eyes and took a deep, calming breath. "I haven't raised her all these years just to have her disgraced and banished. Execution is even a possibility, depending on the whim of the court."

"I didn't know genetically perfect people have judicial whims." As soon as McCoy said it, he was sorry. This wasn't the time for a dig at Empyrean society. When Elizabeth looked at him, he saw the hurt in her eyes and the determination.

"When your ship left here eighteen years ago, while I waited for Anna to be born, I made a promise to myself and to her. I didn't want her to face the same frustration and disappointment I did. I wanted her world to be different. I wanted to reach a level of power here where I could *make* things different. I haven't worked this hard to get where I am just to throw all that accomplishment away, to throw my *life* away."

Her intensity didn't surprise him, but it did unsettle him. He was still trying to assimilate the concept that Anna was his child. He didn't know how much more he could handle, and he didn't know what she might ask of him. "There's nothing I can do about all that. What's done is done."

"I'm not asking you to change the past, Leonard. I'm asking you to change the future."

"How?"

"By taking Anna away from Nova Empyrea aboard your ship."

He scrambled to his feet. "Now hold on a minute," he protested. "The *Enterprise* isn't *my* ship! I've got a captain to answer to, not to mention Starfleet and the Federation! And I'm in no position to take care of a child."

"Anna's not a child—she'd be an adult if she stayed here, and she'd be an adult if she leaves."

"I don't care how genetically perfected she is, Beth. She's still going to need a parent for guidance, and I don't know if I'd be much good at that."

"You underestimate us. I assure you, you won't have to 'take care' of her."

"I don't know that I can dismiss my paternal responsibilities all that easily. Besides, aren't people going to wonder why Anna just up and disappeared?"

Howard Weinstein

"No one needs to know the details. And I can manage the aftermath. Whatever happens, it'll be better than what's going to happen if she stays. You'll be saving her from the indignity of a hearing and a sentence, and you're the *only* one who can do that."

For several moments, all he could do was shake his head in time to the rhythm of the doubts bubbling through his thoughts. "I don't know if I can, Beth."

She stood and took his hand, clasping it between hers. "I know I've just dumped a huge weight onto your shoulders. I'm not asking for any promises, Leonard."

"That's good, 'cause I can't give you any."

"But you'll try," she said. It wasn't exactly a question; it was more like a plea.

"I'll try." He took out his communicator and flipped it open, relieved to hear the familiar electronic chirp. "McCoy to *Enterprise*—one to beam up."

Chapter Nine

WITH ITS BRICK AND STONE paths and patios, its display
coves with wood and stone benches, and tall, shelter-
ing trees, the statue garden had long been Anna's
favorite retreat. The statues themselves, set in eclectic
groupings ranging from classical to abstract, had all
been crafted by Empyreans. The benches were arranged so that visitors could either look directly at the
artworks or simply sit among them.

For Anna, no matter what her mood, the statue
garden was a place where she always felt at home.
When she wanted to be alone, it was the perfect place
to find solitude. When she needed to have a heart-to-
heart confessional with a dear friend, they could sit
cross-legged on a bench, facing each other under the
outstretched tubular form that looked to Anna like a
leaping panther.

She knew there were other nooks where lovers met
and embraced, though she had yet to come here for a
romantic rendezvous of her own. And when she

wanted to get together with a group of her best pals to laugh or sing or argue about whatever was on their minds, this was where they would meet.

Perched halfway up a gently inclined hillside, the statue garden hugged the natural contour of the slope. Curving around the hill as it did, it was one of the few vantage points to offer views of both the city to the north and the seashore to the east.

Today, as daylight faded into a comfortably warm evening, Anna found four of her friends at their usual place, clustered around a small campfire burning in an open stone hearth. There was Paolo, with his fierce dark eyes and flashing smile.

And Eleni and Alexei, both fair, resembling each other enough to pass as brother and sister. That impression was quickly erased by the fact that their limbs seemed to be habitually entwined, more or less passionately depending on where they were and whom they were with. Among friends, they were joyfully uninhibited, and everyone was certain they would spend the rest of their lives together raising a boatload of willowy towheaded children.

And moody Ethan, with his unruly mop of chestnut hair and a face too regal and serious for someone not yet eighteen and his unsettling habit of asking one question too many, no matter what the subject. He'd always been that way, and Anna had known him longer than any of the rest of their group of friends, since she'd been enrolled in the same art class with him at age six. She could still remember him—at six—arguing with their teacher about the merits of realism versus abstract art.

By the time Anna made her way up to the seaside overlook, the others had already been there long enough to begin their ritual of sharing a bottle of wine, a couple of long loaves of bread, and the assortment of homemade jams Paolo made as a hobby. They were also well into the debate of the day. Anna was not surprised to find the pending treaty negotiations with the Federation to be the chosen topic.

"—I mean, the Great Empyrean Experiment hasn't exactly crumbled since those Federation people came here," Alexei was saying as Anna joined them. He acknowledged her arrival with a wave.

Paolo, always assuming the role of host no matter where they gathered, already had a cup of wine and a hunk of bread ready for her. She took them and sat on one of the blankets laid on the grass without interrupting Alexei's continuing statement.

"They've been here as long as we've been alive. Just because the old people are scared of anything Outside, that's no reason to go back to the way things were before."

Eleni spoke up. "Do you really think the old people are afraid?"

"Don't you? Of *course* they are," Ethan said, his jaw taut with resentment. "They're afraid of anything not written in stone like the Ten Commandments. They're afraid of anything new and different. They prove it every day, don't they? Aren't we just prisoners on this planet?"

Paolo continued munching on his bread, as if unwilling to let Ethan's intensity spoil the pleasant evening. "Does that mean you want to leave, Ethan?"

"I didn't say I *wanted* to leave. I'd just like to have some choices. Curiosity shouldn't be a crime, should it?"

"It's hardly a crime."

"I don't know about that, Paolo," Eleni said. "It almost got me into big trouble once."

Paolo eyebrows arched. "Oh?"

Eleni glanced around at her friends, then looked down, signaling uncertainty. Paolo leaned forward, pouring some more wine for her. "Come on, Eleni. You can't tease us like that. Is this some deep, dark secret?"

"It *was.*"

"Even from me?" Alexei asked, looking hurt.

Eleni nodded solemnly. "I've never told anyone— not even you, Anna." She took a deep breath, held it for a moment, then let it out in one quick puff, like a reluctant bather unable to avoid a headlong leap into the deep end of a cold pool. "When I was twelve, I snuck into the Federation compound."

Eyes widened in disbelief. Eleni found everyone staring at her.

"You?!" Paolo hooted. "You never broke a rule in your life!"

Jarred by her revelation, Alexei frowned at her like she was a stranger. "Why would you sneak in there?"

She shrugged. "I told you . . . I was curious. They were from Outside, these mysterious people, and I wanted to meet them."

"How did you get in?" Anna asked, fascinated.

"It wasn't as hard as you think. It was drummed into our heads that we were supposed to stay away from there. So we *did.* But I made a discovery: When nobody *expects* you to do something, they don't actually try all that hard to *keep* you from doing it."

Anna leaned closer, overcome by her own curiosity, especially now that she'd met Dr. McCoy and Ambassador Rousseau. For as long as she could remember, Anna had wondered what those people in the mountaintop complex were like. It was almost unbelievable that mousey Eleni, best known for being inseparably attached to her boyfriend, had done something Anna had long fantasized about doing herself. "What happened once you got in?"

"Well, I wandered around the grounds a little bit. I guess I was a little afraid of actually going *inside* the buildings. Nobody knew I was there yet. I even thought about just leaving before anybody could catch me."

"What happened then?"

Eleni smiled at the memory. "Somebody caught me."

"My God! You must've been *terrified,*" Anna said.

"Not really. The man who found me was, well, *gorgeous,*" Eleni said with a playful waggle of her eyebrows.

Anna smirked. Paolo, Alexei, and Ethan pursed their lips in disapproval, and Eleni glared at them. "You boys are so predictably *vain.* Like nobody who's not Empyrean can be gorgeous?"

The young men exchanged glances of alliance. Alexei seemed most threatened, so he voiced their unified response. "Possible, maybe . . . but not *likely.*"

"Well, he was this big, bearded *bear* of a man," Eleni continued, doing what she could to aggravate the boys' discomfort. "His name was Jacob Simon. I fell in love with him instantly." She turned sweetly to see Alexei squirm.

Anna played along, trying to hide her smirk, continuing what had become a sort of interview. "So what did he do?"

"He took me inside. The administrator in charge wanted to turn me over to the government. *That* was when I *really* got scared. I imagined all these punishments and tortures. I *begged* Jacob to help me."

"Did he?" Anna noticed that the boys pretended to be indifferent.

Eleni nodded. "At the last minute. He asked them to let me go out the way I came in and not tell anybody I'd been there. And that's what they finally decided to do."

"What were they like?" Ethan asked, trying not to sound too interested.

"Well, they were *different.*"

"From us?"

Eleni nodded again. "And from each other. Some were fatter, some thinner. Some weren't very tall. A couple of the men were bald."

"So," said Alexei, "you're saying they weren't as perfect as we are."

She gave him a sardonic look. "Perfection isn't always perfect."

"What's *that* supposed to mean?"

"Figure it out."

"Hey, hey," Paolo said, waving his hands like a referee. "We're getting off the topic. So, did you ever do it again?"

"No."

"Did you ever see Mr. Bearded Bear again?" Alexei asked, baiting her.

"No. Though I still *want* to."

Alexei looked alarmed and more than a little threatened. "You do? Why?"

"Because they know things we don't. If they're still here when I'm done with school—if Jacob's still here—I'd jump at the chance to work with them."

Paolo waved his hand in a dismissive gesture at odds with the genial expression on his face. It was one of those times Anna didn't know what to make of him and wondered if he was as nice as he seemed. "Oh, Eleni," he said, "they couldn't possibly know anything we don't know. They're—well, let's be honest—compared to us, they're *flawed.*"

Ethan's simmering anger flared. "Sometimes you're such an idiot, Paolo. If we're so perfect, we shouldn't be afraid of stuff that's Outside."

Paolo's amiable grin faded, and he stood up, looming over Ethan. *"That's* idiocy. There are plenty of reasons to keep Outside out, and they've got nothing to do with being afraid."

Now Ethan got to his feet and they argued face-to-face, voices rising with each exchange. "There's only one reason: *fear!* And it's stupid—"

"It's not stupid to protect ourselves—"

"Isn't it stupid to duck challenges and avoid diversity? With everything I'm learning about science, I'd like to apply my ideas and talents to a wider world than one little planet."

"We've already *got* plenty of diversity. We don't need the insanity and warfare and physical defects that Outsiders pass around the galaxy like some virus!"

"Empyrea was a good idea that's going bad—"

"You better watch who hears you say that," Paolo warned.

"If you think I'm going to live my life afraid of who might not like what I've got to say—"

"Ethan's got a point," Alexei said suddenly, absorbing Paolo's accusing look. "Things are going to be different when our generation starts running this world." He stopped as abruptly as he'd started when Paolo and Ethan *both* turned to stare at him like he was several kinds of fool.

"Unfortunately," Ethan said, "they're *not* going to be any different when we're in charge. This treaty is going to be rejected, and that'll be that."

"I'll drink to that," Paolo said, hoisting his cup with a mean smile.

But Ethan shook his head in disgust and, without another word, stalked off down the dark path. Alexei took off after him, skipping sideways as he turned back toward Eleni. "I can't let him go like that. I'll see you at your house later. Okay?"

"Go," Eleni said as she stood next to Anna.

Quite satisfied with the outcome of the argument, Paolo knelt on the ground, packing up the refreshments in his basket. "It would be interesting to see who'll be right about the future—except I *know* it won't be Ethan. Can I walk you two home?"

"No, thanks, Paolo," Anna said. "We'll see you in school tomorrow."

Eleni and Anna left him behind and headed down the path, walking in silence for quite a while. They stopped when they reached an overlook and leaned on the stone wall, watching the moonlit waves rolling onto the beach a few hundred feet beneath them.

"He's madly in love with you, you know," Eleni said, without preamble.

The flat statement caught Anna off guard. She blinked a couple of times, trying to figure out who and what Eleni was talking about. *"Paolo?"*

"No, silly," Eleni said with a pained expression. "Ethan."

That didn't make any more sense to Anna. "Ethan?"

"Ethan."

"I don't think so, Eleni. Ethan and I have always been best friends, but . . . no. You're wrong about him."

"You obviously don't notice the way he looks at you."

"He *doesn't* look at me. He doesn't look at *anybody* lately, unless he's arguing with them."

"That's exactly what I mean. He *doesn't* look at you *differently* than he doesn't look at anybody else."

Anna stared at her friend. "Maybe it's hormonal, but you're starting to make less and less sense when you and Alexei aren't joined at the hip or some other body part."

"Suit yourself, Anna," Eleni said with a shrug. "But if you haven't noticed, you're the *only* one."

Anna watched a whitecap foaming in the moonlight, tracking it from its most distant visible point all the way to its crashing end on the sand and rocks below. "Even if you're right, I don't know. Ethan is just too dark. Those moods! He's always going on about something."

"He's always been like that. It's never stopped you from being friends with him."

"There's a big difference between being friends and, well, you know." She couldn't even say the word.

But Eleni could. "Lovers."

Anna pretended she hadn't heard it. "I don't know if I could stand being around all that intensity all the time. Could you?"

"He's passionate. It could be exciting, especially the first few times."

The blush warming Anna's face made it clear she knew exactly knew what Eleni meant. And she chose not to reply, but only partly out of embarrassment— and partly because the notion did have some appeal. There was another long wave-watching silence. Then: "Eleni, you're crazy."

"Maybe."

"Come on. Let's go home."

Chapter Ten

"WELL?" McCOY PROMPTED. *"Say* something already."

Kirk stood at his cabin window, his back toward McCoy, who sat patiently in a soft chair. But he could see McCoy's reflection as the doctor waited behind him. "Like what?"

"Hell, I don't know. Congratulate me on my sperm motility."

Kirk had just been told about McCoy's revelatory visit with Elizabeth March. In all honesty, he had no idea what to say, how to react. He turned to face his friend with a shrug. "Congratulations on your sperm motility. This must've been a hell of a shock for you—I know it is for *me.*"

"I should've told you about this in my quarters, not yours."

"Why? Some kind of weird protocol?"

"No. I've got a better liquor selection. And I could really use a drink about now." McCoy leaned back and rubbed his eyes. It was the end of a long and very tiring day; he'd managed to get past wishing it had never happened. Now he just wanted it to be over. "I can see you're having a hard time making sense of all this."

"I don't know, Bones. I've had my share of youthful flings around the galaxy."

"I know—I witnessed most of them. But this wasn't just a youthful fling, Jim."

"What? You were planning to stay on Empyrea eighteen years ago?"

"Probably not. I don't know. Maybe. It didn't matter. I wound up not having that choice." He sighed and shook his head. "Who knows, maybe it was temporary insanity. The wounds from my marriage hadn't healed. And Beth March had this—this *magnetism,* this eagerness to connect with somebody from anyplace *but* Nova Empyrea. And, boy, did we ever connect."

"That's obvious," Kirk said, not without sympathy. "The question is, what do we do about it?"

"We?"

"Of course. I'm not going to let you go through this alone."

McCoy responded with a weak smile. "I appreciate that, Jim."

"First question: Do you want to stay out of this, or do you want to help?"

"Of *course* I want to help!"

Kirk raised a cautionary finger. "Fools rush in, Bones. Think about it: You're not under any ethical or moral obligation. Other than the obvious and unwitting contribution, you didn't create this . . . situation. Elizabeth March did that, all on her own."

"Anna's not a 'situation,' she's a child. And there's no reason she should suffer for the sins of the mother, not if there's something I can do to help."

"*We* can do."

"We," McCoy said, accepting the correction. "Are *we* going to run aground of the Prime Directive on this?"

"You mean, if you take Anna away on the *Enterprise?*"

"Yeah."

Kirk formulated a careful reply. "Well, you know I believe in a . . . *flexible* . . . interpretation of the Prime Directive."

"I've noticed. So what does your flexible interpretation tell you in this case?"

"I think that taking Anna and keeping the March family skeleton in the closet doesn't have any significant effect on the natural development of Empyrean society or culture. It's not like this is some primitive civilization without knowledge of spaceflight or life on other planets."

"I take it that means I've got your blessing?"

"If you want it—if you *really* want to get involved in this—you've got it, Bones."

"I *am* involved, Jim. How can I run off without at least trying to help?"

"So what're you going to do?"

"Go back down there and tell Beth I'll take Anna with us when the ship leaves Empyrea."

"Not that I want to throw any *more* monkey wrenches into the works," Kirk said slowly, "but do either of you know if Anna is *willing* to leave?"

McCoy stared, feeling like a complete dunce. Tossed as he'd been by the day's emotional maelstrom, that question had never even occurred to him. He'd been too busy searching his own soul. But Kirk had asked a key question, and McCoy needed to learn the answer. One thing he did know, and it scared the hell out of him: *You can't save somebody if they won't grab the lifeline.*

* * *

92

"What do you mean, you don't know?" McCoy faced Elizabeth March, his face furrowed by an incredulous frown.

"Leonard, how *could* I know? It's never come up over breakfast: 'Say, Anna, just supposing I committed genetic fraud and your father was some guy from another planet and *wasn't* syringe 112-B from the reproductive bank, how would you feel about escaping from Nova Empyrea before we get caught and both get thrown into prison, banished, or executed?'"

McCoy shied away from her glare as he realized she was right. "Well, there's only way to find out. We've got to tell her the whole story and see how she feels."

Elizabeth sighed. Her shoulders slouched as she faced up to a moment she'd dreaded for eighteen years. "So I guess you're not willing to knock her out with a surprise sedative, beam her up, and have her wake up when the *Enterprise* is several hundred light-years from here?"

"That wouldn't be my first choice, no."

"I didn't think so." Elizabeth closed her eyes for a moment. "Will you be there when I tell her?"

"If you want me to."

She reached over and clutched his hand in hers. "Then let's get this over with."

They found Anna alone in the dark sunroom, playing a melancholy piece on her guitar to the accompaniment of night sounds drifting in through the open windows. With McCoy standing by in silent support, Elizabeth sat with her daughter on the wicker sofa and told her the truth. No embellishments, no excuses.

Maybe it simply becomes easier to say hard things the second time around. Whatever the reason, McCoy admired the way Elizabeth said what she had to say without hesitation or apology. As he listened, he realized that she had regained her balance and drawn on admirable reserves of strength to get through this. And he found himself increasingly concerned with Anna's reaction.

He watched her closely, looking for signs. He watched her eyes, her mouth, her posture. But he saw nothing obvious to indicate whether she was stunned or disappointed or angry or ashamed. Or just numbed. Was she aware of his scrutiny and trying to hide her feelings? Considering the magnitude of what her mother was telling her, was it humanly possible for her to absorb that much of a jolt and still maintain an unnatural poise?

Empyrean or not, she was just an eighteen-year-old kid. The foundations of her existence were being shattered. The darkest of worries and fears filled McCoy's head and fluttered in his stomach. *Can she handle this?*

And then Elizabeth was done. The revelations were complete. They waited for Anna to say something. But she sat there in silence, her breathing calm and even. McCoy felt like asking if she understood all of it—the past and the present, the causes and consequences of what he and Beth had done. But he was certain she did understand, and he felt less uncomfortable following Elizabeth's lead. Beth knew her own daughter. He didn't. He kept his mouth shut.

"So," Anna finally said, still calm, "now that you've told me all this, what am I supposed to do?"

"If you go away with Dr. McCoy, you won't have to face the worst."

"Is it my choice?"

"Anna, there *is* no choice."

Anna suddenly jumped up, her face flushing with rising anger. "You had a choice! You made it before I was born—before I was *conceived*—and you stole *my* choices at the same time!"

"I'm sorry—"

But before Elizabeth could get past those two words, Anna rushed from the room, leaving her mother and McCoy in the void no words could fill. The sounds of the night outside seemed unbearably loud.

"Well," Elizabeth eventually whispered, "that didn't go too well."

"Can you blame her?"

Beth rubbed her eyes. "I guess not. I kind of hoped she'd be stronger, take it in stride."

"Would you have taken it in stride if you were her?"

"Enhanced emotional stability *is* part of the Empyrean character," she said, avoiding the question.

"Give the girl a break," McCoy said as he sat down next to her. "Don't forget, she's got my imperfect chromosomes, too. She needs some time."

"Time is something we don't have a lot of. She's going to have to accept her fate—and be on that starship of yours when it leaves."

McCoy knew the question that Elizabeth did not want to hear. He also knew it had to be asked. "What if Anna doesn't agree?"

"I don't agree at all," Ethan said flatly, "not one bit." He and Anna sat on the carpeted floor of the library's circular atrium that formed the open core of the ten-story research complex. They leaned back against the top-floor railing, ignoring the elevator car dropping down the transparent tube behind them. From there, they had a clear view of the large windows that overlooked the rest of the university campus.

"That doesn't surprise me," Anna teased. "You never did know anything about musical composition."

"Then why did you ask me?" He squinted at her, trying to see through her playful facade.

"Maybe I just wanted to see how predictable you are."

"Oh? And how predictable *am* I?"

"Well, for one thing, I knew exactly where I'd find you at this time of night."

"Okay, then," he countered, "speaking of predictability, you are *never* anywhere *near* the library at what you call this time of night."

"But I am tonight. So maybe I'm not as predictable as you think."

"You are," Ethan said with a dismissive wave of his hand.

Anna flashed a challenging half smile. "You think you're so smart. What *would* I be doing if I wasn't here?"

"Sitting by yourself in that sunroom of yours, playing your guitar or maybe the piano or your cello."

The look of surprise on her face made it obvious he was right. "How do you know?"

"Sometimes I walk by your house . . . and listen."

"You do? I never saw you."

"That's the general idea. I don't mean to bother you or interrupt." He looked away, his voice softening. "I just like to hear you play, even if I *don't* know anything about musical composition."

Anna looked at him for a lingering moment, searching for something to help her understand him, finding him looking back with much the same purpose. Then she got up and walked over to the window and watched the lights twinkling on the paths and roads below. She waited for Ethan to join her, hoped he would. After a few moments, he did.

"Ethan . . . what would you think if one of our friends turned out to be . . . genetically illegal?"

He cocked his head. "Huh?"

"Not pure Empyrean."

"Hmm!" His eyebrows went up as he pondered her question, which seemed to come out of nowhere and catch him genuinely off guard.

She watched his eyes. This one of the few times she

could recall when Ethan did not have a ready response, even if it was just to volley back with a question of his own. He'd become so serious lately—even cynical—and now she saw something quite different in those eyes: a sense of wonder and amazement, as if she'd pointed a spotlight into some shadowed corner of his psyche. Instead of being upset by this unexpected illumination, he seemed intoxicated.

"Forbidden love with an Outsider . . ."

His sentence fragment made her frown. It was her turn to be surprised: He sounded like a dated, old romance novel. Quite without seeking it, she'd uncovered a previously unknown facet of his personality. She wasn't at all sure she liked it. It just wasn't *him.* "What about it?" she prompted with a bit more impatience than she'd intended.

"Well, I never really thought about it . . . I mean, living with a secret like that. Would this person have known his heritage while he was growing up?"

"Speaking hypothetically, of course—"

"Of course."

"No, she—I mean, *he*—just finds out as an adult. Maybe at our age."

"Do you know something about somebody?"

"No!"

"Then what suddenly made you think about this?"

She looked away from him, nibbling her lower lip as she watched a vehicle driving slowly past the library. "Nothing. I mean, something . . . what Eleni told us today."

"You mean about sneaking into the Federation compound?"

"If she could do it, who's to say an adult couldn't have done it—"

"And had an affair with one of the Federation scientists?"

Anna nodded. "It's possible. Isn't it?"

"Well, I guess so. But Eleni's innocent little adventure happened when she was barely twelve. That's a lot different than an adult getting pregnant by an Outsider and having that child. An adult would know the consequences, an adult would know she couldn't keep that secret forever. Wouldn't she?"

He looked directly into her eyes. This time, she couldn't look away, though she wanted to and tried to. *Does he know? Can he tell?*

"Yes, an adult would know," she said. "But I'm not talking about the mother. I'm talking about the child. What would you think of him?"

"If something like this actually happened? It wouldn't be his fault. I certainly wouldn't hold it against him. In fact, I'd think of him as a symbol of all the possibilities for variety, all the choices *we* don't get just because we're Empyreans locked into this prison planet."

Ethan's habitual contentiousness had edged back into his voice. Anna found that comforting. She let him go on.

"It *is* possible an Empyrean could've mated with an Outsider or could someday if it hasn't happened already. That's exactly why the conservatives want to close down that science complex: to make sure it *doesn't* happen *ever*. And you know what scares me the most?"

"What?"

"If your little hypothetical forbidden romance *did* happen and the secret came out now, that would be the worst possible thing. It would play right into the old geezers' hands, give 'em just the ammunition they need to shut down negotiations with the Federation— hell, those talks are just for show anyway—it's already a foregone conclusion—"

"Ethan, maybe it isn't."

"And it'll be a hundred years—*more*—before any Empyrean leader even *thinks* about opening contact with Outsiders again."

"Don't you think some of our leaders really want that treaty renewed?"

He looked at her sadly. "No."

Ethan stayed to continue studying. By the time Anna left the library, it was well past midnight and the campus streets were deserted. She walked alone, his pessimistic words still going around and around in her head. She tried to think of an argument to counterbalance what he'd said, but she couldn't.

In all probability, he was right. If the truth of her origin came out now, the conservative backlash would seal the fate of the limited Empyrean experiment. Not only would the Federation outpost be shut down, but it *would* be generations before another Empyrean government might scare up the nerve to try anything like it again.

Maybe it would *never* happen again.

And maybe her mother was right. Maybe she had no choice.

When Anna got back to the presidential mansion, she found McCoy and Elizabeth still there, still awake. Unsure of how he should behave toward Anna, McCoy stood by as her mother greeted her with a prolonged hug.

"I was worried about you," Elizabeth said softly.

"I'm sorry I ran out like that." Anna shrugged. "I didn't know what else to do."

"I was just making some tea for us. You want some?"

Anna nodded. She and McCoy followed Elizabeth into the sunroom, where a lamp cast a gentle halo of light in the midst of darkness. They sat around a small table while Elizabeth filled delicate cups with the steaming, sweetly aromatic herbal tea.

"I never knew you were such a rebel, Mother."

Both McCoy and Elizabeth were relieved to see Anna smiling.

"You approve of that?" Elizabeth asked.

"As a matter of fact, I do. Maybe that's why I ran. It's not easy finding out that your government-issue mother used to break all the rules."

Elizabeth raised a dissenting hand. "Now wait a minute. I didn't break *all* the rules—"

"But you sure broke the *biggest* rule."

"Well, I guess I did that." Then her smile faded. "If I hadn't, I wouldn't have you. Or, at least, I'd have a different you. So I can't say I'm sorry, but now we're paying the price for what I did."

"I know."

McCoy let out a breath, trying to relax. "We knew we had to tell you the truth, but we were worried that you wouldn't be able to handle it. That was quite a bombshell we dropped on you."

"I'm okay—" She paused awkwardly just before saying the word *doctor.* "I'm not sure what to call you. *Doctor* seems kind of formal. Dad? Daddy? Father?" She spread her hands, surrendering to the uncertainty of the situation.

McCoy smiled, trying to put her at ease. "Leonard'll do just fine."

"Besides, you two will have plenty of opportunity to work all that out."

"That's right," McCoy agreed. "As soon as we get to the *Enterprise,* I'll call some friends back on Earth and see what we can do about getting you into a university."

Anna's expression darkened. "Uhh, Leonard, Mother, there's something—"

"Wouldn't want all that genetically perfected intellect gathering cobwebs," McCoy continued. But there was something about the look in Anna's eyes that made his voice trail off. "I'm sorry, Anna, I didn't mean to jump the gun."

"No, I'm the one who should be sorry," Anna said. "Sometimes I just assume that people can read my mind, which is ridiculous."

"Ahh," McCoy kidded, "a flaw! That'll help you fit in with us *un*perfected folks back on Earth."

"I'm not going back to Earth."

McCoy and Elizabeth both stared as if they hadn't heard what she'd said or as if they'd *wished* they hadn't.

Elizabeth spoke first. "Anna, we thought you agreed. It's the only choice we have."

"No, Mother, it *isn't*. Empyrea is my home. I haven't done anything wrong—"

"No, *I* did," Elizabeth said.

"No, you *didn't*. You fell in love and had a baby. That shouldn't be wrong, no matter where my father was from. I'm staying here, no matter what the consequences."

Elizabeth tried to squelch the sick feeling rising in the pit of her stomach. "Anna, you can't—"

"Mother," Anna interrupted, "let me say what I have to say. Maybe it's genetic, but I've got the same feelings about our isolation that you had when you were my age. Here we are, the best human beings who've ever existed and what does our government do? It keeps us bottled up like some experimental curiosities too fragile to be let out of the lab where we were born. I resent that!" She swung her arm up toward the sky. "We should be out there, helping the rest of humanity reach its full potential the way we have."

Elizabeth held her daughter's shoulders, gazing directly into her eyes. "Anna, sweetie, I agree with you. In the best of all possible worlds, you'd *be* out there. But this is the *real* world, and we Empyreans aren't as perfect as we'd like to think."

"*Your* generation isn't. But mine wants to be different, and we *will* be. You had the guts to tell me the truth. Now I have to do the same thing for you. There's a growing underground of young people—nothing formal, yet, though that's just a matter of time. We're going to change this society."

"Are you talking about some kind of revolution?" McCoy asked, wondering if genetically perfected humans still carried the all-too-human penchant for violence.

"In a way, but not what you're thinking. We're not going to shoot our way to the future. We *are* the future—it's only a matter of time until we take over Empyrea. Our weapon is patience. As we become the leaders, we'll make those changes."

McCoy glanced at Elizabeth, visibly impressed. Maybe there *was* something to this genetic perfection stuff. "She's got a point. Sooner or later, her generation's going to be running the show."

"But you won't be there to see it happen, Anna. At best, you and I are going to be banished. At worst, well, nobody's ever been convicted of genetic fraud. The court could decide this is the perfect time to make an example out of us—to send a message to every Empyrean that this crime strikes at the heart of who and what we are. They could be compelled to invoke the death penalty."

"Mother, nobody has to know about us."

Elizabeth stared at her. "There's no way to fake the reproductive bioscans."

"Maybe so, but who says I have to take them?"

"What *are* you saying?"

"I'm willing to give up my reproductive rights if that's what it takes to stay here and see this revolution through. If I decline the scans, we'll be able to keep our secret."

"Is that possible?" McCoy asked, feeling more like an outsider than ever.

"It's possible," Elizabeth said, "but there's no record of a healthy Empyrean doing what she's suggesting. Anna's not exactly a low-profile eighteen-year-old. If she skips the scans, people are going to ask questions. Do we compound the old lie with new ones?"

"Why not?" Anna asked with chilly nonchalance. "Why should I care about following the rules of a system that doesn't care about me? If you're so worried about the questions people might ask, then I can just disappear, fake my own death. You can wear black for a while—"

"And what will *you* do?" Elizabeth demanded.

McCoy could hear the desperate quiver of hysteria edging into Elizabeth's voice as Anna's side of the conversation took its radical dive away from what both he and her mother considered to be anything remotely connected with rationality.

"I'll go into hiding. I've got friends who'd jump at the chance to help me do something like this."

"Anna! This is crazy!"

"Oh, as if submitting to the whims of some ossified court is sane?"

"Hold on," McCoy said, wading in before the argument between mother and daughter jumped another quantum leap beyond reasonable. "I'm a doctor, not a sociologist or a lawyer. So I'm not even going to try to make a case based on custom or the Empyrean legal code. But maybe there's a *medical* solution we haven't thought of."

A glimmer of faith appeared in Elizabeth's eyes. "Do you really think so?"

"I don't," Anna said flatly, looking as dubious as her mother looked hopeful.

"Now, I'm not offering any guarantees," McCoy said, looking from one to the other. "But, as my Vulcan friend Mr. Spock is fond of saying, there are always possibilities. All I'm asking for is a little time to figure out what they might be."

Chapter Eleven

JIM KIRK had been called many things in his life and his Starfleet career, not all of them complimentary. But he honestly believed that he had never been labeled a know-it-all. Even as a "positively grim" cadet—self-described, with the benefit of a quarter century of hard-earned wisdom and perspective—he had always tried to maintain enough self-awareness to admit that he could not possibly know the answer to all questions in every discipline.

Despite an unbendable determination to excel in whatever he did, he'd always been secure enough to say "I don't know" when he really didn't. Said to the right people—the ones who *did* in fact know—those three little words signaled his willingness to learn from a variety of mentors more than happy to share their own knowledge with any open-minded pupil who came along.

Kirk had always recalled the advice his dad gave him as he packed to leave Iowa for his first year at

Starfleet Academy: "Don't be afraid to be a sponge. Soak up everything you can." No one had ever given him better advice.

Later on, of course, Kirk had also learned when *not* to make admissions of ignorance. Life as an explorer presented challenges that did not always fit neatly with textbook definitions of ethics. The value of a well-executed bluff could be inestimable, whether in poker or one of the many perilous situations to which he and his ships had been exposed.

From the start, Kirk had seen it as an elementary, nonthreatening fact of life: Other people would always possess information and skills he did not. His early acceptance of that concept served him well once in command. Whatever his flaws as a person and a commander, he had no trouble at all delegating responsibilities to talented officers as confident in their expertise as he was in his own. In their areas of specialty, he'd never found any reason to question Scotty, McCoy, Uhura, or the rest of his seasoned crew.

As for Spock, well, over the years he'd served with Kirk, he had proven countless times that he alone was the equivalent of a shipload of veteran officers. Now, on the *Enterprise* bridge, with the night shift on duty, he and Kirk huddled at the science console for an informal briefing on the problems he and Engineer Scott had found during their examination of the Federation outpost on Empyrea.

After all their time together, this captain and first officer worked with each other so effortlessly that Spock instinctively pitched such briefings with a balance of technical information he knew Kirk would find neither confusingly arcane nor insultingly simple. With a subtle deference to rank and friendship that Kirk appreciated but never commented upon, Spock often left it to his captain to draw and voice the significant conclusion.

"So," Kirk said, "this glitch in the outpost power system is . . . minor?"

"At this point, it appears to have been an isolated malfunction, one that was easily corrected."

"And it was in the fusion reactor at the ground-based facility?"

Spock nodded. "Though the power source on the planet additionally provides energy for the orbital platform as well as for the satellite network."

"Via microwave uplink?"

"That is correct, Captain."

The corners of Kirk's mouth curled into a mischievous smile. "Don't act so surprised, Spock," he teased, knowing full well that Spock hadn't appeared the least bit surprised. "I was paying attention to your briefing."

"I did not mean to imply otherwise."

"Is this problem going to stay isolated and minor?"

"That is our expectation, though a final determination depends on several factors, the analyses of which are not yet complete. Mr. Scott's able staff should have useful results by oh-seven-hundred."

"Okay. Then let's set a meeting in the briefing room—you, me, and Scotty—oh-seven-thirty. Unless something comes up sooner than that."

"Very well, sir. I shall inform Mr. Scott."

"And I'm going to call it a night," Kirk said, already edging toward the turbolift. "It feels like it's been a very long and very strange day."

Because there was no need for Spock to remain on the bridge during his off-duty hours, he stood and moved to the turbolift with Kirk. "I take it you are referring to Dr. McCoy's disclosure?"

The doors slid open and they entered. "Deck five," Kirk said, instructing the control computer. As the doors shut and the pod moved smoothly down the turbolift tube, he shot a guarded glance toward the Vulcan. "You know about that?"

"He informed me upon his return from the planet earlier this evening."

"Oh." Kirk sounded surprised. Though both his best friends had mellowed over the years, their relationship was still a prickly one, and the matter of McCoy's late discovery about Anna March seemed the sort of thing he might keep private. "I would-'ve mentioned it to you," Kirk began a little awkwardly.

Spock rescued him. "I, too, found Dr. McCoy's decision to apprise me of his situation . . . unexpected. He seemed quite interested in any biomedical suggestions I might be able to contribute to his search for a solution to his dilemma."

Kirk's eyebrows rose as the turbolift came to a stop and the doors opened. They stepped out. "He asked you for advice?"

"Indeed," Spock said as they strolled toward Kirk's cabin. "Another unexpected turn of events."

"Sort of the theme of the day," Kirk said with a tired smile. "He must be getting desperate."

"He is."

They arrived at Kirk's door and it opened. "Well, Spock, I guess I'll see you in the morning."

"Technically, it is already morning."

"Don't remind me."

Before Kirk could enter, they heard the whistle of the intercom page and the voice of Lieutenant Lisa Putman, the young woman handling the communications console overnight. "Bridge to Mr. Spock."

Kirk nodded toward the interior of his quarters and Spock accepted the nonverbal invitation. They both crossed to Kirk's desk, where Spock activated the small intercom screen. "Spock here, Lieutenant."

"Sir, we're being hailed by Dr. Ortega, the Empyrean liaison. He insists on speaking with you immediately."

"What's a few more minutes without sleep," Kirk

mumbled in resignation. "Pipe it down here, Lieutenant."

"Aye, Captain."

A moment later, the fresh-scrubbed Putman disappeared from the desktop screen, replaced by Ortega's angry face and peremptory voice. "Commander Spock, I thought you and Engineer Scott were instructed to deal with that plasma flow fluctuation problem right away."

Spock exchanged a glance with the captain. "We did so, Dr. Ortega. At the time of our departure for the *Enterprise,* all readings were nominal."

"Well, they aren't now. Rather than leave this to chance, I did some troubleshooting myself. The source of the problem is, quite clearly, Federation modifications made to the facility-management software."

"Indeed," said Spock mildly. "Are you quite certain of that, Doctor?"

"I am, Commander. If you and your engineer would care to beam down, I'll be happy to show you the program errors. They caused subprocessors controlling four flow regulators to shut down and overrode the safety backups."

"Hmm. Most curious," Spock said in a soft voice, mostly to Kirk. "Very well, Doctor. We shall transport down presently and meet you at the control center. Spock out."

The comm screen winked off.

"If you weren't a Vulcan," Kirk said, "I'd say you looked distinctly unenthusiastic about informing Mr. Scott of this little bit of news."

With typical equanimity, Spock touched the intercom switch again. "Spock to Mr. Scott."

A moment later, Scotty's image appeared on the small screen. He was out of uniform, to be expected at this time of night, but it was obvious he hadn't yet gone to sleep. He wore his Starfleet robe and was seated at his desk. "Aye, sir. Scott here."

"I regret disturbing you at this hour."

"That's all right, sir. I was wide awake."

"Scotty," said Kirk, "you need your beauty sleep."

"Maybe so, Captain, but I've got to keep on my technical journals sometime. A wee nip o' Scotch, a few journal articles, and I sleep like a baby."

Kirk smiled. "Whatever works for you, Scotty. Unfortunately, there's a problem——"

Scott's jaw tightened. "Let me guess. My good friend Dr. Ortega called."

"A logical deduction," Spock said. "He claims he has discovered errors in Federation-originated software——"

"And he's blamin' the plasma flow malfunctions on *that?* Of all the bogus——"

"Mr. Scott," Kirk said quickly, preempting a lengthy streak of Gaelic cursing, "go take a look——and try not to throttle Dr. Ortega."

Scott exhaled a simmering breath. "Aye, sir. Scott out."

"Spock," Kirk said, "Scotty's pride notwithstanding, could Ortega be right?"

"It is possible, Captain," Spock said after a moment of thought. "Federation scientists are certainly capable of error——as are the Empyreans, *local* pride notwithstanding."

As Spock left, Kirk felt considerable sympathy for his first officer and chief engineer. *It's never easy dealing with somebody who's totally convinced you're wrong.*

"Right here and here," Ortega announced smugly, scrolling quickly through lines of mathematic instructions buried in the programming responsible for operating the power-generation systems.

109

"No way," Scott said with an emphatic shake of his head.

"It's right there on the screen. You can't argue with what's there," Ortega insisted. "Are you going to claim those aren't blatant programming errors?"

"Doctor, those're mistakes a second-year engineering student wouldna make, let alone experienced, highly trained experts. And how d'you explain the fact that this fusion generator—obsolete or not—has been workin' just fine for years with that kind o' software bug?"

"Maybe they just changed the programming recently. I really don't know, Engineer." Ortega waved angrily toward the computer monitor. "What I do know is that we have irrefutable evidence of Federation incompetence. How do *you* explain *that?*"

With a flash of angry frustration in his eyes, Scott seemed ready to explode. But he didn't. "I canna explain it, but I *know* there's got to be another reason f'r this."

"When you find your phantom explanation, I'll gladly listen to it. Until then, I want the rest of this program combed for additional errors that could affect these operating systems, and I want them eliminated. We can't have malfunctions jeopardizing shutdown procedures."

Before the boiling Scott could say anything, Spock stepped between him and Ortega. "We shall see to that, Doctor. Rest assured that any other currently existing anomalies will be found and corrected."

With a curt nod, Ortega pushed his chair away from the console and stood. "So far, we've been lucky. The malfunctions have been minor. But luck runs out. It's your job to make sure there are no *further* malfunctions of *any* kind." Then he turned on his heel and marched out of the control center.

When they were alone, Spock faced Scott, though

not without a hint of sympathy in his eyes. "Mr. Scott, your insistence on responding to Dr. Ortega's contentiousness in like fashion is not constructive."

"Beggin' y'r pardon, sir, but I didna mean for it to be bloody constructive," Scott said through clenched teeth. "It just doesn't make any sense. The people workin' here, well, they just wouldna *make* those mistakes."

"While I cannot sanction such an all-inclusive statement, I do agree with it in principle."

Scott's eyes widened in surprise. "Y'do?"

"Yes. The elementary nature of these errors makes Dr. Ortega's assumed scenario extremely unlikely."

"Then why didn't y' tell *him* that?"

"Further dissension would have served no useful purpose. And we do not as yet have any viable alternatives to Dr. Ortega's conclusion, precipitate though it may be. One fact is clear: This operating software does contain errors. If we begin with the contention that Federation personnel did not make those errors through incompetence or accident, then we must propose other hypotheses."

"Such as?"

"A Federation scientist made the programming errors *intentionally.*"

"With all due respect, sir, that's ridiculous."

"In all probability. But let us assume, for the moment, that it is not ridiculous."

Scott shook his head. "Why would somebody do that on purpose?"

"Sabotage," Spock suggested.

"Why in the name o' heaven would one o' the Federation people sabotage their own observatory? What would they have t' gain by discrediting their own project?"

"I cannot think of a logical reason, but there may be emotional motivations to which we are not privy."

"What about the *Empyreans?*" Scott said, warming up to the exercise in detective work. *"They've* got reasons if they want this observatory shut down."

"True. Anything that casts a negative light on the performance and presence of this outpost makes treaty rejection more likely."

Scott's brow furrowed. "When y' told Ortega we'd do what he wanted, y' said we'd look for all *currently existing* program errors."

"That is all we are able to do," Spock said innocently. "We cannot look for errors already corrected by someone else. Nor can we anticipate and chronicle errors not yet made."

"Ahh, but if future errors *do* crop up, we'll be able t' prove they weren't there before, because we'll be leavin' 'em with a clean slate," Scotty said with a sly smile. "You were already thinkin' that somebody pulled off some intentional sabotage, weren't you?"

"That possibility had crossed my mind. We will indeed correct all errors we find, and we will then have an up-to-date record of operating software. Should any other problems occur, we will know without doubt that observatory personnel were not responsible, because they do not currently have access. And the perpetrator may leave telltale evidence."

Scott nodded and smiled. "I do love a good sting."

"A 'sting,' Mr. Scott?"

"Y'know, a setup?"

"Ahh. For purposes of entrapment of a guilty party. A staple of the literature of crime and detection. Then, a 'sting' it is."

"But what if Ortega's the one responsible? He's sure made it clear he wants this outpost gone."

"Sentiments that do make him an obvious suspect," Spock agreed. "Perhaps too obvious."

"If he *is* the one who planted the program bugs, we'll not trap him. He knows what we're doin'. He knows *we'll* know if the system's tampered with again.

And that'll put outpost personnel in the clear . . . somethin' *he* wouldn't want t' do."

"An eminently logical chain of deduction, Mr. Scott, one that necessarily decreases Dr. Ortega's suitability as a potential perpetrator."

"Of course, that may be what he's *hopin'* for," Scott pointed out, tipping the deductive seesaw back once again.

"We are getting ahead of ourselves, Mr. Scott. At this juncture, our suspicions of sabotage are speculative."

"Agreed, sir. So let's get to work on this, and maybe we'll find something a little more incriminating."

Chapter Twelve

For the first time in her life, Anna knew insomnia firsthand. Despite her busy existence—some commonly overscheduled combination of school, music, friends, art, dance, and sports crowded every day—or maybe because of it, she'd always managed to fall asleep within five minutes of crawling into bed.

Sleeping wasn't something you thought about. It was just something you did, as automatic as breathing.

Until tonight. Fighting off familiar drowsiness, she slipped on her favorite flannel nightgown and opened her windows a crack to let in both the cool night air and nature's music, the sounds of the wind in the trees and the insects and birds calling across the woods and fields around the mansion. She curled up on her right side, as usual, and expected to be asleep before she knew it.

However, sleep fluttered just out of reach, like an

evasive butterfly. After fifteen minutes of unaccustomed wakefulness, she felt the mattress pressing against her ribs, something she'd never noticed before. She had to change position, something else that was new.

With more than a little dismay, she discovered that no other position felt right. She tried the mirror image, lying on her left side instead of her right. She tried lying on her back, then her stomach. She tried fluffing her pillow, then tossing it aside.

Nothing worked. By the time an hour had passed, Anna realized she was no longer drowsy at all. Fully awake at an hour when she should have been fast asleep, she found herself distracted by outdoor noises she'd always found soothing. The irregular rhythms of the night birds' chatters and hoots, the staccato chirps of the crickets—all the voices of the darkness clashed like an orchestra trying vainly to get in tune.

She got out of bed and went to the kitchen, taking care to be as silent as possible. She didn't want to wake the household help or her mother. She just wanted a snack to quiet her grumbling stomach. Then she planned to try falling asleep again.

After another hour of tossing and turning, she switched her bedside lamp on and read for an hour, hoping the concentration would make her sleepy.

That didn't work either. Her mind raced in a way she'd never experienced before, flitting from one recollection of the day's events to another. There were McCoy and Rousseau and her mother and her friends. There was Ethan and Eleni. Like scenes from a play, she repeated key snippets of the most important conversations over and over, then over again.

She could understand that. The things she'd learned that day—about Dr. McCoy and her mother, about Ethan's feelings for her—had changed forever who she thought she was and who she might yet become.

There were momentous decisions to be made, and the ripples from those decisions would churn not only her life but those of loved ones and friends as well. After this day, nothing would or could ever be the way it had been yesterday, before the *Starship Enterprise* had arrived.

But with all those crucial concerns to occupy her and keep her awake, why was there a song, a popular trifle she'd heard on the music channel, running through her head like some out-of-synch soundtrack? Why was she thinking about—and unable to remember—what she'd had for breakfast? Why was she thinking about how many strokes of her hairbrush it took to get out all the tangles each morning?

Why was she thinking about *trivia?*

Eventually, she gave up both trying to sleep and controlling her thoughts. She curled up in the over-stuffed chair near her bedroom window, opened the delicate wood blinds, and watched the first thin line of dawn glowing on the horizon. Then she got up, got dressed, and tiptoed into the kitchen. There, she stopped to wrap a few of yesterday's muffins in a cloth napkin, bundled them into a tote bag, and left the house.

Anna wasn't sure if her choice of paths through the countryside was intentional or simply unconscious. But she found herself on the hill overlooking Ethan's family pasture. The animals were all in the barns. The morning mist hung low, droplets clinging to the dark green grass twinkling in the first rays of the sun. She thought about the childhood afternoons she and Ethan and their friends had spent on this hill, rolling down in summer, racing down on sleds and skis when the snows came.

Now she stood there alone in the quiet of dawn. Until it was shattered by one sharp, explosive clap of sound ringing out across the pasture. Though she'd only heard that sound a few times before, Anna recognized it as a gunshot. Probably from the target pistol Ethan had asked for as a boy and had been using more and more often lately. He liked to set wooden blocks up as targets on a rotting section of old fence in the north corner of the pasture. It was far enough away from houses and barns that the noise didn't bother people or animals.

She headed that way, down the hill and across the field, then through the old stand of trees that bordered the pasture. Three more shots rang out, each louder than the last, confirming that she was getting closer.

She found Ethan where she expected him to be, reloading the black steel gun with its pearl handle. "Hi," she said as she came up behind him.

He turned, then grinned when he realized it was Anna. "Hi. How'd you know I'd be out here?"

"I told you—you're predictable," she said with a sly look in her eye, knowing he'd remember their teasing from the night before. She glanced at the top fence rail. Nothing standing on it. "Did they fall off, or did you shoot them off?"

"I shot them."

"Getting pretty good at this."

"I guess."

"I can understand target shooting in a range with an energy-pulse weapon, but why do you like shooting with that old replica? It's so noisy."

"So?"

"Didn't those things go out of style a couple of centuries ago?"

"Why do you play old music?"

"Is there an analogy there?"

Ethan gave her a goofy shrug. "Maybe not. I just think it's more of a challenge this way. The weapon's not as exact, the conditions aren't so perfect, like in a range."

"Sounds old-fashioned."

He bristled, taking the observation like a personal insult. "And what's wrong with that?"

"Nothing," she said hastily, startled by his reaction.

"Sometimes I think we're too quick to say all the old stuff is bad. Sometimes we're so busy rushing to where we're going, we forget where we've been."

Anna came closer to him with a reassuring smile. "I know what you mean."

Then the closeness seemed to make them both uncomfortable, and she backed a couple of steps away. He finished reloading, then went to the fence to set up five new target blocks, each about four inches square.

Anna stood where the dirt was scuffed, guessing that to be Ethan's firing line. Raising her hands as if holding the gun, she squinted toward the fence. The targets looked awfully small from here. Ethan watched her with amusement.

"You want to try?"

"Me? I've never shot an old-style gun. And I was never very good with pulse weapons either."

"That doesn't mean you can't try."

"I guess not. Okay. What do I do?"

He placed the gun in her hands, then showed her how to hold it in a two-handed grip, with his own hands on top of hers. The touch of their skin had the same distracting effect on each of them. Glances flitted with an intentional randomness, as if neither wanted to be caught looking at the other's face. Ethan stuttered uncharacteristically as he explained how to aim and pull the trigger, warning about the recoil when the gun fired.

"You got all that?"

She continued looking blankly at the targets, as if she didn't hear his question.

"I said, did you get all that?"

"Umm, yeah."

He released her hands and stepped back. "Try it."

Steadying the gun, Anna aimed and squeezed the trigger. Despite his coaching, the blast and kick caught her by surprise and she let out a sharp, reflexive shriek. To nobody's surprise, the targets survived her one-shot assault unscathed. She and Ethan both stared at the blocks, then at each other, and they started to laugh.

She handed the weapon back to him more abruptly than was necessary.

He looked a little disappointed. "Don't you want to try again?"

"No, thanks. You hungry?"

"Sure. What've you got?"

She unwrapped the muffins and handed him one. "Were you going to shoot some more?"

Ethan shrugged. "That's enough for this morning."

"Want to walk?"

"Where?"

"No place in particular."

"Okay. Just let me pack up."

Munching down the rest of the muffin, he gathered the remaining target blocks and put them and his gun into an old backpack. He rejoined her, and she gave him another muffin. Then they walked across the pasture without speaking, side by side—close, but not *too* close. They seemed determined to avoid looking directly at each other.

"How do you feel about loose ends?" Anna asked after a while.

"Never liked 'em much."

"Me neither."

"Ethan." She exhaled slowly. "I know how you feel about me."

"You do?" he asked as if in peril.

In that one briefly eloquent question, he seemed to

Anna simultaneously relieved and afraid. It wasn't hard to understand his ambivalence. As long as his feelings had been a secret—at least from her—he'd been free to fantasize or suffer in private. Free to do nothing. But now that they were bringing everything out in the open, she had no idea what might come next and no idea what she *wanted* to come next.

"I wondered if you knew," he said.

"Until yesterday, it seems like I was the only one who didn't," she admitted. "I'm kind of thick sometimes."

"That's true."

She frowned at him in mock annoyance. "You didn't have to agree so quickly."

"Who told you? Eleni?"

"Miss Busybody," Anna said with a ironic curl of her lips.

"So now that you know . . ." He swallowed, unsure of what to ask or how to ask it.

Anna saved him. "Do I feel the same way?"

"Yeah."

She stopped walking, closed her eyes, and tipped her head back, letting the sun warm her face. Then she looked right into his eyes for the first time this morning. "I never really thought about this before."

"Never?"

"Well, I thought about it, but not about any one specific person."

"Oh." He looked down. "So I guess that means you don't feel the same way."

She bent forward so she could look up at his face. "I didn't say that."

"Then you do?" he asked, straightening up.

"I didn't say that either." Exasperation edged into her voice. "Why are *men* so *difficult?*"

"Why are *women* so difficult?"

Without warning, she started walking again. It took him a couple of strides to catch up.

"We really *are* old enough to think about a future together, Ethan."

"So? You say that like it's a bad thing."

"It's not bad. I just don't know if I'm ready for it. Are you?"

"I don't know. But thinking about it doesn't mean we have to get married tomorrow."

"This isn't just fantasizing. I don't want to say anything to hurt you, and *I* definitely don't want to get hurt." She shut her eyes and sighed. "Why is this so hard?"

"Why is what so hard?"

"Thinking about love, and about having a future with someone when I don't even know if I *have* a future . . ." The instant she'd said those last few words, she regretted it. She'd let slip far more than she wanted to. Or had she?

His eyes had taken on a glaze at the sound of the word *love* coming from Anna's lips. It wasn't until a few moments later that the rest of what she'd said registered in his brain. His frown combined concern and confusion. "What do you mean?"

She waved off the question. "Never mind."

"Never mind?! You sound like you've got a death sentence hanging over your head."

"That's not what I meant."

"What did you mean?"

"Nothing."

"Anna, you meant *something*—"

"It's just all this stuff with the Federation outpost, that's all. It's just one little treaty, but it's everything."

They came to a fence and leaned their elbows on the top rail. A flock of sheep grazed on the other side, and Anna and Ethan watched them as a welcome excuse to avoid looking at each other again.

"Ethan, how would you feel if you got married and didn't have children?"

"Why wouldn't I have children?"

"Well, say, your wife couldn't for some reason."

After a moment, he said softly, "I kind of always assumed I'd be a father, have a family."

Her questioning became more insistent. "But what if you *couldn't?*"

He had to look at her now, and he did. "I guess if I was with someone I really loved, it wouldn't matter. Why are you asking me this? Are we talking about you?"

"No."

"Is there something wrong? Are you sick?"

"No," she whispered. She rested her folded arms flat on the fence rail, then leaned her head forward, her eyes downcast. Should she tell him? She felt like she had to tell someone or she'd explode. Ethan was her best friend. And he loved her. Maybe she even loved him. Maybe if she told him, she'd know for certain. She took a deep breath and exhaled slowly. "Ethan, you have to swear you'll never tell another living soul."

"Tell 'em what?"

"What I'm about to tell you. No matter what happens, no matter how you feel, no matter what happens to me. Do you promise?"

His mouth felt like dust and his stomach went queasy. He began to regret having those muffins. "I promise."

Then, with a calmness that astonished her, she told him. Everything. Once she began, the words came more easily than she could ever have imagined. Ethan listened in silence, his face a blank mask. As she spoke, she wondered what he was thinking. Whatever it was, there was no going back now.

"So, those are my choices," she said as she finished the story. "I can leave with Dr. McCoy, or I can stay and face punishment and ruin my mother's career . . . I can stay and go into hiding . . . or I can stay, skip the genetic scan, and just pretend I can't have children for some private medical reason. So . . ." Her voice trailed off. Essentially, she'd run out of things to say. And she desperately wanted to know what was going through Ethan's mind now that he knew.

"If you leave," he said simply, "I'm going with you."

"Ethan, you can't do that."

"Try and stop me."

"The captain of the *Enterprise* may stop you."

"Then if I can't go with you now, sooner or later I *will* leave this planet, somehow, and I'll find you."

"Is that a *threat?*" she teased.

"Of *course* not!"

She smiled and brushed her fingers through his hair. "That's very sweet, Ethan. But I think you might change your mind about that after I've been gone awhile."

"I don't think so." He stood quietly, looking at her face. "What about Dr. McCoy? You said he was going to try and find a way to get you past the genetic scan."

Her shoulders slumped in a disheartened shrug. "Trying and succeeding aren't the same thing."

"I made you a promise. Now you have to make me one."

"What?"

"Tell me what happens. Tell me what you decide. I don't want to wake up one day and find out you've just disappeared."

She nodded. They hugged and held each other for a long time, sealing a bond made of equal parts hope and despair.

Chapter Thirteen

"CREDIT WHERE CREDIT IS DUE," McCoy said. He stood in the *Enterprise* briefing room, facing Elizabeth, Anna, and Kirk around the conference table. "What I'm about to tell you was actually Spock's idea."

He was trying his damnedest to appear confident and believed he was failing miserably. He paced, not knowing what to do with his hands, and wished his mouth wasn't so damned dry.

"All right, Bones," Kirk said. "Stop fidgeting and tell us what you came up with."

"Sorry." He gripped the table edge with both hands, giving himself something literally solid to hold onto. "The idea is to get Anna through those genetic scans somehow without anybody finding out there was anything abnormal about her conception and birth. The key is Beth's genetic brand—that's what Anna's missing, and that would be the red flag when she's examined."

"What are you thinking, Leonard," Elizabeth said, "that you can simulate that?"

McCoy nodded. "That's right. It's basically our only hope."

"But is it possible?" Kirk asked.

"I'm not sure. First I'll need to do a thorough genetic workup on both Anna and Beth to get a baseline comparison. Then I'll need to see if I can isolate Beth's genetic brand."

Kirk frowned. "And if you can? Then what?"

"Then I've got to find a way to transfer it to Anna or fake it."

Elizabeth exhaled a dubious breath. "It sounds like a long shot."

"I never said it wasn't," McCoy snapped. He knew he sounded defensive, even desperate—exactly the opposite of how he wanted to sound. His tone softened. "But it could work. Is there anybody who doesn't want to try?"

They all looked at Anna. "Miracles do happen," she said.

Then McCoy turned to Kirk. "Is it okay with you, Jim?"

"I've got no problem with it. Good luck, Bones." He glanced at the mother and daughter McCoy was trying to help. "Good luck to all of you." Then he smiled. "If anybody can pull this off, McCoy can."

With purposeful professionalism, McCoy gathered his raw data on Anna and Elizabeth as quickly as possible, then closeted himself in his sickbay lab for the hard work of analysis. He knew he was racing against a clock, time being measured by the outcome of Mark Rousseau's treaty negotiations. Whatever the results, the *Enterprise* would be leaving soon. He had that long to come up with his miracle.

He'd hardly begun when the door of his adjacent

office slid open and Rousseau entered from the corridor. The doorway between the office and the lab had been locked open and he came through it. "You've been making yourself scarce. I haven't seen you since I left you with Elizabeth after our meeting yesterday."

"I'm not open for social calls," McCoy said curtly, barely looking up from his microscope.

Noting the chill in McCoy's voice, Mark's posture stiffened. "All right, then, this is business, Bones." He held up the electronic PADD in his hand, the treaty document displayed on its screen. "I wanted your opinion on my treaty extension proposal before I send it down to President March and the Empyrean Council."

"I'm sure it's fine."

"I'd like you to read it."

"I really don't have time. Like I said, I'm sure it's fine. Probably a piece of diplomatic genius."

"You don't have to be so sarcastic."

"Sorry," McCoy said, though his tone made it clear he wasn't all that sorry. "Since when do you care about my opinion anyway?"

"Would I ask if I didn't?"

"I don't know, would you? Isn't everything you do beyond reproach? You could've been an Empyrean."

"What the hell is *that* supposed to mean?"

"Forget it. Now get out of here and let me work in peace."

Instead, Rousseau gripped the backrest of McCoy's rolling chair and yanked it away from the lab bench. Then he spun it around so McCoy couldn't help facing him.

"What the hell're you doing?" McCoy growled as he jumped to his feet.

"Trying to figure out when you turned into a lunatic."

"Well, when you do, be sure and tell me."

Rousseau shook his head. "It's like you've been mad at me for years."

"Ahh! You noticed!"

"Don't I at least deserve the courtesy of knowing *why* you're so angry?"

"Not really."

"I thought we were friends."

"So did I," McCoy said pointedly.

"Doesn't that entitle me to a chance to make right whatever you think is wrong?"

"There it is—whatever *I* think is wrong! Like, if you don't agree, it can't possibly be true."

"Give me a chance."

McCoy gave Rousseau a hard look. That was the closest he'd ever heard Mark come to pleading. But he dismissed it, sat down, and rolled back to the lab table. "Forget it, Mark. It's not worth the trouble."

Rousseau stood over him, hands spread in appeal. "Since when is a friendship not worth some trouble?"

McCoy remained determined to ignore both the question and the man. With an exasperated shake of his head, Rousseau gave up, turned, and retreated from the lab, finding Captain Kirk standing in the office, just outside the lab door.

The ambassador acknowledged Kirk with a silent nod but kept going out into the corridor. When he was gone, Kirk entered the lab.

"Taking up surveillance as a hobby?" McCoy asked tartly without looking up.

"I didn't want to interrupt."

"How much did you hear?"

"Enough."

"So?"

"So, I seem to recall asking you if Rousseau's coming aboard was going to be a problem for you."

"And what did I say?"

"You said you'd manage. Is that what you call 'managing'?"

McCoy leaned back in his chair. "As a matter of fact, I do."

"Let me give you a piece of advice, Bones. Whatever bee you've got in your bonnet, let it go."

"Very quaint. Now can I get back to work here?"

Arms folded across his chest, Kirk stood squarely in the center of the room. He had no intention of letting McCoy's snarling scare him away.

McCoy rubbed his eyes and sighed. "You're determined to torture the truth out of me, aren't you?"

"As a matter of fact," Kirk said, planting himself on the edge of the table, "yes. So why don't you just make this easy?"

With another sigh, McCoy threw up his hands. "Oh, all right." Then he jabbed an accusing finger toward Kirk. "Anybody ever tell you that you can be a damn pain in the butt?"

"Consider it a specialty. Now, get on with it, Bones."

McCoy slumped back into the chair. "It happened while Mark and I were here, aboard the *Feynman.*"

"That's what I figured."

"You wanna tell this story, or should I?" McCoy snapped.

Kirk raised both hands in a gesture of surrender. "Sorry. I'll shut up."

"Fat chance. Anyway, it was near the end of those few months we spent at Empyrea. I'd been on the ship for a while by then. And the more I saw of Mark, the more I wondered if this was the guy I grew up with. Somewhere along the way, he started turning into this self-important glory-seeker . . ."

. . . All of a sudden, Starfleet's rules and regs seemed to chafe him like a pair of starched undershorts. I started to realize there'd been a pattern to his life— quitting something he was good at just so he could go and tackle something else.

128

The *U.S.S. Feynman* circled Nova Empyrea in a lazy orbit. McCoy found Captain Rousseau sitting alone in the empty rec lounge, near an observation window, watching cloud formations swirl near the planet's northern pole.

"Quite a storm brewing, Leonard," Rousseau said without turning.

McCoy set his coffee mug down with a clunk and slid into a chair. "Down there? Or up here?"

"I can't believe Starfleet wants us to leave."

"Don't take it so personally. Starfleet doesn't want us tied up in long, drawn-out negotiations, and the Federation just wants a team of professional diplomats in on this. What's wrong with that?"

"It's an *insult,*" Rousseau said in rumbling outrage, glaring at McCoy. "I can *do* this."

"Nobody said you couldn't."

Mark swiveled back toward the window, his voice becoming reflective. "Maybe being a starship captain isn't what I was meant to do. Diplomacy, Leonard . . . going out there without Starfleet brass looking over your shoulder. That's the way to solve problems."

"Mark, this is your first command, for godsakes. You've got to expect some of that."

"With diplomacy, it's results that count, not some foolish adherence to a book of regulations written by people who wouldn't know what to do with a field command if it fell on them."

"Is that what that tall tale was all about?"

"What tall tale?"

"What you told Starfleet to convince 'em to let us stay here a little longer, that you're close to a breakthrough."

"So I exaggerated a little."

"A *lot.*"

Rousseau abruptly swung toward McCoy and fixed him with an intense gaze. "This is my big chance to prove I've got what it takes to be a diplomat."

"Shouldn't you be proving you've got what it takes to be a starship captain? I thought you wanted a heavy-cruiser command."

Mark shrugged. "Maybe I do. But I can't see myself doing that for the rest of my life. I've got to stay one step ahead. If I get this treaty with the Empyreans—"

The whistle of the intercom interrupted him, followed by the lilting voice of his female first officer, Commander Kara Choudhury. "Bridge to Captain Rousseau."

He reached for the tabletop comm panel. "Rousseau here. What is it, Commander Choudhury?"

"We're picking up a distress call, sir."

"On my way. Rousseau out."

McCoy followed him to the bridge and listened as Choudhury gave her report, using a starchart on the main viewscreen to show the relative location of the ship in trouble. "It's a small Areian freighter, sir, at the far range of long-distance sensors."

"Any luck establishing contact?"

"No, sir. They just sent the message once. It's possible they're conserving power."

"It's also possible they broke up out there." Rousseau checked the starchart with a frown. "How long would it take us to get there?"

"Three days, sir."

"Well, I can't believe there's not another ship somewhere that's closer to their position."

Choudhury's dusky eyes blinked in confusion. "So we're not going to respond, sir?"

"No, we're not, Commander. We've got important business right here at Empyrea."

"Well," Kirk said, trying to be nonjudgmental, "that was a legitimate command decision. Maybe not what I would've done, but I don't know all the facts."

"Then here's another fact for you," said McCoy.

"The next day, Choudhury picked up the same distress call . . ."

"I continued routine monitoring, sir," Choudhury said, facing Captain Rousseau as they stood on opposite sides of the command seat.

"I gave no orders for you to do that," Rousseau said with some annoyance.

"Begging the captain's pardon, but you gave no orders for me *not* to, sir."

Rousseau's mouth tightened into an exasperated line. "Same message?"

"Aye, sir. Again, transmitted just once. And again, we've been unable to establish contact with them. Perhaps we should do something, sir."

"And I suppose you have something in mind, Commander?" asked Rousseau as he sat down.

"Aye, sir. Since we're unable to leave Empyrea, we could send a continuous message in that general direction, so any ships passing that way will know the Areian freighter is in trouble. So, even if the freighter can't transmit its own distress call, for whatever reason, we'll be increasing the likelihood that someone will find them and help them."

"That sounds reasonable," Rousseau said. "Very well, Commander. See to it."

"With all due respect, Captain, *sir,*" said McCoy from the back of the bridge, "that's not nearly enough."

Without warning, Rousseau rose up from his seat, gripped McCoy by one arm, and hauled him into the turbolift. "Come with me, Doctor." The doors snapped shut behind them. "Deck 7."

McCoy felt the lift pod drop down from the bridge deck. "Why in blazes are we goin' to deck 7?"

"We're not," Rousseau growled. "Stop lift here."

The computer instantly obeyed, and the pod halted

in its tube, somewhere in the middle of the ship. Rousseau turned on McCoy with an icy glare. "If you ever do that again, if you ever question my authority on the bridge—friend or no friend—I'll slap you with insubordination charges so fast it'll make your head spin."

"Insubordination! All I'm doing is telling the truth!"

"You're my chief medical officer, not my conscience!"

"Well, *somebody's* gotta be your conscience—"

"You listen to me, Leonard," Rousseau hissed, stabbing his finger into McCoy's sternum, "the negotiations with Nova Empyrea have potentially historic benefits. You're the one dealing with the medical data, you know how important this could be! I'm the only one who can complete this mission, and neither Starfleet nor some distress call from halfway across the galaxy is going to stop me! Is that clear?"

"Clear as a bell, Captain, *sir,*" McCoy said, not bothering to hide his disapproval.

"Good. As long as we understand each other." He paused. "Restart turbolift." The pod resumed its smooth descent . . .

"So, what happened?" Kirk asked.

"Well, we heard the Areian distress call once more, the next day. Then that was it. Mark made a point to tell me he'd been right, that some other ship found 'em and took care of 'em. He pushed on with his negotiations, and of course he got his damn treaty. We actually left about a week later. We happened to be passing by the area where that distress call came from . . . and we eventually found it."

"Found what?"

"The freighter—a drifting hulk, with four dead crewmen. Well, I lit into Mark—"

"In private this time?"

McCoy nodded. "Respect for the uniform, if not the man. I called him a bastard; he defended his decision. Insisted we'd been too far away to help—that they probably would've been dead by the time we got there anyway, even if we'd left right away."

"Then what?"

"Then I requested an immediate transfer."

"Did he grant it?"

"Yeah . . . but that's not what I wanted him to do." Kirk squinted in puzzlement. "It wasn't?"

"No. I wanted him to stop me, to admit he was wrong, that we should've answered that distress call. But he didn't do any of that. Apparently, he wasn't the man I thought I knew."

After a moment of pensive silence, Kirk stood up. "Maybe you expected too much."

McCoy gave a Kirk a steady look. "Maybe."

"Nobody's perfect, Bones."

"Honest to God, Jim, I'm not looking for perfect. Just *better*."

"The Empyrean way?" Kirk asked in a dubious tone.

"I guess not."

Considering the "crime" to which Elizabeth March had admitted guilt—genetic fraud—McCoy knew the Empyreans didn't have the answers either. Right now, only one thing mattered to him.

Unless he could come up with a solution, Anna would suffer the consequences.

Chapter Fourteen

IT WAS NO GREAT SURPRISE that Anna found it difficult to concentrate on her schoolwork. At the first opportunity, she slipped away from the campus and made her way up the hillside path to the sculpture garden. But this time, she wasn't looking for companionship. She needed solitude.

She was aware that Dr. McCoy would have his results soon, then she would find out whether she'd be able to continue leading the only life she'd known, here on Empyrea, or whether she would have to set out on a whole new path, far from the only home she'd ever had.

All afternoon and into the evening, she sat on a bench overlooking the ocean shore, letting the rhythmic march of the waves mesmerize her. Maybe she'd been wrong. Maybe she didn't need time alone to think. In fact, she was tired of thinking. All the thinking she'd done over the past couple of days had found her no answers, at least none that solved anything.

Not that the problem she faced was so complex. In reality, it wasn't. It had never occurred to her that something so simple could also be so profoundly overwhelming. It came down to one essential dichotomy: Depending on Dr. McCoy's conclusions, either everything would change or nothing would change. And the outcome was completely out of her control.

"There you are." It was Ethan's voice coming from the cool shade behind her. "I've been looking all over for you."

She said nothing as he came over to join her in watching the waves.

"I guess you haven't heard anything yet," he said.

Anna shook her head. Then she told him about McCoy's idea to generate some kind of simulated genetic brand, intended to fool the Empyrean scanning procedures.

Ethan looked dubious. "Do you really think he can do that?"

"What do you mean?"

"Do you really think their medical science can outsmart ours?"

"I don't know. Maybe. Why?"

"They're not Empyrean. How advanced can they be?"

"Advanced enough to build starships," Anna pointed out, trying to argue the worry out of her voice. "We haven't done that."

"We haven't had any reason to build starships. We don't want to go anywhere," Ethan countered. "If what Dr. McCoy plans to try is possible, don't you think somebody on Empyrea would've thought of a way to do it by now?"

"Nobody on Empyrea ever had a reason to do that either—until now."

"Well," he said with a shrug, "I hope you're right. But if I were you, I wouldn't want that to be my only hope."

"Have you thought of a backup strategy?"

Ethan shook his head forcefully. "Not a backup. I think we should do something bold, *now,* without waiting for Dr. McCoy to pull off some medical magic trick."

"Do something like what?"

"Like kidnap one of the starship officers to use as leverage—"

She didn't like the sound of that at all. *"Leverage!?"*

"Yeah, force them to take not just you, but all the young Empyreans who want to get off this planet—all of us who think we're being limited here, everybody who wants to experience the whole universe."

Anna stared at him. "Are you out of your mind? *Kidnapping?"*

"We're not planning to hurt anybody. Like you said, it's a strategy, a way to exercise some power over our own lives."

"What about taking power with patience, like we talked about?"

"Anna, we don't have time for patience! Look at your mother—now we know that she was a rebel when she was young. She felt the same way then as we do now."

"So?"

"Look what happened to her! Now she's in charge of the establishment she wanted to get rid of back then. The same thing's going to happen to our generation."

"Only if we let it."

"You may not have a choice—you may be gone or *dead.* Are you really ready to put your fate in the hands of some Starfleet witch doctor?"

"He's not a witch doctor, Ethan," she said harshly,

losing what little patience she had left. "You don't know what you're talking about."

"I know I can't just stand by and watch what they're going to do to you!"

"We can't just take hostages and start making demands!"

"So you're going to go along with this medical treatment?"

"If Dr. McCoy thinks it'll work, yes."

He paused, staring into her eyes. When he spoke, it was barely above a whisper. "And what if it doesn't work? What then?"

She managed a weary half smile. "Maybe then you can take a hostage." Her tone made it clear she was kidding. Or was she?

Ethan reached out to hold her, and she allowed him to fold her into his arms. She was too tired to maintain their safe distance. She found it flattering that Ethan felt strongly enough about her to consider something so dangerous, and at the same time, it frightened her. What else was he capable of doing on her behalf?

She knew none of what was happening was her fault. Yet, she couldn't help feeling responsible in some way. And the last thing she wanted was for Ethan to raise trouble to a whole new level of risk by doing something crazy.

"Just wait," she pleaded almost inaudibly.

"Okay. But I won't wait until it's too late. I'll do *something* before that."

He said it with the quiet force of a vow, a vow that sent a shiver of dread down her spine.

"What th' bloody hell," Montgomery Scott growled in response to the door chime that roused him from a restless sleep.

Flipping the covers back, he threw his robe over his

pajamas and trudged barefoot to the door. He felt for the lock release, and the door slid open. He found himself squinting up at someone silhouetted against the soft nighttime lighting in the corridor. He wasn't too sleepy to notice the pointed ears.

"Dr. Ortega called," Spock said.

Scotty raked his fingers through his disheveled hair.

"Again? And at *this hour?"* With a curse grumbled under his breath, he turned and retreated to the sitting area of his cabin. "Whatever it is, it'd better be serious."

Spock followed and the cabin door shut behind him. "Dr. Ortega insists that it is."

With a derisive grunt, Scott slouched over to the food slot for a mug of black coffee, as hot as it came.

"Based on our dealings with Dr. Ortega, skepticism is not unwarranted when it comes to his pronouncements and complaints," Spock said as Scott took his coffee and slumped into the nearest chair. "However, the captain has asked us to beam down for a firsthand appraisal of the exact nature of the problem."

"Bloody hell. Dollars to doughnuts Ortega wouldn't know a power coupling from a pile o'—"

"May I remind you that this could be our opportunity to demonstrate to Dr. Ortega—"

"Y'mean, rub his genetically perfected nose in some of that self-proclaimed superiority," Scott said, brightening a bit. "All right. I'll meet you in the transporter room in ten minutes—unless y'want me t' beam down like this."

"That will not be necessary. Ten minutes." With that, Spock left Scotty to curse by himself and to get dressed.

Ortega was nowhere to be found when they materialized in the lobby of the deserted Federation observatory. Opting for the elegance of one well-chosen word rather than the flamboyance of a scattershot string of them, Scott muttered his favorite Gaelic obscenity.

Spock's left eyebrow went up. "Pardon me, Mr. Scott?"

"Nothin', sir. Just a comment on Dr. Ortega's manners 'n' lineage."

"Ahh. Related, no doubt, to his apparent absence in the face of what he claimed to be a critical malfunction in the suspect power system."

"No doubt. So, what do we do now, sir?"

Spock thought for a moment. "Protocol dictates—"

"Ortega can take his protocol and shove it up the nearest—"

"Where have you been?" came a sharp voice from a corridor off the reception area.

"We have been on the *Enterprise,*" Spock said with prosaic neutrality. "Now we are here following your summons. We came as rapidly as we could."

"Well, in the time it took you to get here, the whole power system could've blown. You now have that much less time to avert a disaster."

"With all due respect," Scott said, forcing out those words of preamble, "I doubt the situation's *that* critical."

"Fortunately, Engineer, it's not your job to appraise the situation, just to fix it. If you fail, you and your Federation will be held responsible."

"Now, look here, Doctor—" Scott began.

But before he could continue escalating the argument with Ortega, Spock interrupted. "Doctor, if you would show us what you observed, we shall endeavor to expedite analysis and repair."

Abandoning all pretense at politeness, Ortega turned and marched down the corridor, expecting the two Starfleet officers to follow. Spock did so right away. Scott hung back long enough for an exasperated shake of his head, then went along grudgingly.

They reached the control room and Ortega took them directly to the bank of systems monitors.

"You see," Ortega said in a tone of voice that made it clear he didn't think they *would* see unless he pointed things out to them.

"What I see," Scott said, eliminating all remaining shreds of diplomacy, "is some genetically perfected exaggeration. All we need t' do is reduce plasma pressure at the flow regulators. There's no need t' claim the sky's fallin'."

Before Ortega could fire back, an alarm siren whooped and a strip of red-alert lights circling the ceiling started flashing. Spock, seated at the main console, tapped several commands into the keypad. "The sky may just have fallen, Mr. Scott."

With a dissuasive scoff, Scotty shouldered Ortega out of the way, glanced at the monitor readouts, then punched up a system schematic.

"One malfunction on top of another," Ortega said, "and this time, they're *not* minor. Look at this: Fully a quarter of the modulator network has collapsed, and it's *not* just due to programming errors." With angry jabs, he keyed an adjacent computer terminal to display a listing of reactor core components. "Four phase converters have failed. And now there's radiation leaking in there, Engineer."

"I *know* what's leakin', Doctor." Scott scanned the diagrams on his monitor, which showed yellow points flashing at five locations deep within the power plant's innards. "At least the bloody containment field's holdin'."

"For now," Ortega said. "If that leakage isn't halted—"

"Keep y'r pants on. We'll stop it."

"If the containment field fails—"

Scott gave the Empyrean a dismissive glare. "And what're the odds o' that happenin'?"

"What were the odds of *this* happening, Engineer?"

"However unlikely," Spock said, "we cannot dismiss that possibility, Mr. Scott."

"It's a lot more likely than either of you seem to think," Ortega snarled, "thanks to substandard, faulty Federation programming and substandard components built by substandard humans."

That was more than Scott could take. "Substandard? *Substandard?*" Without regard to rank or manners, he elbowed Spock aside and hammered at the keypad with the fingers of both hands. It's either that or hammer Ortega, he thought. "I'll give y' substandard."

Within moments, Scott had called up construction plans for the Federation complex dating back nearly twenty years. Seconds later, he had isolated the plans for the power plant's reactor core itself.

"Mr. Scott," said Spock, "exactly what are you doing?"

"Makin' a point, sir." His anger at a boil, he glared at Ortega. "The entire electroplasma system, *everything* you just branded as 'substandard,' the guts responsible for this malfunction—"

Ortega glared right back. "What about it, Engineer?"

Scott jabbed a finger at the spec notes displayed alongside the architectural and engineering blueprints displayed on the largest monitor screen. "It's *Empyrean* designed and built."

That flat statement even caught Spock by surprise, betrayed by his elevated eyebrows. "Are you quite certain of that, Mr. Scott?"

"Aye, sir. That I am. I did some extra research before I went to sleep. I was goin' to tell you in the mornin'. But now seems as good a time as any."

"Wait a minute," Ortega said in a confused mumble. The maddening certainty in his posture wavered as his eyes darted from Scott's satisfied smirk to the computer displays and back again, then from one to the other yet again. "That's impossible."

"The whole system is built around a duophase network," Scott said, authority ringing in his voice. "The Federation switched to *triphase* systems a good fifty years ago, long before this place was ever built. Maybe this wouldna've happened, Doctor, if your system wasn't so out of date that it never even *heard* of triphase circuitry."

This time, the truth on the monitor riveted Ortega's attention and his head shook almost imperceptibly. "I can't believe this," he whispered.

So much for genetic perfection. Scott wanted to say it out loud but contented himself with merely thinking it. "Accordin' to Nova Empyrea's own records, you didn't trust Federation equipment when this place went up, so y'r people insisted on supplyin' Empyrean components f'r key systems. I'll bet you didn't know that until now, Doctor."

Ortega was so shaken, his mouth moved without making a sound for a second or two of imperfect hesitation. "No . . . I—I didn't. I was a kid when this place was built."

"Well, you're not a kid now, Doctor. You're a grown man—"

"And grown men admit when they're wrong," Ortega said softly. "These reactor core components are in use all over the planet, in satellites, not one of them has ever failed."

Scott put a fatherly hand on Ortega's shoulder. "Well, laddie . . . nobody's perfect."

"Dr. Ortega," Spock said, "the physical failure of core components may be attributable to factors other than substandard design and construction."

The befuddled Empyrean blinked rapidly as he tried to concentrate on what Spock was saying. "What do you mean, Commander?"

"You yourself certified last night's diagnostic results. Yet newly occurring program errors are present. This malfunction is clearly independent of the earlier problem and cannot be blamed upon Federation observatory personnel."

"So what are you saying?"

"We submit that someone else is responsible for what amounts to infliction of methodical damage on observatory operating systems."

Ortega stared for a long moment. It was bad enough that a system manufactured here on his world seemed to have failed for unexplained reasons. And now—

"Are you accusing Empyreans of sabotage?"

"We're not accusin' anyone of anything, Doctor," Scott said. "In fact, it might be a good idea f'r everyone to stop makin' unproved allegations."

Spock nodded. "We are suggesting that a wider investigation would seem to be in order."

President March sat at the back of the auditorium as Clements led the symphony orchestra through the final portion of rehearsal. The neoclassical piece they played was bold and brawny, with full and energetic participation of brass and strings. But Clements commanded the lectern with a minimum of motion, the antithesis of the popular notion of the theatrical, arm-waving conductor of musical legend. Instead, his hands moved only at the wrist in precise tempo, with only an occasional larger motion from the elbow to point to the extreme sides of the orchestra.

Elizabeth marveled at the control it must have taken to limit his movements so exactly. She'd watched Clements conduct for years and often wondered how he kept himself one step removed, avoided getting caught up in the passion of the music. Did he really feel it? Did he enjoy it? Or was it a technical exercise for him, not all that different from solving crimes?

At the final note, he allowed himself a down stroke with a small flourish in its execution. Then he turned, as if he'd known Elizabeth had been sitting out there in the darkened theater.

How does he do that? She stood and walked up the aisle.

"It's a rare honor," he said, "having the president attend a rehearsal."

"It's a rare treat, listening to one of your works in progress."

"You need me for something?"

"Yes."

He dismissed the musicians, then came down the steps at the side of the stage.

"I've just been talking to Captain Kirk," she said as they sat in the front row.

"Oh? About what?"

March briefed him on the situation at the observatory, presenting the facts of the increasingly complicated case of documented malfunctions and possible sabotage as Kirk had explained them to her, with Ortega's grudging concurrence. Then she brought her austere chief investigator back to her office for a resumption of the conference with the *Enterprise.*

"I still can't believe an Empyrean would do something like this," Elizabeth said.

"I mean no disrespect," said Kirk, "but is it possible for an Empyrean to conduct an effective investigation of this matter?"

"You mean because of my announced opinions favoring the end of any Federation presence here," Clements said. It was a statement rather than a question, made with steely dispassion.

"You're not exactly impartial," Kirk said. "I don't know that anyone on Empyrea could be."

"My impartiality—or lack of it—is personal, Captain. My investigation is professional. As a starship captain, I'm sure you've been faced with one or two

144

occasions requiring you to put personal feelings aside in order to do your job."

"One or two," Kirk said with a slight smile. "I see your point."

"If it's any assurance, I won't be working in secret, Captain Kirk. You'll be kept apprised. And I'll need to interview Dr. Skloff and members of his staff. Maybe they can shed some light. Is that all right with you?"

"No problem at all, Mr. Clements."

"Good. Then I'll be in touch. Clements out."

Moments after Kirk's conversation with the Empyreans ended, McCoy called from sickbay.

"Jim, can you get down here?"

The desolate rasp of McCoy's voice over the bridge intercom portended doom. That was Kirk's instant reaction: *It's something bad, but what?*

"Sure, Bones. What is it?"

"I—I'd rather tell you in person. I'd like you to be here when I present my test results to Elizabeth."

"Shouldn't that be private?"

"I need you here, okay?"

"Okay. I'm on my way."

By the time Kirk arrived, Elizabeth March had already transported up from the planet and was standing in the sickbay office, her face taut with apprehension. Obviously, McCoy hadn't told her anything yet. The doctor himself looked drawn and exhausted, the bags under his eyes bigger and darker than Kirk had ever seen them. Kirk feared the worst: McCoy hadn't come up with the medical miracle Anna needed.

"Bones asked me to be here," Kirk explained. "Is that all right with you, President March?"

She nodded numbly. Then they both turned to McCoy.

"Out with it, Bones," Kirk said.

"Well . . . it looks like I can do it," he said in a strangely flat voice.

Doubling back on the negative expectations foreshadowed by the look on his face and the sound of his voice, McCoy's unexpectedly positive words took a couple of extra seconds to sink in. Kirk stared at him. "You can?"

"Yeah. I think so."

"Then what's with the hangdog face?"

"Something else. I'll get to it." He paused for a deep breath. "There's actually a way to replicate the maternal genetic brand. And I'll be able to give Anna a hormonal treatment that'll mimic the reproductive inhibitor effect long enough to fool the Empyrean doctors."

Kirk broke into a grin and clapped McCoy on the shoulder. "That's great!"

But McCoy held up a restraining hand. "There's a problem."

"What?" Elizabeth asked.

"The genetic brand shows up in every cell in your body. It's supposed to scan that way in Anna's body, too. My best guess, it'll take weeks to infuse naturally into all of Anna's cells."

"If Anna has to undergo the genetic scan before the brand's completely infused, will the scanners notice the deficiency?" asked Kirk.

"They could," McCoy said. "I don't want to take that chance."

Hope drained from Elizabeth's face. "Your ship's not going to be here that long."

"Bones, is it possible to start the treatment and then let it continue after we leave?"

"It's possible, but there's no guarantee it'll work. If I'm monitoring, there might be something I could do."

"Leonard," said Elizabeth, "is there some way to speed up the infusion process?"

"There may be. It would involve introducing a modified carrier construct, which is normally used to increase production of blood cells or spread replacement genes into cells damaged by radiation or disease."

The medical jargon put Kirk out of his depth, so he asked the one question he could think of. "What's the risk to Anna?"

McCoy went from glum to grim. "Fifty–fifty chance the treatment could kill Anna. The natural biostasis mechanisms that regulate cellular reproduction could be kicked out of whack, inducing runaway cellular propagation—"

"Like cancer?" said Kirk.

"Pretty much. It could also destroy her immune system or cause dysfunction of vital organs."

Elizabeth shook her head vigorously. "No. That's not an acceptable risk. I'd rather have Anna leave Empyrea and never see her again, I'd rather face whatever punishment our courts want to throw at me than live the rest of my life knowing she died trying this."

Kirk looked at McCoy's sad eyes, knowing the doctor felt like he'd failed. "Bones, you did the best you could."

"Too bad that wasn't good enough."

"It's not your fault, Leonard," Elizabeth said. She turned toward the door. "I guess I'd better beam down and tell Anna that our choices have been narrowed considerably."

"Wait," McCoy said. "There's something else."

Kirk recalled the cryptic summons McCoy had used to call him down from the bridge. Was he about to explain it?

"My genetic tests revealed something I didn't expect." McCoy stopped and looked accusingly at Elizabeth, searching past the fear in her eyes. "According to what I found, I'm *not* Anna's father."

Chapter Fifteen

KIRK COULDN'T HELP STARING, but he didn't know whether to stare at McCoy or Elizabeth. "What're you talking about?"

"Just what I said. We're not a genetic match." His glance flicked back to Beth, who seemed more subdued than surprised. "If I did the next test, I'd find out that Anna's father is actually Mark Rousseau, wouldn't I?"

She hung her head, unable to look McCoy in the eye. Kirk couldn't tell if her response was driven by shame, disappointment, or a combination of both.

"I guess so," she said quietly.

"You guess so?!" McCoy exploded. "What do you mean *you guess so?* Don't tell me there were others!"

"No!" she shouted back. "At the risk of sounding like an immodest Empyrean, I doubt very much that many Outsiders could ever meet the standards set by our own men. I just happened to meet two exceptional

148

Terrans when I was rebellious enough to take advantage of the opportunities."

"Did you know I wasn't Anna's father?"

"No. In fact, I avoided finding out. I never really wanted to know. I saw something of each of you in her. I'm very proud of her," Elizabeth said fiercely.

McCoy's anger subsided. "I can understand that pride, even if I've got no genetic part in it."

"If you weren't sure which one was Anna's father," said Kirk, "why did you decide to tell Bones?"

"I knew Mark Rousseau had a family. I thought Leonard didn't. It seemed like this would be simpler if I picked the one who was less encumbered."

"That sounds rather calculating," Kirk said, not bothering to be diplomatic about the chill in his voice. He didn't like it when someone took advantage of a friend.

"Maybe so," Elizabeth shot back. "But my daughter's life is hanging in the balance. And I had another reason for picking Leonard. I had more faith in his coming to the rescue."

"Well," McCoy said, "somebody's gonna have to tell Mark."

Beth bit her lip. "I don't know if I can face him."

"I'll tell him if you want," said McCoy. "It's just one more thing added to all the stuff we've gotta settle between us. Besides, you've got a daughter down there who needs you. Go tell her, and help her do the right thing."

Elizabeth squinted at him. "What *is* the right thing?"

"How the hell should I know?"

"We can still take her back to Earth," Kirk said.

"Thanks, Captain," Elizabeth said. "I hope that'll be her choice, because I don't see any other. I'll call you after Anna and I talk it over."

Elizabeth left, with Kirk just behind her. He paused

in the doorway to look back at McCoy, who had slumped down into his desk chair.

"Bones, are you okay?"

"I should be relieved. Who wants to be a new daddy at my age?"

"You don't look relieved. Maybe you were starting to think of helping Anna as a way of making up for the life you never had with Joanna?"

McCoy glared up at Kirk. "If I want two-bit psychoanalysis, I can talk to myself in the mirror. Now get the hell out of here."

Funny how the truth sometimes becomes a moving target, Elizabeth thought as she found her way to the *Enterprise* arboretum. She was relieved to find no one else there. Before she could face Anna with this latest amended truth, she needed to face herself—and her past.

She sat on the soft thick grass, under the protective boughs of a whitewood tree with golden leaves. She'd never seen a tree like this before and wondered idly what planet it came from. But that bit of botanical curiosity only served as momentary diversion from the question overwhelming her: *How did I get into this mess?*

Not that she needed anyone else to tell her the answer. She knew and remembered, perhaps all too well . . .

With all the impatience of youth and love in her stride, Elizabeth March hurried up the hillside path, hurried through the long shadows of tall trees, ignoring the fiery sunset out over the water. The picnic basket holding tonight's dinner didn't weigh all that much, but she resented it anyway, sure that it was slowing her down. Besides, if she abandoned it by the trailside, what would they eat? She'd promised him a picnic he'd never forget.

She smiled to herself, knowing she could fulfill that promise without any food at all. But her invitation had implied a meal.

She couldn't wait to be with him.

She reached the sculpture garden and saw him across the patio. His back was to her as he stood at the stone perimeter wall, his slender form silhouetted against the darkening sky, looking out toward the sea. Then he sensed her presence, turned, and smiled, and she rushed to him. They fell into each other's embrace and kissed, then just held tight.

"Leonard," she finally said, "you look different."

"I do?" He swallowed self-consciously as she examined him.

She nodded, her eyes narrowed as she tried to figure out what it was. "Your hair."

"I combed it."

"That's it. I'm used to it falling across your face, not all slicked back."

"I just thought, for a special occasion like this—"

"Never mind." She raked her fingers through it, and it wasn't slicked back any more.

With a grin he couldn't suppress, he led her to the blanket he'd already spread out near the wall, with his own basket of bread and wine and fruit. "You hungry?" he asked, lighting the lantern standing on the wall.

"If you are."

"I'm *starving.*"

"You're skinny enough as it is, Leonard. Let's eat."

President March sighed as she lay back on the cool grass, staring up through the branches and leaves, wishing there was a real sun staring back from a real blue sky. Then she closed her eyes, hoping in vain for some relief from the tension gripping her neck.

Could that picnic dinner really have been eighteen years ago? The memories and sensations were still so sharp. She could smell the fresh-baked bread, feel the cool evening air, taste the wine, taste McCoy's lips as they kissed . . .

Not that it mattered, but there was still plenty of food left. McCoy and Beth lay side by side on the blanket, his arm draped over her, her back spooned against him. Holding his hand in hers, she pressed it against the silky smoothness of her neck. Then she guided it down, using his fingers to open the buttons of her blouse. She slid his hand inside and stretched his fingers upon her warm skin.

He snuggled closer and brushed a kiss across the nape of her neck. Then she turned over on her back and smiled up at him, entwining her legs with his. With her hand behind his head, she pulled him down, her lips parting as they kissed again.

"Should we go back to my place or yours?" he whispered.

"Your place? It's a starship. Wouldn't your shipmates wonder about a strange woman bedding down with you for the night?"

"Okay. Your place then," he said.

"Why go *any* place?"

They shared another slow, soft, moist kiss.

"Because I want to make love to you," he said.

"And I want you to."

There was a lingering moment of distressed silence as he realized what she was suggesting. "Here?"

"We're alone."

"We're also *outside.*"

"You're from the South. It's warm there. Didn't you ever make love outdoors?"

He propped himself up on one elbow. "Well . . . once," he said without great enthusiasm.

"You didn't like it?"

"Well, we were . . . interrupted." He paused, concerned that continuing on this conversational track would irreparably shred the mood they'd been building.

"What do you mean? Interrupted by what?"

Because she asked, it would have been impolite not to answer. "Bees," he said.

Her eyes laughed, even though she tried not to. "Bees?"

"Bees."

"That must have been embarrassing."

"Not to mention painful."

There was another prolonged span of awkward silence. "I can see how an experience like that might affect your opinion of, uhh, open-air amour." Beth stroked his ear with a featherlight touch of one finger. "Do you think there's anything I could say to change your mind?"

"Mmm . . . you could try."

"Okay." She thought for a second. "Well, there are no bees up here, not at this time of night."

"Anything else that stings?"

"No."

"Bites?"

"Other than me?" she asked innocently.

"Other than you."

"I don't think so."

"Snakes?"

"Never seen one around here."

He paused for a moment of deliberation. Then, with a straight face, he asked, "Predatory birds?"

Beth giggled. That made him smile.

"Not that I'm aware of," she said, rubbing her cheek against his, letting him take in her scent.

"Well, in that case . . ." He unfastened the last few buttons of her blouse, then slipped one strong hand under the light, cool cloth. He felt the warmth radiating from her, felt her heart beating against his touch. "I place myself in your capable hands."

"Not yet." She sighed. "But I'll take care of that in a

minute or two." Then she shivered, and it wasn't because she was cold . . .

Elizabeth still remembered how they'd surrendered to each other that evening, how they had melted together and thrilled each other beneath a moonlit sky and a canopy of rustling leaves. And she believed she would always remember. Just as she would always remember what happened later: how they'd skipped the tram and walked hand in hand to her street, because that would give them more time together. And how they'd talked about whether he would stay with her that night.

She'd wanted to talk about whether he might stay here for good, remaining when his ship was ready to go. But she found herself unaccountably afraid to think that far ahead, and she didn't know if he was ready for a decision like that. She didn't want to push him. There'd be time for them to think about a future together later.

On this one night, neither wanted to separate. Their passion had made that clear. But McCoy had that southern blood running through his heart, and he simply could not ignore the chivalry that came as naturally to him as breathing. So she'd allowed him to convince her it would be much more romantic to say goodnight, to part and savor the love they'd shared, then greet each other again in the freshness of the morning.

"I don't want you to leave," she'd said.

"And I don't want to. That's why we should."

She'd given him a dubious grin. "Is this some perverse southern Gothic lovers' torture?"

She'd watched him beam up, then walked the remaining block to her apartment, though it felt like she was floating.

How different things might have been if she had followed her impulses and insisted that McCoy stay with her. What happened next might not have happened at all . . .

"Elizabeth."

Even as the voice called softly to her, it was unmistakably Mark Rousseau's voice. It came from the patio alongside her house, and she followed it, though she could still hear McCoy's farewell echoing in her mind.

Rousseau, the young starship captain, enfolded her in his powerful arms, and she felt a flutter of guilt in the pit of her stomach. She hadn't planned to fall in love with *two* Starfleet officers. Hell, she hadn't planned—or expected—to fall in love with *one*.

The two men were so different.

Of course, they were unlike Empyrean men—a distinction that had made them instantly appealing, much to her astonishment. The generations of genetic tweaking here on Nova Empyrea had produced a population of males without the imperfections of other humans. Despite the obvious assets of the men she'd known, none had lit any kind of burning, lasting desire in her. The word that accurately summed up her reactions to Empyrean men was . . . *tepid*.

Elizabeth had felt that way for some time, but her dissatisfactions had remained amorphous until she'd met the visitors from the Federation. In a flash, she knew: By comparison, Empyrean men were domestic, commonplace, almost tedious, in their genetic perfection.

Leonard McCoy and Mark Rousseau were anything but perfect. They were wild, exotic, unpredictable creatures. They had flaws and rough edges. She found them irresistible.

As much as they were unlike Empyrean men, they were equally unlike each other. Elizabeth didn't know much about the forces and events that had shaped these two men. But she knew McCoy as a thoughtful scientist, a nurturing lover, self-effacing, sensitive, and sardonic all at once. For all his self-doubts, he had a core of natural stability and decency that made him strong enough to be gentle. More than anyone she'd ever known, he made her feel safe and wanted. And he made her laugh.

Mark Rousseau, the bold leader and explorer, was by contrast a personified force of nature, a commanding tempest of dreams and drives, fueled by an impatience with the status quo and a gambler's haphazard affinity for taking risks that would intimidate most others. As a package, Rousseau might have been insufferable without his endearing conviction that the best reason for embarking on any great adventure was to bring others along on the journey.

Leonard was a warm hearth. Mark was a roaring blaze.

She loved them both.

But right now, Leonard wasn't here. And Mark was. She invited him in, knowing where they'd end up, where all their trysts had ended up since the second time they'd been together. She couldn't help wondering if there was something wrong with what she was doing, alternating between lovers.

She also couldn't help doing it. A century and a half of genetic management techniques may have made Empyreans stronger and smarter, but the primal imperatives deep within the human soul had remained unaltered. *Chemistry is chemistry. I'm living proof of that.*

Admittedly, at times, Elizabeth felt sneaky. Neither lover knew about the other. Neither one had asked, and she hadn't volunteered. If one or the other did ask, she would try desperately not to hurt either of them. But she would have to be honest and tell the full and complete truth, including her belief that Mark's heart inevitably belonged to his ship and to his ambitions.

But McCoy . . . There was a chance—small but present—that he might give his heart to her and stay.

As Mark Rousseau literally swept her off her feet and carried her up to her bedroom, she doubted with silent irony that all the genetic enhancement in the universe would ever clear up the conflicts and confusion that accompanied love.

Love had gotten her into this predicament. She had no idea what might get her out.

President March opened her eyes again, then sat up. There was no avoiding what had to come next. It was time to call her daughter and bring her to the *Enterprise*.

Chapter Sixteen

ELIZABETH WASN'T THE ONLY ONE with stunning truth to tell.

After Kirk left him alone in sickbay, McCoy summoned Mark Rousseau. Then he told the unsuspecting ambassador the whole story, ending with the verdict of surprise fatherhood. Rendering Mark speechless gave McCoy a small measure of grim satisfaction.

"After all those years," McCoy said as he poured them a couple of brandies, "I thought there was one time when I finally got the girl and you didn't."

"Looks like we both got her," Mark said, finding his voice. It could've been a quip, but it didn't come out that way. He was too shell-shocked for humor.

McCoy found himself taking mirthless satisfaction in seeing Mark Rousseau overwhelmed, and he decided to use the sharp needle. "Yeah, but *you're* the one who got her pregnant."

"Don't get so high an' holy with me, McCoy. It could just as easily have been you."

"Maybe so, but I wasn't the newlywed. When we came to Empyrea, you'd barely been married, what, two years? Didn't that wedding vow mean anything at all to you?"

"Of *course* it did," Rousseau growled, clenching his fists as if contemplating using them on McCoy. "You don't know what I was going through."

"Then why don't you tell me?" McCoy taunted.

"Go to hell, McCoy." Rousseau slumped back in his chair, covering his face with both hands. "I was scared to death I'd be a lousy husband."

"Why? You were a star at everything else."

"Everything else came easily. Marriage didn't. You should know that," Mark said, stinging back. "Erica and I got married, and I suddenly realized I had no clue what to do."

McCoy stared in disbelief. "Are you kidding? The heartthrob of the South?"

"This time, it meant something. Do you remember how many times Erica put off our wedding?"

"A half dozen that I knew about. She didn't know if she wanted to spend her life married to somebody who was gonna be gallivanting across the galaxy."

"Do you know why she finally went through with it?"

McCoy shook his head.

"I got down on my knees and begged," Rousseau said simply. "And I promised I wouldn't stay in Starfleet more than a few years."

"So that's why you were so desperate to show what a great diplomat you could be. But that still doesn't explain you and Elizabeth."

Rousseau sighed. "By the time our ship found Nova Empyrea, Christopher had been born. I was terrified of being a father—"

"Something else you weren't prepared for?"

"Were you?"

"Nobody is. It's a wonder all kids don't turn out to be messes and monsters."

Rousseau managed a concurring smile. "I was also terrified of what I was missing, being away from home while he was a baby."

"So your solution was to warp across the galaxy and have an interstellar affair?"

"My God, Bones! You were there. You know what Elizabeth was like—the magnetism! And not just her—*all* those Empyrean women. I never *claimed* to be infallible!"

"Oh, no?" said McCoy sarcastically. "You sure acted like it."

"Maybe that's just how *you* saw me. Sorry I had to disappoint you."

"What about Anna? Are you going to disappoint her?"

"Anna's not my responsibility," Rousseau said, his tone blunt.

"You're her *father,* for heaven's sakes!"

"A quirk of biology, and Elizabeth's choice." Mark stood up as if to leave. "Whether Anna stays, undergoes your treatment, or leaves with the *Enterprise,* that's not my concern."

"The *hell* it isn't!"

Rousseau shook a finger in McCoy's face. "I'm here for one purpose: to get that treaty extension."

Without warning, McCoy launched a roundhouse punch that connected squarely with the side of Rousseau's face, dropping one extremely surprised ambassador to the floor, flat on his back. He blinked back startled tears while McCoy flexed his right hand gingerly and winced in pain.

"Serves you right," Rousseau said.

"I'm a doctor—it's my hand. Whatever I broke, I can fix. And whatever it was, it was worth it! I've wanted to deck you for years, you arrogant, self-impressed, self-centered sonofabitch." Standing over Rousseau, McCoy let all his pent-up fury pour out. "When we were kids, I thought you were the greatest thing since sliced bread. I envied you, I worshipped you, I wanted to *be* you! And I wish to God I knew what happened to you!"

Mark propped himself on one elbow, rubbing his bruised cheekbone with the other hand. "Maybe nothing happened to me. Maybe you just saw the parts of me you *needed* to see. I'm sorry I disappointed you. Idols don't ask to be idols, and they don't ask to be born with feet of clay. That's just the way things are."

With that, Rousseau got unsteadily to his feet. McCoy's angry glare softened to sorrow. He looked at Mark and shook his head. "Go get your damned treaty—while I try to figure out a way to save your daughter's life."

The wedge that time and distance had plainly driven between him and McCoy bothered Rousseau more than he was willing or able to admit. After a futile hour spent trying to fine-tune his draft treaty extension, McCoy's contemptuous diatribe still echoed in his mind. It still stung far more than any fist hitting him in the face.

Rousseau knew that he had always possessed an effortless charm, no matter what the company around him. He took no credit for it. It was simply a gift, and he'd learned to rely upon it early in life. *Probably a gift I've long since taken for granted.* Somewhere along the way, he now realized with dismay, it had become easier to choose his words with diplomatic care when dealing with strangers than with friends.

Professional instincts had replaced personal ones. As he made his way to the *Enterprise*'s arboretum for a little solitude, he was unsettled by one further realization: He had more confidence in his ability to achieve the treaty renewal than to patch things up with McCoy.

The door to the arboretum slid open. The moment he entered, he heard the sweet jangle of guitar strings coming from the midst of the trees and shrubs. Someone was playing an elegant but simple folk melody with a lively verse and a melancholy refrain. He followed the crushed-gravel path that seemed to lead to the source of the music.

In a central green bounded by willow trees, he found Uhura sitting on a bench, playing by herself. He paused under cover of the leafy canopy, unsure whether his presence would be considered welcome or an intrusion. Without stopping her song, Uhura looked up, smiled, and nodded for him to join her. With a return smile, he sat at the end of her bench. When she finished, he applauded.

"Sixteenth-century English?" he ventured.

"That's right. I'm impressed."

"Well, I was very interested in all kinds of music when I was young," he said modestly. "Even thought of it as a career for a while there. Then I found some other roads to explore."

She held out the guitar, her gesture inviting him to take it.

He hesitated. "Are you sure?"

"I'm offering."

"Not everyone is so willing to have their instruments manhandled by strangers."

"No fellow musician is a stranger," she said, giving it to him. Then she laughed. "As for the manhandling, well, I know where I can get a phaser on short notice."

With his thumb, he strummed at tuneless random for a few moments, as if acclimating himself to the feel of his fingertips on the strings, the distance between them, and the effort required to press them firmly to the fingerboard. When he seemed satisfied, he began a tentative pick with the individual fingers of his right hand, though the notes he played still lacked the cohesion of a musical piece.

After a minute of that, both hands fully at home on Uhura's guitar, he merged effortlessly into the fast-flowing river of notes that were the hallmark of upbeat jazz. Then, almost imperceptibly, he added a strong, driving bass line that Uhura found irresistible. She couldn't help drumming along in time on the top of her guitar case.

Rousseau's melody bounced along its joyous way, then tumbled to a close. And it was Uhura's turn to applaud in lusty appreciation.

"That was wonderful, Mr. Ambassador!"

"Please, just call me Mark," he said, handing the guitar back to her.

"Unless I miss my guess, you're a big fan of old-time twenty-first-century jazz, with some African rhythm fused in for good measure."

"You've got a great ear, Commander."

"Call me Uhura, everyone else does. And you're quite a jazz guitarist."

He ducked his head sheepishly. "Not so good. I never really took guitar-playing seriously. I seem to pick up one of these every ten years or so."

Uhura's eyebrows arched. "You're kidding."

He shrugged. "Nope. I was a brass man—probably for the bombast period, then woodwinds and keyboards."

"It sounds like diplomacy's gain is music's loss, Mark."

"Coming from you, I take that as a high compliment. I understand you've always been the source of the *Enterprise*'s most beautiful music."

"Oh, I don't know if I'd go that far. I just try to make sure my shipmates remember that music hath charms," Uhura said with a sly half smile. She began quietly playing another simple folk tune. "I hear you and Dr. McCoy had a little tiff earlier today."

His eyebrows arched in surprise. "I didn't realize news traveled that fast in a ship this big."

"Big ship, small family," she said, then added mystically, "Besides, I *am* the communications officer. Anything you'd care to talk about?"

"Music hath charms, indeed," he said wryly. "Ahh, it's not a burden I'd want to dump on you."

"No burden."

He turned his hands palms up in a gesture of philosophical acceptance. "These things happen. Friends drift apart."

"Is that really what this was about?"

"I'm not sure. Maybe it's also about how well people *really* know each other versus how well they *think* they know each other."

Uhura's lashes batted up, revealing dark eyes and a searching gaze. "So who's guilty of misjudgment?"

"Probably both of us. Now he knows I'm not the man he thought I was."

"And what do *you* know?"

"That McCoy's probably a better man than I ever was or ever will be."

"Did you tell him that?"

Rousseau let out a short, ironic laugh. "That's a burden I lived with for a long time, people thinking the world of me. I'd never lay that on someone else. Better to be underestimated, don't you think, Commander?"

"Mmm, I don't know about that."

"Oh, sure it is. Then you aren't likely to disappoint people, and it's that much easier to amaze them. Let's face it: You were much more impressed with my guitar technique after I told you I'd never played before."

"Maybe. So, now you've lowered Dr. McCoy expectations."

"You can say *that* again. I think he's got higher expectations of one-celled organisms than he does of me."

"Then you may never have a better chance to show him he's wrong."

Mark sighed with resigned sadness. "I'm not so sure he *is* wrong. If you knew exactly what we argued about—"

She gave him a sideways glance veiled by her lashes for an extra trace of mystery. "Who's to say I don't?"

The rhetorical question caught him off balance. "Do you?" he asked with genuine uncertainty.

"I know enough. After all, I am—"

"—the communications officer," he finished with a grin. Then he stood and inclined his head in a gracious bow. "Thanks for the company, Commander."

"Anytime."

"You know, I came in here wanting to be alone. I'm glad I wasn't."

"Same here."

As he left the arboretum, Rousseau knew there were some people he should find and some things he should say. But he couldn't help wondering if he had the courage—and he wasn't sure he wanted to find out.

Chapter Seventeen

Captain's log, Stardate 7596.1.

Dr. McCoy continues his efforts at refining a genetic treatment for Anna March. Meanwhile, the Empyrean investigation into problems with the observatory reactor continues. Following last night's emergency, First Officer Spock and Chief Engineer Scott have stabilized the reactor core's condition. Now, we wait to see if other malfunctions develop.

WITH UNCHARACTERISTIC HESITANCE, Mark Rousseau entered the *Enterprise* observation lounge and approached Anna and Elizabeth March. They were seated in a semicircular booth behind a screen of ornamental shrubs, their voices subdued as they spoke quietly near the windows.

"Mind if I join you?" he asked without his customary ebullience.

Elizabeth offered a diffident shrug as her reply. Neither affirmative nor negative. Rousseau accepted that as the most encouraging greeting he could expect, considering the circumstances. He sat on the outer edge of the curved seat as Anna filled a third glass from the pitcher of sparkling orange beverage she and her mother were sharing.

Rousseau took it gratefully. "Thanks, Anna."

"You're welcome . . ." Her voice trailed into an awkward pause. "I hadn't even figured out what to call Dr. McCoy. Then I find out he's not my father, you are, and I don't know what to call you either."

"Just Mark will do." He took a sip of his drink to wet his dry mouth.

Elizabeth noticed the discolored swelling under his eye. "Where'd you get that?"

He managed a wan smile. "McCoy's bedside manner . . . his way of persuading me to alter my perspective." Before he could continue his confessional, he needed a deep, stabilizing breath.

"Is that why you're here?" Elizabeth asked.

He nodded. "Not that I have a lot of parental rights here—not that I deserve them—but, for what it's worth, Anna, I don't want you risking your life on this medical treatment either. You've got a place with my family back on Earth, and you always will." He made a conscious effort to brighten his expression. "You know, you'd fit right in with my other kids. My son's a couple of years older, and my daughter's going to be eighteen next year."

Anna looked him straight in the eye. "Mark, I don't want to disrupt your family. The last thing you need is some mystery child barging in."

"Anna, it wouldn't be like that at all."

"Well, that's how I'd feel. Your kids and your wife might feel the same way."

"Then we could keep your identity a secret."

"You mean lie?" The corners of Anna's mouth twisted with disapproval.

"Not really. Just say you're the child of an old

friend coming to Earth to continue your studies. That's not a lie."

"Selective truth then."

Elizabeth appreciated what it took for Mark to come here and reach out, and she was annoyed with her daughter's prickly response. "Anna, this isn't easy for any of us. Mark's only got your best interests at heart, and we—"

"*My* best interests," Anna cut in. "Meanwhile, everybody *but* me is making *my* choices and decisions."

"I thought we agreed—"

"*You* all agreed, Mother. Nobody gave me a chance to *disagree.*" Anna stood and slid out of the booth. "Well, I've made up my mind. I'm not going to have to disrupt the Rousseau family, because I'm *not* leaving Empyrea."

"Anna!"

"Mother, I'm an adult. My life is my responsibility. The decision is mine and Dr. McCoy's. If he thinks there's any reasonable chance this medical treatment will let me pass the scans and live my normal life here where I belong, then I'm going to take that chance."

Elizabeth jumped to her feet, determined not to go along with what she considered to be lunacy. "Anna, you can't be serious—"

Now it was Mark who interrupted, placing a firm hand on Elizabeth's shoulder. "Let's see what McCoy says."

She whirled. "I don't care *what* Leonard says! I'm not allowing Anna to risk her life like that!"

"Is it a risk? Sure, it is," McCoy admitted, facing Anna and her mother and father in his sickbay office. "The question is, is it an acceptable risk. Now, I've managed to fine-tune the accelerated genetic-branding procedure a bit."

"Before," Elizabeth said critically, "you said there

was a fifty–fifty possibility she could die during the procedure."

"Well, now it's more like sixty–forty in favor of successful treatment."

Beth glared at him. "You're not making that up, are you?"

"I'm a doctor," he growled, "not a goddamn odds maker. I'm giving you my best opinion."

And then Anna faced the parents who cared so deeply about her fate and the physician who would hold that fate in his hands if she convinced them to sanction her choice. She spoke up in a voice filled with quiet passion. "Mother, I know you want the best for me. You all do. But I want to live *my* life, not somebody else's life. And my life is here, where I can fight for this world to be what it *should* be, what *you* wanted it to be when you were my age, Mother."

Elizabeth felt tears coming to her eyes, the sting of emotion rising in her throat. She looked into her daughter's face, hoping Anna wouldn't notice. She was determined not to cry. It would have been easier to look away from Anna, but she couldn't, not now. Not when Anna stood before her, asking for what amounted to a benediction.

Asking with a clear-eyed courage that compelled respect.

Asking her mother to go along with her choice—a choice that Elizabeth knew might be suicidal.

Anna was not demanding. She issued no ultimatums, made no threats.

"Let *me* make the choice *you* got to make, Mother."

Elizabeth exhaled slowly, looking from McCoy to Rousseau, then, finally, to her daughter. "You've earned the right to make your own choice, Anna. I can't stop you . . . and I shouldn't. Mark?"

He replied with a gesture of silent surrender.

Then Elizabeth turned to McCoy. "The decision is Anna's and yours, Leonard."

They all faced Anna again, her posture signaling her certainty. "Let's do it."

With a solemn nod, McCoy touched the intercom. "McCoy to Chapel. Those preparations for Anna's treatment—"

"Already done, Doctor. Ready to begin any time you are."

"Thanks. McCoy out."

Anna, Elizabeth, and Mark all looked at him in wordless surprise. He shrugged.

"I just had a feeling, that's all. I know determination when I see it."

As McCoy reviewed the medical data and procedures in final preparation for his treatment of Anna, he couldn't help feeling a foreboding chill. Was he really so certain of those odds he'd quoted to Elizabeth?

"Are you okay, Bones?"

The voice—Kirk's voice—echoed as if in a vast cavern. It sounded so far off, so incorporeal, that McCoy didn't even blink in response. Not until it spoke again did he swivel his desk chair slowly, consciously reestablishing reality in his sickbay office.

"I said, are you okay?"

"Huh? Yeah . . . yeah, I'm okay." Then McCoy turned gruffly defensive. "Why shouldn't I be?"

"No reason. Are you sure you're ready for this?"

"Of course I am. If you're trying to bolster my confidence, you're doing a lousy job, Jim."

"Sorry. I'm just concerned about you, that's all."

"Why?"

"Because you've been on an emotional roller coaster for the past week, and I can see what Anna's safety means to you."

McCoy stood up. "Look, Jim, she's a patient; of *course* I care about her safety. I wouldn't be doing this procedure if I didn't think the risks were manageable.

And she's *not* my daughter, so I'm not carrying that baggage into the treatment room."

"Are you sure about that?"

"No, goddammit, I'm not. Anything else you'd like to ask to unnerve me?"

Kirk put a steadying hand on McCoy's shoulder. "I've got faith in you, Bones. We all do."

McCoy's blue eyes gave Kirk a level gaze. "What if you're all wrong? What if *I'm* wrong?"

"You're giving Anna the chance she wants. No matter what happens, that's not wrong."

"Tell me that again when it's all over," McCoy said softly.

"All readings stable, Dr. McCoy," Dr. Chapel said.

McCoy already knew that; they were right up there on the biofunction monitor above Anna as she lay on the bed in the sickbay operating theater. He also knew Chapel's telling him was her way of reassuring him. And he appreciated it.

He acknowledged with a nod. Anna was already unconscious, hooked up to the life-support apparatus covering her torso like medical armor. What they would be doing to her was not surgery, technically speaking. But they would be introducing a foreign substance into Anna, one that would be carried into every cell of her body. McCoy and Chapel were all too aware of the possibilities for life-threatening disaster. McCoy wanted Anna on full standby life support from the moment treatment began. That way, if anything did go wrong, there'd be no time wasted in implementation of emergency countermeasures.

McCoy licked his lips. His mouth didn't always feel so dry before an operation. *Why now?* "Got the serum, Dr. Chapel?"

She held up a vial of purple liquid. "Serum ready, Doctor."

"All right then. Let's get this show on the road. Begin infusion."

Chapel tipped the vial nozzle down, then inserted it into a hypospray. She showed it to McCoy. He nodded again. With smooth skill honed during her nursing days, Chapel placed the hypo against Anna's neck. McCoy heard the familiar hissing sound as she squeezed the trigger, injecting the serum until the vial was emptied. Then they both stepped back and glanced at the biomonitor.

There was no initial reaction, and McCoy let out a relieved breath. "Well, so far, so good."

"I'll stay here with her, Doctor," Chapel said. "If you want to go out and tell President March and Ambassador Rousseau that everything's all right . . ."

"Thanks, Christine." First, he reached for a small towel and wiped away the beads of perspiration that had popped out on his forehead. Then he went out to his office.

Rousseau and Elizabeth jumped reflexively to their feet the moment he came in. Kirk was with them, too.

"Relax," McCoy said, managing a smile for their benefit. "Everything's fine. I really don't expect any complications."

Elizabeth didn't look assured. "It's the complications you *don't* expect that worry me, Leonard."

"Look, Beth," McCoy said, diplomatically letting the comment pass, "it's going to be a couple of days till we know if the treatment's taking. I'd suggest going on back home; you'll be a lot more comfortable there. And Mark, why don't you go work on that draft proposal of yours. I'll give you both progress reports every hour."

They showed no signs of leaving.

"President March," Kirk said, trying to help, "we can have you beamed back up to the *Enterprise* at any time if you feel the need."

"There's really no reason for everybody to be underfoot," McCoy said.

"I don't feel much like going home alone," Elizabeth said.

"And there's no way I'm going to be able to concentrate on work," said Mark.

Elizabeth turned to Rousseau. "Would you like to know more about Anna? Because I'd love for you to know her like I do. I can tell you all about what she was like growing up."

Mark smiled. "I'd like that. You've got pictures, I suppose?"

Elizabeth couldn't help smiling back. "She's my only child. Have I got pictures! It would take a whole cargo shuttle to haul 'em up here."

McCoy stepped between them, putting his arms around their shoulders. "That sounds like a good idea, you two beamin' down together. I promise I'll keep you posted."

"Leonard," Elizabeth said, "I'd like you to come, too."

The invitation caught McCoy off guard. "I—I'd like to," he stammered, then glanced back toward the operating room, where Chapel stood in the open doorway. "But I'm not sure I should leave."

Elizabeth cocked an eyebrow. "You *said* everything was fine."

"Doctor," Chapel said, "I won't leave Anna's side while you're gone."

"If we need you, Bones," said Kirk with a grin, "we know where to find you."

"Because I was never absolutely sure which of you was Anna's father," Elizabeth said, "I kind of always thought of you *both* as her father. Now that I do know, I'd still like for both of you to know about her. Come on, Leonard."

"Well . . . okay." McCoy slipped out of his lab coat

173

as Kirk handed him his uniform jacket. Before he left, McCoy wagged a finger at Chapel. "Any sign of trouble—*anything at all*—you get me up here. *Instantly.*"

"Understood, Doctor."

He watched from out of sight, from the shadows behind a massive tree trunk, as McCoy, Rousseau, and Elizabeth beamed down together, materializing in the gardens near the presidential mansion. The sun had already dipped below the roof of the house, and it was cool and dark beneath the big trees.

He gripped the energy-pulse weapon tightly and took careful aim. A bright blast from the weapon took the three of them from behind, and all fell to the ground unconscious.

Ethan emerged from the shadows, a tight-lipped smile briefly crossing his face. The time for talk had passed, as he had told Anna it would.

Now it was time for action.

Chapter Eighteen

ELIZABETH REGAINED CONSCIOUSNESS FIRST, feeling the cool dampness of the slate path against her cheek. She rolled onto her side, then sat up too quickly. She fought the swirling vertigo spinning inside her head and had to brace herself with one hand to keep from keeling over.

Steadied in that position, she made a concerted effort to take stock of her situation and organize her thoughts, an effort complicated considerably by the fog filling her head. First, the present: She knew who she was. She knew where she was: She could tell by the familiar trees that she was sitting in the garden grove near the presidential mansion. She knew it was evening: There was a chill in the air, the sun was down, the path lights had come on.

Next, the immediate past: How had she come to be here? Where had she come from? Recollections: fragmented, oddly distant—the starship. *Enterprise.*

Anna. Sickbay. McCoy and Rousseau. *Now I'm getting somewhere . . .*

Beaming down. To here. Then what?

She looked around. There was Mark Rousseau, a meter away, moaning, rolling over, looking up at her with unfocused vision. And McCoy—

Clarity blew back into her mind like a cold wind through a door suddenly thrown open. *Where the hell is McCoy?* The silent shout of panic rattled in her mind. Maybe he had crawled off. Still not sure she could stand without falling, she tried to get up and succeeded, eyes searching frantically around. There was no sign of him, no sign of where he might have gone.

She went over to Rousseau, squatted next to him, and touched his face. "Mark! Mark, are you all right?"

Propping himself on one elbow, he shook his head to clear it. "I think so."

His speech wasn't quite slurred, but his enunciation lacked its accustomed crispness. Whatever hit them had obviously affected him more than Elizabeth.

He squinted at her. "Wha' happened?"

"I don't know. Somebody ambushed us. McCoy's gone."

"How long?" Rousseau got to his knees, resisting the wave of nausea rippling through his gut. "Got to look for him."

She gripped his arm. "We're in no shape. We've got to get our police on it."

"We have to call the *Enterprise*."

"Can you stand up?" When his only response was a blank blinking of his eyes, she shouted the question at him again. "Mark, can you stand up?"

He winced at the loudness of her voice. "Yes." Then he actually made the attempt. He staggered, then forced himself to stand without swaying. His speech had regained its edge. "Not as gracefully as I'm accustomed to, but I think I can get as far as your mansion." He held out a hand, as much to help her up as to steady himself.

"Okay. Let's go."

As soon as she was able, President March summoned an Empyrean investigation team to the site of McCoy's disappearance. Then, with more than a little trepidation, she and Rousseau contacted the *Enterprise*.

"I can have a search party down there in five minutes," Kirk said from the starship's bridge after assuring President March that Anna's condition remained stable.

"No, you can't, Captain," President March told him. "Our laws forbid it."

Kirk's jaw tightened as he squelched the reflexive impulse of an angry response. "Considering the circumstances, I'd think you might make an exception."

"I know Dr. McCoy may ultimately be responsible for whether my daughter gets through this treatment safely, Captain, but I'm not above the law. And I resent the implication that we Empyreans are incapable of conducting a proper search."

"Elizabeth," Mark Rousseau said as soothingly as possible, "I'm sure Captain Kirk meant no such thing."

"Of course not," Kirk said, making a hasty jump into the diplomatic opening the ambassador had provided. "I just thought our tricorders might be helpful in scanning for clues."

Elizabeth accepted the tacit invitation to reduce the tension a bit. "We do have our own scanning devices, Captain. But if you'd care to beam a few tricorders down, I'll offer them to our forensics team."

"We'll do that," Kirk said.

"And we'll give you updates every half hour or sooner if we find something."

"I'd appreciate that," Kirk said formally. *"Enterprise* out."

Kirk pounded a frustrated fist on the arm of his chair the moment the comm channel was closed. *"Dammit."* He swiveled to face Chekov at Spock's science station.

Chekov knew that look in Kirk's eyes; the captain had no intention of sitting by passively when one of his crew was in trouble. "Keptin, ve could initiate a sensor scan of the area vhere Dr. McCoy disappeared."

"Would the Empyreans be able to detect it?"

"Vith our sensors at full strength, they could. Their technology is not that far behind ours, considering how long they have been isolated."

"What about less than full strength?"

Chekov punched the numbers into his computer. A moment later, he had the calculation he sought. "It is possible to reduce scanner power levels and to reconfigure sensor frequencies so they blend into natural background radiation patterns—"

"To a point where they'd be undetectable by planetary sensors?"

"Aye, Keptin."

"At that low level, would we still be able to pick up McCoy's life form readings if he was wandering around the woods down there?"

"Vandering the voods or someplace else relatively unobstructed, I believe so, sir. But our ability to scan below the planet surface—"

"Like in a cave?"

"Aye, sir. That ve probably could *not* do."

Kirk nodded distractedly. "Well, precipitating a diplomatic incident by violating Empyrean sovereignty isn't likely to be helpful at this point—"

Chekov looked disappointed. "Then ve do nothing, sir?"

"I didn't say *that,* Mr. Chekov. I said I don't want to cause an interplanetary incident—*yet.* But I'll be *damned* if the Empyreans think I'm about to stand by and do nothing when McCoy's missing, maybe hurt. Initiate low-intensity sensor sweeps of the area around the mansion, and *make sure* they don't catch us."

"Aye, sir."

I'm blind, McCoy thought the moment he snapped back to consciousness. He knew his eyelids were open, but he only saw darkness. Then he felt the binding around his face. *Just blindfolded . . .*

Where the hell am I? he wondered, struggling to orient himself, both mentally and physically. *At least I'm alive.* Beyond that, he knew he was lying on his back, his hands resting on his chest, bound tightly by bands around his wrists. He tried to move his feet; they were shackled, too.

He felt a sensation of motion headfirst. He heard footsteps coming from the direction of his own feet. So he knew whoever was with him was pushing him along from that end, probably on some sort of antigrav cargo sled. The feet sounded like they were scuffing against dirt and hard ground rather than pavement. *Outdoors?*

McCoy listened and concentrated. There was no wind, no warmth of sun against his skin and clothing. *Could be a calm night.*

But he heard no sounds typical of nocturnal nature —no birds calling from treetops, no leaves rustling, no insects humming or chirping. And the air didn't feel or smell like outdoors. He inhaled deeply and sensed the clammy, musty odor of damp rock. *Must be in a cave or a tunnel.*

McCoy realized he was strangely unruffled, considering his predicament. The moments spent concentrating on rational analysis helped distract him from dwelling on just how dire his straits might be.

He licked his lips. He was a little surprised that he wasn't gagged, and he wondered why. Whoever captured him seemed to have planned ahead sufficiently to ensure that an ungagged mouth was not merely an oversight. Wherever he was, if McCoy was being given the opportunity to shout, in all likelihood there wasn't anyone around to hear him.

Instead, he wriggled sideways slightly and attempted to swing his legs over the edge of whatever he was lying on. He felt forward motion stop.

"Going for a stroll, Dr. McCoy?"

The voice was male and with a timbre that identified the speaker as young. Maybe eighteen years old, McCoy guessed. Not unkind or intimidating, but definitely controlled. This kid seemed comfortable with what he was doing. "I was thinking about it, yeah."

"You might have some trouble with those ankle shackles."

"You wouldn't happen to know somebody with a key."

"As a matter of fact, I do."

"You?"

"Yes."

"You have me at a disadvantage, son," McCoy said.

"Actually, I have you at *several* disadvantages, Doctor."

"Well, I was referrin' to the fact that you know my name and I don't know yours."

"No harm there, I guess. It's Ethan."

"Where're we headed, Ethan?"

"You'll know when we get there."

"They got here without incident," said Clements, standing in the now-floodlit garden with Mark Rousseau and President March. He glanced at the readout on his scanner, a handheld device similar in size to a Starfleet tricorder. "That much we know. The *Enterprise* confirmed no problems in transport."

A dozen other Empyrean forensic investigators were busy scouring the gardens, the paths, and the surrounding woods and lawns, looking for any shreds of evidence that might help them figure out what happened to McCoy.

Elizabeth nodded. "And I'm *sure* all three of us arrived here. We didn't have a chance to say anything before we were stunned. But I was in the middle, and I could tell out of the corners of my eyes that Mark and Leonard were both where they were supposed to be."

"The residual ionized radiation footprints of the transporter materializations confirm that, with ninety-nine percent certainty. They're what they should have been after three people beamed down here using Federation equipment," Clements said. "Now, you're sure it was just a second or two after you materialized that you were stunned?"

Rousseau and Elizabeth exchanged a glance of agreement. "As sure as we can be," Rousseau said. "It was certainly no more than that."

Clements grunted. "Well, it's pretty clear that someone was waiting for you, waiting to stun you with an Empyrean energy-pulse weapon. Two of you were left unharmed. It seems likely that Dr. McCoy was taken as a hostage."

"A hostage!" Elizabeth shook her head, both baffled and horrified. "This is impossible. This just doesn't happen here!"

"Maybe it didn't before," Mark said grimly, "but it looks like it does *now*. Mr. Clements, have you had any luck tracking where they went after they grabbed McCoy?"

Clements regarded Rousseau with the disdain of a

professional lecturing an amateur. "Luck, Mr. Ambassador? Luck doesn't enter into the investigation. And you used the word *they,* implying more than one perpetrator involved in this incident."

"You don't think it was more than one person?"

"It's not my job to draw conclusions unsupported by evidence. And so far, the *lack* of contrary evidence does in fact lead to the likelihood that one person did this—in my opinion."

"What makes you say that?" Mark asked.

"The more people involved, the greater the probability of making a mistake that would leave some damaging hints behind. As of now, we have yet to find any such hints."

Mark Rousseau exhaled a frustrated breath. "One person. Why would one person want to kidnap McCoy?"

"Leverage, Doctor."

McCoy snorted, a gentle scoff. "I think you're overestimating my value, Ethan." He was still blindfolded cargo, riding along on the sled. Ethan's was still the only voice he'd heard as well as the source of the only set of footsteps. It seemed pretty certain that it was just the two of them on this journey—*to wherever.*

It wasn't long before they reached their destination. McCoy felt the sled stop, and Ethan removed the blindfold. McCoy sat up and saw that they were in a cavern about twenty feet high and thirty around. It was clearly an intended destination, previously made ready for their arrival.

McCoy glanced around and noticed pole-mounted lamps casting a pale yellow glow, a freestanding heater taking the chill off the damp air, four cots set up, some containers of survival supplies and packaged food, and a couple of camp food warmers ready for cooking. In addition, there were at least twenty large shipping crates piled up along two walls. Those were sealed, and McCoy had no idea what was in them.

McCoy sized Ethan up visually for the first time. *Sturdy, good-looking kid. He's definitely got some purpose in mind . . . something that means a lot to him. But is it selfish? Or idealistic?* "All the comforts of home?"

Ethan shrugged. "Some people believe physical suffering enhances the purity of revolution. I'm not one of them."

"So, you're a revolutionary, are you?"

"Potentially, in a manner of speaking," he said, hedging as he removed a tarp, revealing sophisticated field communication equipment.

"If you don't mind my asking, how do I fit into your revolution?" McCoy asked as Ethan bent over and loosened the connecting chains on his ankle and wrist shackles but didn't remove them.

"You don't, exactly. I've decided some things are more important than revolution in the societal sense."

McCoy tested his circumscribed freedom. The extra give allowed limited use of his hands and would probably make it possible for him to shuffle along, though not fast enough to let him attack or escape. "Personal things?"

"You could say that."

"Ahh. Then my guess would be, this has something to do with Anna March."

Ethan looked up abruptly. "Anna? Why Anna?"

"You tell *me,* Ethan. You're her age. You're smart."

"We're all smart on Empyrea."

"I hope you're smart enough to know taking me as a hostage isn't going to get you what you want, whatever that is."

Ethan gave him a hollow smile. "That's open to interpretation, Doctor." Then he turned away to start heating up two containers of stew.

"This *isn't* open to interpretation, son. Starfleet doesn't bargain for hostages, no matter who. That's the rule, and Captain Kirk's going to follow it."

"Rules can be broken. Are you hungry?"

"I could eat."

A few moments later, the food warmer beeped, indicating the stew had reached the desired temperature. Ethan opened the door, took out the containers, opened their tops, and handed one to his prisoner along with a spoon.

McCoy took it gratefully. He was a lot more hungry than he'd admitted. "Not bad for field rations," he said as he swallowed his first mouthful.

"Thanks."

"They're going to be looking for me, y'know," McCoy said.

"Well, they're going to be frustrated, then."

"I'm not talking about Empyrean search parties."

"Neither am I, Doctor," Ethan said with polite confidence.

"The *Enterprise* can scan this whole planet, inside and out."

"I know that. I also know these caverns are inside geologic formations that are going to cause so many ghost images they're not going to know *what* they're looking at, much less be able to find out where you are."

McCoy frowned. He was annoyed that the kid was so damned blasé, but he refused to give Ethan the satisfaction of knowing that. "You think you've got it all covered, don't you?"

"I do have it all covered. The only way they'll find you is if I want them to."

"Hmm. Okay. Let's just say, for argument's sake, that's true. What're you doing all this for?"

Ethan poured two cups of water from a canteen. "You were right."

"About what?"

"This is about Anna. I want the *Enterprise* to give safe passage to Anna, me, and any other young Empyreans who want to leave our planet."

"I hate to rain on your parade, son, but Anna doesn't *want* to leave. She's undergoing treatment on the *Enterprise* right now. She insisted on it—"

Ethan waved a dismissive hand. "I know all about your treatment. That's not going to give her the life she wants. It's just a way of making her continue to live a lie—her *mother's* lie. Plus, I don't think your treatment's going to work. I just hope and pray it doesn't kill her."

That McCoy took as an insult. "Since when are *you* a doctor, kid?"

"I'm not. But I'm Empyrean."

McCoy rolled his eyes. He was getting damned tired of that superior local attitude and fervently wished for a divine dose of comeuppance for the whole damned colony. In a softer corner of his heart, he also hoped Ethan would live long enough to learn his lesson and to put it to good use after all this was over.

"It's not just me," Ethan went on. "There's a whole movement growing here, a lot of young people who aren't going to stand for another generation of this isolation. We've got something to prove to the galaxy and just as much to offer."

"I thought you had plans for changing things peacefully by growing into leadership."

"We did, but some of us don't think that's going to work. And I'm tired of waiting. We've made other plans." He gestured toward the unmarked supply boxes. "Those crates contain weapons."

"You're gonna start a civil war?" McCoy's eyebrows arched in surprise.

"Sometimes violence is the only way to bring change."

"That's not the Empyrean way."

"It wasn't, but maybe it should be."

"Back on Earth, humanity's been spending the last three hundred years trying to do away with that attitude," McCoy said with a derisive snort of disapproval. "If you're that anxious to throw away all that progress, then you Empyreans aren't as genetically perfected as you think."

Ethan spooned some stew into his mouth, chewing thoughtfully. "Well, resorting to violence was a choice I was never happy about. Now I've got another one."

"So, instead of a shooting revolution, you think I'm your ticket to political asylum."

"That's right."

"That's *wrong.* It'll never happen, Ethan. And the longer you hold me here, the worse it's going to be for you when they find us."

Ethan remained unfazed. "We'll see, Doctor."

"Why are you doing this?" McCoy asked again, extra intensity in his lowered voice, his eyes narrowed.

"I told you."

"Bull. This isn't about politics or asylum or even getting off this planet. That's not what's driving you."

"Okay. Then you tell me, Dr. McCoy. What *is?*"

"Love," McCoy said flatly.

The flicker in Ethan's gaze was minute. Had McCoy not been looking for it, it would have passed unnoticed.

"You love Anna," he continued, "and you think this is the only way to save her."

Ethan looked away for the first time.

Ha! McCoy thought as a triumphant grin lit his face. *Now I'm getting somewhere!* "I *knew* it."

Ethan yanked a weapon out of a holster hidden under his jacket. Not a modern energy-pulse weapon, but his old-style revolver, dead-aimed at a point between McCoy's eyes. "If I were you, Doctor, I don't think I'd be laughing."

But McCoy didn't flinch. "I'm not laughing at you,

son. Well, maybe I am, but not *only* at you. I'm laughing at you, me, and every other male ever driven to acts of temporary insanity by love."

Finally sensing some doubt in this kid, McCoy decided to raise the stakes in their verbal joust. Perhaps not the wisest course of action, considering the gun in Ethan's hand, but a risk he'd already decided he'd have to confront sooner or later. "Y'know, hostage taking only works if you're ready to go the distance."

"And kill you?" Ethan said with chilling composure and no hesitation at all.

"That's right," McCoy said, determined to maintain his own studied casualness. "Are you willing to do that?"

Ethan's return gaze was solid ice. "I know the answer, Doctor. For your sake, let's hope you don't have to find out."

Chapter Nineteen

RAMON ORTEGA stepped out of his steaming shower and toweled himself off, watching his reflection in the fogged mirror. Was it boastful to see his own image and fancy himself a Greek god stepping out of the mists of time? He chuckled to himself; perhaps that *was* a bit much.

By any human standards, he did have an ideal physique: proportions perfect, limbs lithe and sculpted, muscles taut and rippling, though without any bulging excesses. His face was handsome and flawless, yet with dimples that lent a boyish quality to his smile.

The simple truth was, these physical characteristics were nothing special here on his world, not compared to the rest of the Empyrean population. They were just *him*. He'd never really given his looks much thought, nor his intellect, not until these Outsiders intruded, with all their comparisons and raw sensitivities and chips on their shoulders, especially this Scott fellow.

"Ray, are you out of the shower?"

It was his wife's melodious voice calling from the hallway.

"Yes, Kat," he said.

The door opened and she came barefoot into the bathroom, greeting him with a light kiss on the lips. Beneath her fluffy robe, Katrina was as physically perfect as he was, as brilliant a neurosurgeon as he was a physicist and engineer. In other words, well within the norm for Empyrea. He wondered what the Federation people would think of her. Would they dislike her as much as they seemed to dislike him just because of who and what he was? He sighed. *Probably.*

"You're going to be late," she said.

"I'm never late."

"You're working with the Outsiders again today?"

He nodded and wrapped the towel around his waist. "If nothing else goes wrong, this should be the last day."

"Finally shutting down the reactor core?"

He answered with a distracted nod.

"Good," Katrina said. "When all this is over with, maybe you'll sleep better than you did last night."

Ortega winced. "I didn't keep you up, did I?"

"You know me. I can sleep through anything. But I was aware that you seemed to be tossing and turning an awful lot."

"That pretty much describes last night. Sorry, Kat."

"You were still rehashing that equipment failure, were you?"

He nodded sheepishly.

"Ray, that wasn't your fault."

"I know. But it wasn't *their* fault either, and there I was blaming them. Blaming Federation workmanship . . ." His voice trailed off and he shook his head, the recollection bringing a fresh blush to his cheeks. "It was very embarrassing finding out we're behind the times on something we thought we were so good at. I was mortified, and I doubt I endeared myself to those two starship officers."

"You don't talk much about them."

"What's to talk about?" he shrugged.

"Do you like them?"

"That's a strange question, Kat. I don't have to like them."

"Do they like you?"

"I don't think so."

"Hmmm. I like you." She hugged him from behind as he stood before the mirror and brushed his thick, dark hair. "Why wouldn't they?"

"I honestly don't know. But they seem to have their reasons. They're very insecure. It's as if they constantly have to prove themselves or prove that Empyreans aren't superior to random-gene humans."

"But they're *not* Empyrean; that's not their fault either."

"I know that, but they don't seem to."

She slipped out of her pink robe, hung it on a hook, and stepped into the shower chamber. She turned on the hot water and adjusted the nozzle to deliver a mist spray. "I wonder why they have so much trouble accepting themselves for what they are, the way we accept ourselves?"

"I don't know, Kat. Maybe it's easier to accept yourself when you don't have quite so many flaws to overlook."

"I wonder how I'd react if the situation were reversed, if I were an Outsider who came here and had to be compared to us?"

"Probably the same way they're reacting."

"Defensively?"

"Yeah."

She turned the water pressure up and began humming. As Ramon listened, he tried something he'd never done before in his life: seeing himself as an Outsider would see him. It was a difficult perspective to imagine, as difficult as it was to imagine that an Empyrean could have done such cleverly malicious damage to the observatory's power systems. He'd been sworn to secrecy while the investigation went on, so he couldn't tell Katrina how much that unsettling possibility had contributed to his sleepless night.

Confusion was not an emotion Ramon Ortega had encountered often in his life. Yet, here he was, pondering: If Clements's investigators did find a colonist responsible for the troubles with the observatory's computers, then his faith in Empyrean technology would at least be somewhat restored, but his faith in the integrity of his people would be shaken badly. If, on the other hand, the suspicions of sabotage were ruled groundless, then Ortega would have to swallow the painful concept of the fallibility of Empyrean technological know-how.

Either way, Empyrea would be disgraced. In all honesty, he did not know which outcome would be worse.

Jim Kirk swiveled his seat to face the bridge science station. "Mr. Chekov?"

The Russian looked up slowly, as if he'd rather avoid meeting the captain's gaze directly. He knew what Kirk was going to ask. "Sorry, sir. Still nothing on Dr. McCoy."

Kirk's mouth tightened into a frustrated line. "Can we increase sensor power and still sneak past Empyrean scanners?"

Chekov sighed. "There is no vay to be certain, sir. Ve do not know the exact capabilities of the Empyrean scanner system. Ve can only estimate. If ve go beyond the power levels ve are already at, ve vill risk losing our margin of error."

"McCoy may not have a margin of error," Kirk said with quiet intensity. "I think it's time we took that risk, the Empyreans be damned."

At the communications console, Uhura turned abruptly toward Kirk. "Captain, we're being hailed from the planet."

Sulu brightened. "Maybe the Empyreans have found Dr. McCoy."

"The signal is not on any official channel," Uhura said.

Kirk nodded. "Then let's find out who it is."

"*Enterprise,* come in please," said a young man's swaggering voice from the bridge speakers.

Kirk stood in the center of the bridge. "This is the *Enterprise.* Identify yourself."

"I'll speak only to Captain Kirk."

"You are speaking to Captain Kirk."

"This is the Empyrean Liberation Front."

With a skeptical hitch of one eyebrow, Kirk glanced around at his bridge officers, who seemed equally mystified. He noted that Uhura was already working quickly on her analysis of the incoming signal. "What the devil is the Empyrean Liberation Front?"

"You don't need to know anything about us, Captain. All you need to know is that we have your Dr. McCoy."

"If you expect me to simply . . . *believe* you—"

Ethan sat at the communications nook in his cavern hideaway, pointing an Empyrean stun gun at McCoy's chest as he sat five feet away. They both listened to Kirk's voice, each interpreting in his own way.

"—you're going to be disappointed. If you've got McCoy, let me talk to him."

"We can accommodate that request. Stand by,

Captain." Ethan cut off the channel and looked seriously at McCoy. "You can tell him you're okay. If you try to tell him anything about your location or me, I'll stun you."

McCoy shrugged. "I never argue with a loaded weapon, well almost never."

"Then we understand each other." Ethan opened the channel again. "Here he is, Captain. Go ahead, Doctor."

"Jim—"

"Bones?"

"Yeah. He told me to tell you I'm fine."

"Are you?"

"Give or take."

"Where are you? What's this Empyrean Liberation Front?"

Finger on the trigger, Ethan tipped his weapon toward McCoy's chest.

"Uhh, I'm afraid those questions are off-limits, Jim."

"Shut up, Doctor," Ethan ordered. "Now, Captain, listen closely—"

"No, *you* listen," said Kirk sharply. "Starfleet does *not* bargain for hostages. You release Dr. McCoy immediately, then we'll talk."

"Don't insult our intelligence, Captain. If I release Dr. McCoy, you won't give me the time of day."

"If you *don't* release him," Kirk countered, "we'll find you and 'liberate' him ourselves with consequences you're not going to like."

"Save your threats, Captain. We've taken ample and effective measures to make sure you *can't* find us. I'm sure you've been trying, and I'm sure you've had no success."

Chekov's head snapped up from the science console, anger flashing in his eyes. Kirk suppressed a smile. *We don't like our intelligence insulted, either.* If there was a way to get to this arrogant SOB, his crew would find it.

"Confident, aren't you," Kirk said casually. "All right, just for argument's sake, what do you want in exchange for McCoy?"

The answer was instantaneous and not at all what Kirk had expected. "Political asylum aboard your ship and safe transport away from Nova Empyrea for any Empyrean citizens who want to leave."

"That's impossible. We're not in the business of violating local laws."

"Take our proposal to President March, Captain. You may find that laws can be changed."

"Call us when you're ready to surrender. Kirk out."

"I hate to say I told you so," McCoy said. "But I did."

A distracted frown furrowed Ethan's forehead. "I didn't expect immediate compliance, Doctor. But I can tell you this: There are some very frustrated officers on the *Enterprise* bridge right now."

"What makes you so sure?"

"Because I know that their sensors can't get through this rock with any accuracy, and I know how effectively my signal source was disguised."

"Maybe so," McCoy said without a shred of distress. "But you *don't* know Commander Uhura and Commander Chekov. Our people may not be genetically enhanced, but we've got experience you can't even imagine. They don't give up on problems until they solve 'em."

Kirk stared at Uhura. "Commander, you've got to have a *clue* at least."

"Sorry, Captain." She shook her head. "That signal was so scrambled, it could have come from anywhere on the planet."

"If it was scrambled, then there's got to be a way to unscramble it."

"I agree, sir. But it's going to take some time."

"Then you and Mr. Chekov had better get started. I want a full analysis of that signal. And the next time this Empyrean Liberation Front contacts us, *we* better be ready to track them down."

Ortega made it to the science complex a few minutes early and was waiting in the lobby when Scott and Spock transported down from the *Enterprise*. In the control center, he observed as they went through the computer simulation of the shutdown routine one more time. They didn't ask for his participation, and he didn't volunteer, all of which seemed to suit both sides. His role would be supervisory.

They had apparently taken to heart Ortega's initial policy pronouncement that this was a Federation installation, so Federation personnel were to be responsible for its maintenance, repair, and removal. The discovery that it was an Empyrean-built system that had broken down hadn't changed anything. In fact, Ortega believed Mr. Scott to be reveling in the role of savior, rescuing the Empyreans from their own misguided conceit.

I think if I tried to help, Ortega thought, *Scott would tackle me and sit on me to keep me out of it.*

As for Spock, well, he was another matter. Once Ortega had met the *Enterprise* science officer, he thought it would be useful to learn all he could about Vulcans. After all, no one on Nova Empyrea had ever met a Vulcan face-to-face. First, he'd found and reviewed all the information on Vulcans in Empyrean data banks. When he was done with that, he'd then requested and been given updated files from the *Enterprise* library computer.

The genetic superiority of Empyreans over Earth humans seemed of no consequence to Commander

Spock. Nor did Ortega's initial negative appraisal of Spock's mixed lineage. Ortega respected Spock's apparently imperturbable nature, not to mention his ability to focus on the task at hand without the prickly emotionalism Scott insisted on displaying from time to time.

To Ortega, the excitable engineer's behavior often bore significant resemblance to birds and animals that puffed up their feathers and fur in order to frighten off would-be rivals for territory and mates. All in all, rather primitive and pointless, because Scott was neither bird nor beast, and he and Ortega were most certainly not rivals.

This morning, Scott seemed mercifully disinterested in such displays of purported dominance. Ortega took that as an indication that the *Enterprise* engineer was as anxious to get this job over with as Ortega himself was to see the two Starfleet officers back on their ship for good.

Still, for all their flaws, there was much Ortega found admirable about them. Spock possessed a keen intellect coupled with a breadth of knowledge that Ortega had to admit was as impressive as that of many Empyreans. And Scott, for all his volatility, was plainly gifted as an engineer, with as sure a touch and as much instinctive analytical skill as Ortega had ever seen.

"Well, that's it, Mr. Spock," Scott said, "everything reads normal. We're ready to start shutdown procedures."

"Very well, Mr. Scott. You may do so at your discretion."

"Initiating now, sir. Let's hope whoever's been toyin' with us isn't lullin' us into a false sense o' security—"

Without warning, Scott's sentence was cut short by the flashing red lights and piercing siren of the emergency alert system. The engineer swore under his breath. "What in the name o'—"

Spock had immediately slipped into the seat before an adjacent monitor station. Ortega stood just behind them, eyes darting from one monitor screen to another.

"Hmm," said Spock, scanning the data readouts faster than the human eye could follow. "The phase converters are no longer responding to input commands."

"Switching over t' manual override," Scott said tersely, keying the backup systems. He waited a moment for a response.

"Manual overrides inoperative," the computer announced in a stilted voice, its metallic lack of concern at odds with the situation.

Scott flashed a concerned glance over at Spock. "Sir, we've got to reestablish some kind o' control over those converters."

"Agreed. If we do not, the transfer coils will overload."

Scott felt a presence over his shoulder but didn't need to turn. "Stop hoverin' back there, laddie. In case y' hadn't noticed, we could use a wee bit o' help here."

Instantly, Ortega swung a leg over the back of the empty chair between the two starship officers and sat at the newly activated terminal.

Chapter Twenty

Captain's log, supplemental.

Awaiting word from Mr. Scott and Mr. Spock on the shutdown of the observatory's troublesome reactor core. We have had no further communication with the mysterious Empyrean Liberation Front. We still do not know if they will agree to release Dr. McCoy, and we have as yet been unable to locate the source of their original signal.

"CAPTAIN, I'M SORRY." President March sat at her office desk, looking bewildered. Clements, her chief investigator, stood beside her, watching the grim faces of Kirk and Ambassador Rousseau on March's communications viewer. "We've never heard of any Empyrean Liberation Front. Clements, do you know anything about any subversive group that might be responsible for this?"

"Not as such," he said blandly.

From the *Enterprise* command chair, Kirk tried to

read Clements's lack of expression. "Not as such?" he repeated. "Is that a yes or a no?"

"There's been no history of clandestine political opposition in all the time this colony has existed."

"There is a first time for everything," Chekov muttered from Spock's science console, not loudly enough to be heard off the bridge.

Kirk cast a brief, sympathetic glance toward his Russian security chief, then turned his attention back to the image of the Empyreans on the main viewscreen. "That doesn't sound like an unconditional denial to me, Mr. Clements."

"I can categorically state that we were unaware of any dissident group calling itself the Empyrean Liberation Front prior to your telling us about it, Captain Kirk."

Kirk nodded, mulling the Empyrean investigator's extremely careful choice of words. "I see. Now that you *are* aware of it, what do you intend to do about it?"

"We'll do what we would in response to any threat, internal or external: investigate. And if we can confirm its existence, formulate a strategy for dealing with it."

"That's all we *can* do, Captain," Elizabeth March added. "We're well aware that Earth has a long history of this sort of thing. But if you knew us well, you would understand how out of character it would be for Empyreans to form this sort of underground group—no matter what their beliefs or disagreements with government policies."

"That's true, Captain," Rousseau interjected. "They may be less than enthusiastic about welcoming Outsiders, but they've always made room among themselves for open discussion of dissenting opinions. Or at least, they used to."

"Maybe some Empyreans decided discussion wasn't enough," Kirk said. "If their opinions weren't affecting policy, they may have decided that more radical action was their only choice."

"Captain," March said, "you keep referring to this liberation front as a group."

"What else would it be?"

"It could be one unhappy individual," she said.

Kirk's eyebrows arched in disbelief. "A one-man wrecking crew?"

"Captain Kirk," said Clements, "there's nothing this 'liberation front' has claimed to have done that could *not* have been done by one Empyrean."

"Then a whole *government* of Empyreans should have no trouble tracking him down," Kirk said. Though Clements's expression remained neutral, there was a brief flare of irritation in his eyes. Kirk noted it with pleasure: *Good. That barb hit a nerve.*

"Elizabeth," Clements said stiffly, "there are several leads I should pursue immediately."

"Go ahead."

With a curt nod toward Kirk and Rousseau, Clements headed for the door.

"Well, then," Kirk said to March, "I'd appreciate regular progress reports. And we will of course let you know if we hear from them—or *him*—again. If that's all—"

"Uhh, Captain," Elizabeth said, lowering her voice, "if I could have a moment."

Clements paused imperceptibly in the doorway, then continued on as the door slid shut behind him.

Even though she knew she was alone in the office, March waited a cautious extra few seconds before speaking in a confidential tone. "How is Anna?"

"There's been no change in her condition, President March. No problems as far as I know."

The tension in her posture relaxed ever so slightly. "Thank you." Then she sighed. "I'd still feel a lot better about this if Leonard was there. I never should have had him and Mark come down here."

"Elizabeth," Rousseau said, "you're not to blame for what happened. You said it yourself: There's been no history of any kind of terrorism on Empyrea. There was no reason for any of us to think it would start now."

"Maybe there *was* a reason, and I just didn't see it. Maybe I've become so out of touch with my own people . . ."

"Even the best leader can't know *everything,*" said Rousseau.

But she barely heard him. "Maybe popular sentiment about this treaty renewal is a lot more explosive than I thought. What if just by letting you make your proposal, I set off the trigger?"

"You didn't. But even if you did, it's not over yet. And one crazy Empyrean—or a whole gang of them—well, they're not going to win without a fight."

"A fight? Mark, I don't even know which side I'm on anymore."

Rousseau stepped in front of Kirk, dominating the image on Elizabeth's viewer. "Then I'll tell you. You're fighting for your daughter's life and for fairness and for justice. And that's all anyone *can* do."

Elizabeth shook her head. "What about Leonard?"

Rousseau managed a smile. "Whoever's got him, I'm sure McCoy's doing some fighting of his own—in his own way."

"There *is* no Empyrean Liberation Front, is there?" McCoy sipped the last of a mug of tasty broth, then glared at Ethan over the cup's rim. "Other than you, I mean."

"Just because you haven't seen it doesn't mean it's not there," Ethan said with forced bravado.

"How'd you like to bet on that?"

Ethan's brow furrowed as his resolve seemed to weaken. "What makes you so sure?"

"Well, the name, for one thing."

"The *name?*" Now the young man seemed downright insulted. "What's wrong with the name?"

"*Empyrean Liberation Front?*"

"So? There've been lots of freedom fighters in Earth history who've used 'liberation front' in the names of their groups."

"*E*–period–*L*–period–*F*–period?"

"So?"

"You still don't get it." This wasn't the first time McCoy had seen someone so bright overlook something so obvious. And he knew it wouldn't be the last—if he got out of this situation alive.

"Get what?"

"The acronym—ELF—spells *elf!*"

Ethan stared, then blinked, then the corners of his mouth curled into a small, involuntary smile. "Oh."

"Not as imposing as you might've wanted, hmm?"

"No. I guess not."

"So, did you just make it up on the spot when you called the *Enterprise?*"

"Kind of. I guess I've been concentrating on the details of the overall plan. That was one detail I forgot about."

"Are you sure that's the only one, son?" McCoy asked kindly, hoping to take advantage of this moment of unexpected humor. The effort backfired.

"As a matter of fact, I *am,* Doctor," Ethan said, the brass returning to his voice. "Just because we don't have a proper political name doesn't mean there's no group behind all this. These weapons, this base, this isn't my personal fantasy."

"I didn't mean that it was," McCoy said, trying to placate Ethan. Too late. "I'm just wondering if you've gone off on your own crusade."

"There's a lot of discontent on the planet. You and anyone else who underestimates that are going to pay a heavy price."

McCoy shook his head, marveling at Ethan. "When

this first started, I thought you had to have some doubts about what you're doing."

"And now?"

"Now I'm not so sure about that," McCoy said, chuckling.

"What's so funny?"

"I was just thinking about how much easier life is when you're young."

Ethan gave him a look of severe reproach. "There's nothing *easy* about being young, Doctor. If you think there is, then you've got a lousy memory."

"No, I don't, son. Now, you don't have to tell me if this fits you, but when *I* was young, I knew all the answers. Or, at least, I knew the answers were lying around, waiting to be found if I *looked* hard enough for 'em. Then, the older I got, the fewer answers and the more questions I had. Eventually, you've got all questions and *no* answers. And *that's* what's easy about being young."

Elizabeth March gasped as she turned and saw Clements standing unexpectedly in her office doorway. "Clements! I thought you were going to—"

"—pursue leads," he said, completing her sentence. "I did." He held up a small scanner-recorder and keyed its playback mode. He listened dispassionately, watching her face.

Elizabeth's eyes widened in surprise as she heard her own voice, the whole conversation she'd just had with Captain Kirk and Ambassador Rousseau, the conversation she'd believed to be private. When it was over, her surprise darkened into anger. "How dare you eavesdrop on my personal communications!"

"I had suspicions. It was my job to check them out."

"Suspicions! You violated the sanctity of the office of the president—"

"—and the president has apparently violated Empyrean law."

"*What* law?" she challenged, a challenge that knocked him off balance at least for a moment.

"I'm not sure—yet," he said with careful emphasis. "But I do intend to find out. It appears Anna is undergoing some kind of medical treatment aboard the *Enterprise*. You could tell me about it—"

"There's nothing to tell."

"—or I could conduct a much wider, much more *public* investigation."

"Since when is it your job to undermine the presidency?"

Clements slipped the recording device into his pocket. "I could ask you the same thing."

"Clements, it's not like you to do something like this on your own initiative."

"You're right, Elizabeth. It's not. I was approached by other leaders who are dead set against this treaty renewal—"

"And I'm sure they told you to ruin me, no matter what it took."

He shook his head. "No. Just to investigate your apparent favor toward the Federation. And I must admit, I haven't come up with much to explain your policy. There's a clear majority against any further involvement with these Outsiders. But you seem intent on resisting that majority."

"Majorities can be wrong, Clements," she said dryly, regaining a measure of sound footing. "My only intent is to see that opposition opinions get a fair review. As for you, resorting to spying on me, I thought you were more clever than that."

"So did I," he said with a hint of a smile. "And I wouldn't call it spying. That has such . . . *negative* connotations. Consider it justifiable surveillance."

Her anger flared again. "Justifiable? To *whom?*"

"To other members of the government. I don't work

for you personally. I work for the executive branch. And right now, you'd have a hard time finding a lot of allies in your own cabinet."

"I'm not the first president to believe in an unpopular policy, and I won't be the last."

"That's true. But so is this: When I find out what's really going on—and I *will*—you may not *be* president much longer."

Her jaw muscles grew taut. "Go ahead. Investigate all you like. But don't expect any cooperation from me. And don't be surprised when I try to have you removed from your post."

Clements's lips stretched into a tight, cold smile. "I was beginning to wonder if you had any fight left in you, Elizabeth."

"I do."

With a respectful nod, he left her office. She slipped back into her desk chair. And then she started to tremble.

Chapter Twenty-one

IN HIS *Enterprise* command chair, Captain Kirk sat at the virtual heart of ship and crew. Despite the activity and the familiar blend of bridge sounds around him, he found himself mesmerized by the viewscreen image of the planet continuing its deceptively tranquil rotation.

For most of the millennia that humans and other intelligent beings had been observing the cosmos, planetary and stellar motions had been accepted as models of stability. So regular, so imperturbable—the foundations of calendars and cultures wherever sentient life evolved.

Such immutability had given primitive people something to believe in as they wrestled with the mysteries of a universe beyond their comprehension as well as the more commonplace dangers inherent in the daily struggle for survival. No matter what animals had tried to eat them that day, what hostile tribes had attacked, no matter how much or how little food they'd found or harvested, the sun, moon, and stars maintained their cycles. The constellations came and went with nights, days, and seasons. *Something to believe in.*

Over time, of course, modern science had developed. Questions were asked, theories arose, and instruments were invented to test new ideas. Bit by bit, examined from new and ever-broadening perspectives, those universal constants had been revealed instead as pieces of some great, roiling celestial kaleidoscope. *Anything* but constant.

In truth, the only *real* constant was change.

So much for cosmic stability, Kirk thought. As he worried about Spock and Scotty at the science outpost, McCoy held hostage, and Anna March down in sickbay, he couldn't help wondering how much easier it must have been to deal with the earthly trials of life when people still believed in that clockwork universe and its protective, secure structure.

"Captain," Uhura said, interrupting his musing, "the Empyrean Liberation Front is signaling us."

Kirk snapped upright in his seat and glanced toward Chekov at the science console.

"This time, ve will locate them, Keptin," Chekov said with steely determination.

"I'll keep them talking as long as I can. Uhura, open the channel."

"Captain Kirk," Ethan's voice said from the speakers, "this is the Empyrean Liberation Front. We've been monitoring your communications with the Empyrean government."

"Oh?"

"Surprised, Captain? You shouldn't be. I told you we were a force to be reckoned with. We're aware that you've been discussing us with them. And we can assure you, the government has no better chance of finding us than you do. So, if you're counting on them to retrieve Dr. McCoy for you, you're going to be disappointed."

"If you made this call just so you can gloat—"

"We're not gloating, Captain. Just advising. And reminding you that we've got a guest you would like returned."

"A 'guest'?"

"We think it's a less provocative word than *hostage*, less menacing. We want to be absolutely clear about this: It's not our intention to hurt Dr. McCoy or anyone else."

"How comforting. Then let him go."

"We'd be happy to as soon as you and the Empyrean government agree to our demands, which are really not excessive at all."

"Excess is in the eye of the beholder," Kirk said flatly. "Let *me* be absolutely clear: *Any* demands, no matter how innocuous, are excessive as long as you're holding a Starfleet officer against his will."

"We're sorry you feel that way, Captain Kirk. We hope you'll change your mind. Time is on our side. Liberation Front out."

Kirk glanced at Uhura, who signaled that the channel had indeed been cut off from the Empyrean end. Then he rose from his chair and moved to the railing near the science station. "Well, Mr. Chekov? Was he on long enough to get a fix?"

"Still analyzing, sir." Chekov's hand skipped across his keypad, adding to and sifting the data reports scrolling across his monitor screen. Then the screen wiped itself blank, replacing the numbers with a grid. As Chekov watched his handiwork with satisfaction, a three-dimensional depiction of the Empyrean globe appeared, rotating to the west. The computer rapidly selected a grid square, tinted it green, and enlarged it. Kirk looked on with deepening interest as locator circles appeared, then blinked as the computer homed in on a desolate section of mountains halfway across the continent from the colony's capital.

Chekov turned with a clenched fist and a tight smile. "Got him, Keptin."

"The source of the communications signal?"

"Aye, sir."

"Are you sure?"

"Ninety-seven percent certainty. Initiating focused sensor scan of that location now." Then, as Chekov studied the scanners' findings, he began to frown. "Damn."

"What is it?"

"Ve have located them, but ve cannot beam Dr. McCoy out or beam a rescue party in."

"Why not?" Kirk stepped up through the gap in the railing and leaned over Chekov's shoulder for a closer look.

"They are two to three hundred meters below the planet surface. A network of caverns. The combination of mineral deposits vould disrupt transporter integrity. Ve could not guarantee safe beam up."

Kirk made a sour face. "Then we'll just have to beam a rescue team down to the planet surface and go in there and get him."

"Sir," Chekov said, "there is something to be said for stealth."

"Is that an option, Commander?"

"Aye, sir. There may be a vay to reconfigure our transporter to punch through the geological interference."

"How?"

"Boosting power to the phase transition coils, tightening the resolution of the main imaging scanners—"

Kirk's eyes narrowed. "You can do that without Scotty?"

"Keptin," Chekov said, looking mildly insulted, "I have learned a few things from him."

"All right, Mr. Chekov. See what you can do," Kirk

said with a wry half smile. Then the smile faded. "But just in case, get a heavily armed rescue party of twenty ready to beam down and go in their front door."

"Aye, sir," Chekov said as he leapt up from his seat and rushed into the turbolift.

Ramon Ortega slammed his open hand down on the console. "*Dammit!*"

The noise drew the immediate attention of both Scott and Spock still working feverishly at their own terminals in the observatory's main control center.

Scott came over as Ortega slumped back in his chair. "What is it, laddie?"

Ortega made a defeated gesture toward his monitor screen, displaying large yellow letters: REMOTE OPERATIONS CONTROL SYSTEMS DISENGAGED. Scott stared in disbelief. "Mr. Spock, y' better come over here," he said in a voice hollowed by horror.

But Spock was already there. "Fascinating," he murmured.

Scotty spun toward him. "Sir, it's not fascinatin'—it's a *disaster!* The control-logic circuits've failed—these consoles're useless! Without 'em, we've got no way t' access all those malfunctioning systems inside the containment module."

"Indirectly, no, we do not," Spock said, his accustomed Vulcan detachment unshaken.

Scott couldn't believe what he *thought* he was hearing. "Are y' daft, man? Nobody c'n go *in* there! The plasma conduits're down. The pulse injectors've got to be fused open by now!"

"Commander Spock," said Ortega, "the radiation levels inside the containment module would be lethal in a very short time."

"I do not plan a lengthy sojourn."

"Sir," Scott said with an emphatic shake of his head, "you *canna* go in there."

"With protective equipment available from the *Enterprise,* some limited exposure is possible and survivable." He glanced from Ortega to Scott. They were both looking at him like *his* control-logic circuits had malfunctioned. He spoke quickly and precisely. "Gentlemen, we have little choice. We are facing a situation involving random yet sequential system sabotage. For all we know, the person or persons responsible for this have also disabled the containment field—"

Ortega was a step ahead. "If that containment field disintegrates, this radiation could kill thousands of Empyreans."

"That is why the time for debate is past. Unless either of you has a more efficacious solution to this problem—"

"We've got to contact the captain," Scotty insisted.

"Agreed," Spock said as they moved to the communications console. "But quickly, Mr. Scott."

When he heard Spock's compressed briefing, Kirk found the situation and the science officer's conclusion equally bleak.

"Scotty?" He hoped his chief engineer would offer a second opinion he liked better. But none was forthcoming.

"I'm afraid Mr. Spock is right, sir. There's no other way."

"Let me get this straight," Kirk said, eyes wide with skepticism. "Systems are going down like dominoes—"

"And in no particular order," Scott reminded him.

"—and there's enough radiation collected inside that containment structure to wipe out half the capital if it escapes, and somebody's got to *go in there?*"

"Aye, sir," Scott said with a solemn nod. "And even

our best radiation suit's only goin' t' provide short-term protection."

"*How* short-term?" The more he heard, the more disenchanted Kirk became about a situation for which he'd had little enthusiasm to start with.

"We canna be sure, sir. With the remote systems down, we don't know exactly what's goin' on in there."

"And how long will this damage control take?"

"Also unknown at this time, Captain," Spock said.

"We won't know *that* either until we get in there," Scott added.

"We?" Kirk frowned. "Does that mean two of you have to go in there together?"

"No, sir," Scott said. "One of us should be able t' handle the job. And I'm volunteering."

That drew a sharp look from Spock. "Captain, with all due respect to Mr. Scott's superior instinctive abilities as an engineer, I as a Vulcan will be better able to tolerate exposure to radiation levels of this intensity."

"Captain, the haggis is already in the fire, and Mr. Spock'll be, too," Scott protested. "The ship's first officer canna—"

"Mr. Scott, colorful metaphors notwithstanding," Spock said, cutting him off, "there is a more compelling justification for me to be the one who works inside the containment core. Should my attempt be unsuccessful, your greater knowledge of such systems and your gift for engineering improvisation render you less initially expendable."

"He's right, Scotty. If he gets cooked in there, you're the best man to come up with a last-second alternative."

"Last second is *right,*" Scott said grimly.

"I assume you've already got a plan?"

"We do, sir," Spock said.

"And you'll be beamed out and directly into decontamination when you're done?"

"That may not be possible, Captain. The radiation may interfere with the transporter's molecular reintegration—"

"Nothin' I canna compensate for, sir," Scott cut in with a glare of admonishment at Spock. "When he's done, I'll get him out o' there. I've got a couple of ideas to make sure o' that."

Kirk's lips thinned into a concerned line, and he exhaled slowly. He hated putting Spock—or any *other* officer—at risk for a mess caused by a combination of the Empyreans' own overweening conceit and some as-yet-unknown saboteur.

"Captain," Spock prodded, "we must proceed expeditiously."

"All right. Get what you need from the ship. And contact me before you go in there, Spock. That's an order."

"Dr. Chapel!"

The voice of Lieutenant Liftig, the male nurse attending Anna March, boomed from the adjacent ward into McCoy's office. Christine Chapel's head jerked upright, and she realized she'd dozed off at the desk while she'd been studying Anna's charts.

How long had she been out? She had no idea.

Ever since McCoy's disappearance, Chapel had been virtually living in sickbay, staying awake around the clock as best she could to monitor Anna's condition, getting by on naps in a spare diagnostic bed. If anything happened to Anna in McCoy's absence, Chapel knew she would never be able to forgive herself, even if McCoy could.

She rushed into the wardroom and knew even before she saw the diagnostic monitor over the bed that something had gone terribly wrong. Liftig hovered over the thoracic life-support apparatus covering Anna.

"Renal failure," he mumbled, brushing a lock of dark hair off his forehead. "Compensating."

"Oh, my God," Chapel whispered. "Organ dysfunction is the first sign the treatment's going wrong."

"What should we do, Doctor?"

"Run a renal diagnostic, assess damage, make sure there's no other possible cause."

Liftig nodded and reached for the diagnostic tricorder. "Right away."

Chapel felt a cold sweat breaking. Beyond the battery of tests, she didn't know *what* to do for Anna. Maybe it wasn't the treatment, maybe Anna's kidney failure *was* caused by something else, maybe the damage was minimal and reversible.

Maybe it was time for a miracle.

"A clever adaptation, Mr. Scott," Spock said with genuine appreciation. He watched the chief engineer plug a communications module the size of a deck of cards into an auxiliary input in the utility pouch of Spock's silver-gray protective suit. "You say this subspace transceiver has a power output two hundred forty-seven times that of the standard communicator?"

"Give or take."

"Will that not overload the location transponder?"

"I've beefed up the transponder circuits and put in four redundant backups. Even with that, the little beastie'll only work for a couple o' hours before it burns out," said Scott as he turned it on. "But you're not goin' t' be *in* there for longer than that. And while it's workin', it'll act as a homing beacon that should be able t' cut through the ambient radiation and keep the transporter locked onto you."

"Most ingenious."

Scott's staff had beamed down all the necessary equipment. As Ramon Ortega watched Spock prepare for the dangerous work awaiting him inside the containment structure, he found himself fighting off the nagging thought that perhaps he had misjudged these two Federation officers.

Scott secured Spock's helmet seal, then leaned over a computer console to confirm that the sensor telemetry from Spock's protective suit was registering properly, both here and up on the orbiting *Enterprise.* Satisfied that the transmission link was functional, the engineer gave a nod. "Y're ready t' go, Mr. Spock."

"Thank you, Mr. Scott," Spock said, his voice filtering through the suit's communications gear.

Scott flipped open his communicator. "Scott t' *Enterprise.*"

"Kirk here," came the reply. "Go ahead, Scotty."

"Captain, we're about t' start the damage control procedure."

"All right." Kirk let out a deep breath. "Good luck. Spock, be careful in there."

"That is always my intention, Captain."

"Kirk out."

With that, Spock entered the isolation chamber that provided a safe buffer between the control room and the containment structure. The bulky door slid shut behind him, the environmental insulation seals hissing into place. He stood at the master panel that manually operated the doors and safety systems. When it flashed a green light, he pressed the button that unlocked the inner door. It opened, and he strode through. The door slid shut behind him, and Spock was gone.

While Nurse Liftig continue running diagnostic tests, Chapel retreated to the office and activated the desktop intercom screen. "Chapel to Captain Kirk."

A moment later, Kirk's image appeared on the viewer. "What is it, Doctor?"

"I don't suppose we're any closer to finding Dr. McCoy, sir?"

"We're a little closer. Why?"

"Anna March has just suffered renal failure."

Kirk stiffened. "Because of that genetic branding treatment?"

"I'm not sure yet, Captain. But I think so. And if it is, then this could be the first in a series of organ failures."

"Can you do anything for her?"

Chapel shook her head in frustration. "I don't know, Captain. I can try but I could also make things worse. I've reviewed Dr. McCoy's notes. Nobody's done this before. Even he wasn't sure about how to treat all the possible complications."

"He picked a fine time to improvise," Kirk said with intentional sympathy.

"If there's any way to get Dr. McCoy back—"

"—now would be a good time," said Kirk, finishing their mutual thought. "I know. Do what you can down there, Christine. So will we. Kirk out."

Chapel swallowed past the lump in her throat. What she could do wasn't much.

On the bridge, Kirk swiveled toward the communications station. "Uhura, try to raise this liberation front."

Uhura's nod acknowledged the gravity of the situation. "Aye, sir."

Then Kirk stood and moved to the railing near the science console, to which Chekov had returned to continue his efforts at transporter reconfiguration. "Getting anywhere, Mr. Chekov?"

The look on Chekov's face made it clear he desperately wanted to answer in the affirmative, but he couldn't. He shook his head. "Ve're closer but still not there, sir."

"Then we're out of options. Mr. Chekov, report to the transporter room with your rescue team. Stand by to beam down on my order."

Chekov stood and nodded. "Aye, sir."

THE RETURN

ately whispered answer, her mind affirmative, but he
couldn't, he dared not hear it. "Yes, Spock, but I'm not
here..."

"Not in the literal sense, Mr. Chekov," came an
almost apologetic reply, "but your presence here greatly
influences the equations going on around me."

Chekov sighed and nodded. "I see, sir."

Chapter Twenty-two

COOL AND GREEN, the eerie glow of the emergency
illumination deep inside the Sternn fusion core was at
ironic odds with the ever-more-threatening explosive
potential collecting all around Spock. Radiation levels
continued to rise inside what had become a virtual
runaway reactor.

With a tricorder in one hand and a magnetic tool in
the other, he stood before a set of access panels that
opened three meters long and two meters high. The
guts of the power plant's computerized brain and
heart lay exposed, a mass of circuitry and power
conduits out of which he had to make some sense
before it was too late. Some indicator lights blinked
ominously, while others were dark.

"Whoever perpetrated this sabotage was quite thorough," he said out loud, knowing he was being
constantly monitored by Scott on the *Enterprise* and
Ortega in the observatory control center. They could

listen, even offer advice, but they were otherwise helpless spectators.

"Is there any pattern to the malfunctions?" Ortega asked, hunched in front of his useless console.

"None that I am able to discern," said Spock with all his usual objective detachment. "That, unfortunately, makes it difficult to anticipate how the sequence will progress, which in turn reduces the probability of getting ahead of the failure curve and interrupting it."

"Mr. Spock," Scott said from the computer terminal in the transporter room, "I think I've got a way to buy y' some extra time."

Spock glanced at his tricorder, then gingerly inserted his magnetic stylus into a subprocessor node. "I am open to suggestions, Mr. Scott."

"She's goin' t' blow if we don't vent some o' that energy buildup, and I think we c'n do it by diverting some o' the power overload to the orbital platform and the satellite network."

"In essence, utilizing those pieces of equipment as safety valves."

"Aye, sir."

"An intriguing notion," Spock said, "but the resulting overloads will damage or destroy them as well."

"That's probably true," Ortega said, "but explosions of small facilities in high orbit pose much less danger to the planet than a disaster here at the reactor core. And if sacrificing the orbital equipment might give you a better chance to shut this reactor down, then I'm all for it."

"Me, too," Scott said.

"Then I concur as well," Spock said. "Let us hope the appropriate operating system has not yet failed." He took a moment to scan the innards of the control-computer module, locating the circuitry he needed. With surgical precision, he wielded his instrument. "I am pleased to report that it remains functional. I am going to activate the emitter arrays . . . now."

Ortega chewed his lip as he switched his computer to a channel monitoring the links between the power core on the ground and the satellites and orbital station. Both showed sudden jumps in energy reception. The external sensors directed at the Sternn core showed a corresponding drop. "It's working," he said, his clenched fist happily punching the air. "Emitter arrays and reception transceivers all functioning properly."

"Thank you, gentlemen," Spock said. "I shall endeavor to make the best use of the additional time we have gained."

There was no need to say it, but all three of them knew that probably would not amount to much at all.

When McCoy heard Jim Kirk's voice over Ethan's communications system, he had two simultaneous reactions: elation and foreboding.

Though he knew he was in no immediate danger, captivity was not his favorite place to be. If the *Enterprise* was calling Ethan rather than waiting for the "Empyrean Liberation Front" to make the next move, maybe McCoy's crewmates were ready to launch a rescue. Maybe Kirk had finally reached the limits of his patience.

Or maybe something had gone terribly wrong with Anna's treatment regimen and they desperately needed McCoy to save her life. *Why am I such a damn pessimist? Please, God, not that. I can stick around her a little longer . . .*

"So, you're ready to accept our conditions, Captain," Ethan said, making sure there wasn't the slightest hint of subservience in his voice. He held his old-fashioned gun pointed at McCoy's chest, implying that McCoy was not being invited to participate in this conversation.

"No, as a matter of fact, we're not. Despite your best efforts, we have figured out where you are."

"You're bluffing, Captain."

"What makes you so sure of that?"

"If you knew where we were, you'd have beamed a rescue party down by now. Taken advantage of the element of surprise."

"How do you know we *haven't* beamed a rescue party down? Maybe this little chat is nothing but a distraction."

"Nice try, Captain. One, your transporter can't get directly through the mineral deposits between here and the surface, and two, I've been monitoring the area and there's been no transporter activity."

"Are you ready to stake your life on that?"

"That's what this is all about."

There was a pause. Then Kirk said, "What about the life of another young Empyrean?"

Those were the words McCoy dreaded hearing. He no longer cared about the gun aimed at his heart, and he spoke up before Ethan could react or reply. "Jim, is it Anna?"

"Shut up, Doctor!" Ethan jumped up and took a menacing step toward his prisoner. They were ten feet apart when his finger cocked the hammer of his revolver.

McCoy ignored the threat. "Jim, answer me!"

"She's suffering from multiple organ failure, Bones. Chapel's doing what she—"

With a savage chop of his free hand, Ethan cut the comm channel off and glared at McCoy. "Damn you! I told you to shut up!"

From the moment the signal was interrupted, Uhura tried repeatedly to reestablish contact with the Liberation Front comm station. "They're just not responding, Captain," she finally said.

Kirk nodded. He no longer cared about the

Empyrean's diplomatic sensibilities or the fuzzy limits of Federation regulations. He cared about McCoy and Anna. As for precipitating an interplanetary incident, there seemed no time like the present. He pressed the intercom button on the arm of his command seat. "Kirk to transporter room. Mr. Chekov?"

"Aye, sir."

"Take that rescue party down there. Stay alert; we don't know how many people they've got, and we don't know how they're armed. Phasers out, on heavy stun."

"Aye, Keptin. Ve vill find Dr. McCoy and ve vill bring him back."

Clad in fatigues, Chekov led his security team of twenty down to the Empyrean desert, near the entrance to the network of caves where McCoy's captors were known to be hiding. Just as the geological formations in the subterranean rock interfered with attempts to transport beneath the surface, so they also made subsurface tricorder readings erratic.

Chekov frowned at the scanner in his hand, then looked up to address the rescue squad gathered around him. "As ve expected, ve are detecting life forms in these caverns. But ve cannot tell how many, and ve cannot tell exactly vhere they are. Ve vill split into four teams of five each and go down the four main tunnel branches. The further underground ve get, the better our tricorders should operate." *I hope,* he said to himself.

"Phasers on heavy stun," he continued. "Ve must assume that the members of this Empyrean Liberation Front are armed and dangerous. Remember, our primary mission is the rescue and protection of Dr. McCoy. Ve are not looking for a fight. Ve do not know if ve have surprise on our side, so be prepared to fire first if that is necessary to secure our objective. Any questions?"

There weren't any.

"All right, then. Let's go."

"Ethan," McCoy snarled, "don't you *understand?* Anna's *dying*—"

"Why should I believe you—"

"—and I'm the only one who can *save* her!"

"Why should I believe you!?" Ethan's shout echoed sharply off the cave walls.

McCoy took a deep breath, deliberately calming his own fury. The stakes were rising. Emotions were frayed. He was still shackled at the wrists and ankles. Ethan was finally showing the strain as he realized that the situation he had so carefully created might be spiraling out of his control. And, last but certainly not least in order of importance, Ethan was the one with the loaded gun. McCoy was going to have to proceed very, *very* carefully.

"Saving Anna's life is the most important thing to you, isn't it, son? That's the reason you launched this whole circus in the first place." McCoy kept his voice soft, but he was not asking questions. He was almost certain he knew the answers. But he needed to hear them from Ethan if he was going to get anywhere with this seat-of-the-pants attempt to get out of here and back to the *Enterprise* before it was too late.

Ethan swallowed hard. "They can't just beam you up, you know."

"I think you're right about that."

"Then maybe I'm also right about Anna. Maybe your Captain Kirk's lying about that too."

"Ethan, he's not lying. This is *not* some kind of trick."

"How do I know that?"

"All right, dammit!" McCoy knew he was losing his temper and wanted to kick himself for it, but he couldn't help it. "So what if it turns out to *be* a damn trick? What's the worst that happens? This 'liberation front' thing ends, and you find out that Anna's going to be fine. But if you're *wrong* and it's *not* a trick, Anna's not going to be around to hear your apology."

For the first time since this ordeal had begun, McCoy saw fear in Ethan's eyes. Not fear of death or injury, but fear of doing the wrong thing. Fear of the burden of guilt. McCoy pounced.

"Are you prepared to live the rest of your life, however long that might be, knowing *you* kept me from saving *Anna's* life?"

Ethan bit his lip. But he still could not bring himself to answer or move.

"Well, hell, if you're not letting me go, then I'm *leaving,*" McCoy said, not bothering to hide his disgust. With a glance at the gun still pointed his way, he turned and shuffled toward the cavern entrance and tried to control the nervous chattering of his teeth.

"You'll never find your way to the surface."

"Then take me up there," said McCoy without looking back. "If I get lost and Anna dies, how're you going to feel?"

"Doctor, stop right there."

McCoy shuffled on. The entry was just a few feet away.

"If I shoot you with this, you won't be stunned. You'll be dead."

"I know what a gun can do, son."

"Then don't force me—"

"You kill me, you'll also be killing Anna. I don't think you can do that."

"Dr. McCoy," Ethan said, desperation in his voice, *"stop!"*

McCoy forced his feet to move another painful step. Then he heard the metallic click release of a trigger being pulled. His heart stumbled for a beat, he heard the deafening thunder of the gun, he braced for a bullet tearing into his flesh—

—then heard the twang of a ricochet off the rock facade overhead and saw the bullet burrow itself into the silt of the cavern floor.

His heart started again. He resumed his shuffling toward the opening that would lead him out of here. Then he felt something hard, heavy, and sharp hit him between his shoulder blades. He sucked in his breath reflexively before he could process the physical fact that it wasn't a bullet. The object landed at his feet and he looked down. It was small, no bigger than his thumb. It was the electronic key that worked the locks on his shackles.

"How did you know I wouldn't shoot you?" Ethan asked as McCoy freed himself.

McCoy looked up with a wan smile, wondering if any color had returned to his face. "I didn't."

"Neither did I," Ethan said sheepishly.

"Oh. Well, let's just say I hoped genetically perfected people have better things to do than shoot demented doctors in the back. Now get me up to the surface as fast as you can."

Ethan rushed past. "Come on, there's a short-cut."

On the *Enterprise* bridge, Uhura turned in her chair. "Captain!" She had a huge, relieved smile on her face. "It's Chekov. They've found Dr. McCoy. He's fine, and they're beaming up now."

"Good," Kirk said, unable to suppress his own grin. "Call sickbay. Tell Dr. Chapel the cavalry's on its way."

"Aye, sir."

"Oh, Commander."

Uhura glanced back toward Kirk. "Yes, sir?"

"Did Chekov say how many of these Empyrean Liberators were holding Dr. McCoy?"

"One, sir."

Kirk's eyes widened. *"One?"*

Uhura nodded. "One."

"Well," said Kirk, wondering about the single individual who had managed to wreak so much havoc, "I'll be damned."

Chapter Twenty-three

ESCORTED BY CHEKOV and a pair of dusty security guards, McCoy and Ethan beamed aboard the *Enterprise* before the rest of the search team. Kirk, Elizabeth March, and Mark Rousseau were waiting to meet them in the transporter room. But McCoy had no sooner materialized than he was off the platform and out the door at a full run. "No time for small talk" was all he said, his voice trailing behind him.

"Don't worry," Kirk said to the others as they hurried toward sickbay. "If anybody can pull her through, McCoy can."

Elizabeth glared at Ethan. "How could you do this?"

"I did what I thought was best for Anna," he said in a sullen tone, "and for all of us who don't agree with the isolation we're forced to live under."

"Ethan, you may not believe this, but I don't like this isolation policy any better than you do."

"How *can* I believe it? You're in charge of the government that enforces that policy."

"That's what this treaty renewal is all about."

"A renewal you might have doomed with all this nonsense," Rousseau rumbled at Ethan. "Liberation fronts, kidnapping . . . What the hell were you *thinking?*"

Kirk found himself almost feeling sorry for Ethan. Almost. Though the kid seemed to be facing hostility from all sides, he managed to maintain his dignity— no small accomplishment, under the circumstances. Kirk admired that kind of composure under fire, though not enough to pardon what Ethan had done in the first place. If only the kid had not taken the old admonition to stick to your guns quite so literally.

Out in space, orbiting at twenty-eight thousand kilometers above the surface of Nova Empyrea, one of the string of satellites linked to the Federation observatory exploded. Remaining on watch in the transporter room, Scott saw the burst of sparkling metallic shards on the wall-mounted viewscreen.

Canary in the mine shaft, he thought. This first satellite to fall victim to the power overload streaming out of the planet-based reactor was just a harbinger of greater calamity if Spock's damage-control work did not succeed and *soon.*

As he stood by, awaiting word from Spock, Scotty desperately wanted to pace. But he didn't dare take his eyes off the monitors feeding him data on Spock's radiation exposure level and on the critical condition of the Sternn reactor itself.

Some people grew more patient with age. Not Montgomery Scott. The older he got, the crankier he got. *If I'm not careful, I'll be turnin' into McCoy,* he'd thought on more than one recent occasion. But nothing tested his forbearance more than a wait like this, marking time until a near certain catastrophe, unable to intervene.

If anybody could save young Anna March, it would be Dr. McCoy. And if anyone could stave off disaster at the Empyrean observatory, it was Spock. Over the years, Scotty had seen each of them confound the most dire of expectations with remarkable frequency. Though it wasn't something he'd ever said out loud, he privately considered them both to be members in good standing of the *Enterprise* miracle workers' club, that select group of officers like himself upon whom Kirk relied with total confidence.

But it was the nature of miracles that they didn't happen every day. Sometimes, they didn't happen when they were needed the most.

Scotty checked the scanner displays, which gave only grim news. The reactor's runaway power output had not abated, and Spock was nearing the limits of safe exposure to the deadly atmosphere inside the containment module. Then, with no warning, something new showed up on the monitors: The stream of dangerous surplus power they'd been diverting up to the satellites and station in orbit took a precipitous drop, right down to nothing.

But before Scott could figure out what this development meant, he heard Ramon Ortega's voice coming over the communications link to the main observatory complex, a channel they'd kept open during the emergency.

"The emitter array just went off-line here," Ortega said.

Scott let out a deflating breath. "So much f'r our safety valve."

McCoy stepped back from Anna's sickbay bed, watching her chest rise and fall in steady but shallow rhythm. He listened to the pulse of the respirator assisting her breathing as she lay unconscious, caught in that medical nether world between life and death. Then he looked at Christine Chapel standing next to him, her face pale, her shoulders slumped in a posture of weary defeat. They were alone in the treatment theater.

"Well, that's that," he said, trying not to sound as disconsolate as she looked. "We've done what we could. The rest is up to Anna and the good Lord, if there is one."

"Are you sure there's nothing we overlooked?" she asked.

"Of course I'm sure," said McCoy with a glower and a sharp tone he immediately regretted. He rubbed his eyes. "Sorry, Christine. I didn't mean to snap. It's been a long day." Then he glanced at the glowing digital chronometer on the bioscan display. "Make that a long *two* days. I did not get what you'd call a lot of rest in that cave."

"I know."

McCoy squinted at her as he took her arm and led her over to a couple of chairs along the wall. "What am I saying? I hear you didn't get much sleep either while I was gone. That wasn't very smart."

She forced a thin smile as they sat down. "I learned from you."

"Yeah, well, if anybody should know I'm not always the best role model," he said ruefully, "it's *you*. Look, I should've been here when you needed me. I'm sorry."

"I'm the one who convinced you to leave the ship. I should've done a better job monitoring Anna's condition."

"Now who in the hell told you *that?*"

She looked across the room toward Anna. "Nobody had to tell me."

He glared at her, and she tried to lower her gaze. But he tipped her head back up with his hand beneath her chin, and there was no avoiding the intensity in his eyes or in his raspy whisper. "You listen to me, Doctor. I'm the one who concocted this crazy treatment for Anna, and I'm the one who told everybody I knew what I was doing. *I'm* the one who didn't take the time to brief you on every aspect of what might happen. *I'm* the one who thought I'd be right back. So if anybody's to blame for her being at death's door, it's *me.*"

"But I was responsible for her while you were gone."

"And you did every blasted thing you could for her. I couldn't have done any more. We knew this was risky. If Anna dies, part of me is going to hate myself till the day *I* die. But part of me is going to know the risk was accepted with informed consent, and we did the best we could."

Christine shook her head, seeking some reassurance from a man whose medical experience vastly outweighed her own—a man she'd always admired despite, or maybe because of, his very human frailties. "How can you not wonder if there was something *else* we should have done, something we didn't think of?"

McCoy's blue eyes didn't flinch. "You can't."

Those who knew Vulcans well were aware that they were much more complex than their stoic demeanors might indicate. In times long past, they had been warriors, driven by passions as fierce as any beings in the galaxy. To this day, for all the millennia they had devoted to cultivating logic and controlling emotions, the heart of that ancient warrior still beat in every Vulcan. The passions of old had merely been redirected, not banked. It was not in a Vulcan's proud nature to surrender.

But neither was it in the Vulcan intellect to struggle in futility against objectively insurmountable obstacles. These days, in the war between stubborn emotion and implacable logic, a hard-won philosophical middle ground made it possible for Vulcans to live at peace with themselves.

A human might think in such terms as these: Fight like the devil, but have the dignity to know when the fight is lost.

Spock knew. Time was up. His radiation readings told him he had reached the end of his margin of safety here inside the vandalized reactor. He had failed to shut down the furnace that was still churning out of control. Whether by sinister intent or by sheer luck, the mysterious saboteur had drawn Spock into an escalating game that had appeared to have rules but, in the end, did not.

Spock would never admit to humans—not even to his best friends—that the strictly logical approach favored by Vulcans had limits. But there were rare occasions when he had to make that admission to himself. This was such an occasion. Logic habitually led him to approach problems as puzzles to be analyzed and solved intellectually. This saboteur had succeeded in making him believe he was just a short step away from unraveling the pattern of planned malfunctions.

He recalled an ironic, idiomatic human phrase that aptly described what he had actually been doing: *pursuing the wild goose.*

Time was up. And yet—

"Mr. Spock." It was Scott's voice ringing inside his helmet. "I've got to get you out o' there."

"No. Wait."

"What do you mean *wait?* You're past the point—"

"I must make one last attempt."

"T' do *what?*"

Perhaps there was still time for a belated leap of illogical improvisation. "To do what the saboteur never believed we would try to do: to remove the fuel pod."

"Aye," Scott said conditionally, "that'll pull the plug all right, but—"

"That's impossible, Commander Spock!" It was Ortega, bursting into the conversation from his console in the observatory control room. "The radiation has to be at its worst in that part of the containment module. The fuel pod is not designed to be removed while it's powered up. Even if you could get to the tank, the electromagnetic containment fields inside it would kill you once you opened it. And even if you survived that, the pod matrix is too big and too heavy for one man to carry."

"I do not intend to carry it, Dr. Ortega. And if my idea is feasible, it will not be necessary to open the tank and suffer exposure to the containment fields."

"Then, beggin' y'r pardon, Mr. Spock," Scott demanded, "what the hell *are* you plannin' t' do?"

"I will place your transporter location transponder on the fuel pod structure and you will beam the pod containing the fuel pellets themselves out into space."

"I don't know how all that radiation'll affect the transporter, sir," Scott said. "And without that transponder on you, I may not be able t' beam *you* out."

"I will remain close to the fuel pod tank during the transport procedure. The ambient radiation levels should drop by a considerable percentage immediately upon removal of the fuel pod—"

"But there's no guarantee it'll drop enough for the transporter to get through all the radiation that's still goin' t' be there," Scott argued.

"Besides which," Ortega said, "we may never get to that point. As I understand your transporter system, it converts solid matter into a subatomically debonded matter stream, then transmits that stream within an annular confinement beam."

"That is correct, Doctor," said Spock.

"Well, the fuel pellets inside the pod are going to be destabilized during transport," Ortega said. "Their volatility is what makes them work as a fuel to begin with. Destabilization could be enough to start an explosive chain reaction. And if that happens, whether it's here or aboard your ship, it's going to be a disaster."

"Mr. Scott," Spock said with virtually no hesitation, "if you compress the passage interval through the transporter's pattern buffer and increase power to the energizing and phase transition coils, that should speed the sequence as well as strengthen the integrity of the matter stream. The risk of chain reaction detonation should be minimal."

Alone in the transporter room, Scott nodded, lost in a moment of purely technical consideration. "Aye. I think y're right." Then he stopped abruptly and shook his head to clear it. "Mr. Spock, we're talking' about a hot potato that could destroy this ship! We canna do this without the captain's orders—"

"Mr. Scott, there is no time for debate," Spock said. "I am in command of this mission."

"If this doesna work," Scott said, "there may be nothin' left to court-martial."

"That is a risk we must take. The responsibility is mine alone, and the facts are incontrovertible: I cannot sustain much more exposure here. And this is the only means by which we may be able to shut down the reactor before it will most certainly explode. You will consider this a direct order. Reprogram the transporter control sequence as we discussed. I am moving toward the fuel pod tank now. Are you maintaining a tracking lock?"

"Mr. Spock!" Scott protested.

'Maintain tracking lock," Spock commanded in a tone that brooked no dissent.

"Aye, sir," Scott said unhappily. "Reprogramming . . . tracking lock maintained . . ."

* * *

The lights on the *Enterprise* bridge suddenly flickered, then resumed their usual brightness.

Kirk straightened in his seat. "What the devil was that?"

Sulu glanced at the indicators on his helm console. "A power drain off the main engine circuits, Captain."

"Source?"

"It's the transporter system, sir," said Chekov from the science console.

"What the hell is Scotty doing?" Kirk wondered aloud. He punched the intercom button on his armrest. "Kirk to transporter room." He waited a moment, but there was no reply. "Kirk to transporter room. Mr. Scott, are you down there?"

"Aye," Scott mumbled to himself. "I'm here. But I may *not* be after all this is done with."

He knew his diversion of emergency power to the transporter would register on the bridge. But he did not activate the intercom. At risk of insubordination, he'd decided to let Kirk's call go unanswered. There was no time for explanations now and no going back. He could not afford to split his attention from the job he'd agreed to do.

With an unwavering gaze, Scott watched the monitor array on the transporter console and waited for word from Spock. He felt beads of sweat popping out on his brow, but his hands were steady, poised.

Spock found the heavily plated alloy door that sealed the chamber containing the fuel pod. He keyed the mechanism, and the door slid up and out of the way. The air crackled around him as he took the location transponder from his radiation suit and fastened it to the vertical oblong tank that held the pod.

235

"Spock to Mr. Scott. The transponder has been attached. Lock on and energize."

With one hand, Scott activated the transporter. With the other, he manually modulated the extra power surging through the unit. Precise as it was, he didn't trust the computer to handle this. He would have to rely on his own intuition. "Come on, come on," he urged in a whisper, like an encouraging parent. "Grab onto that thing down there . . ."

Spock stood one meter away from the containment tank, aiming his tricorder up to where he knew the reactor's fuel pellet receptacle was mounted. If the transporter was going to work, it should have locked on within a second or two. But the tricorder told him that the pod remained inside the tank, secure in its bracket. Something had gone wrong.

"Mr. Scott, did you energize?"

"Aye, sir!" came the agitated reply. "There's too much interference f'r a positive lock. The circuit's rejecting the automated sequence—"

"Override the safety protocol, recalibrate, and reenergize."

"What d'you *think* I'm doing here—taking a bagpipe break? If the imaging scanners don't hold their resolution, we won't get that fuel pod out o' there. All we'll do is destabilize it, and it'll detonate right next to you." Scott lapsed into silence for a few seconds, then grunted. "There. She's holdin', but I don't know f'r how long. Reenergizin' *now!*"

He activated the transporter once again. As he did, he, Spock, and Ortega each monitored from his own vantage point. The difference was, they were only observers. It was Scotty's hands that were busy juggling fate.

As each man held his breath, their synchronized instruments told them the transporter had found its target, and they recorded the start of the orderly molecular disintegration of the fuel pod. No one was certain what would happen next.

From an engineering standpoint, Scott knew what was *supposed* happen. He also knew that there was nothing more he could do about it. This would either work, or it wouldn't. It would happen within the span of less than five seconds. And a few milliseconds in the middle of the autosequence would determine whether they succeeded or died.

The lights dimmed as the transporter's energizing and phase transition coils pulled three times their normal requirement of power from the *Enterprise*'s mighty warp-drive engines. In less time than it took to blink, the matter stream swirled through the pattern buffer—and the ship did not explode. Yet.

The targeting scanners had already been set for maximum range and dispersion. The transporter's emitter array did its job: The molecules that had once formed the displaced fuel pod rematerialized as a sparkling plasma cloud forty thousand kilometers out in space.

Finally, Scott allowed himself to breath.

"Well done, Mr. Scott," said Spock.

Scott's answer came only after a moment of dazed relief. "Thank you, Mr. Spock." Then his eyes widened. *Spock! My god! I forgot about Spock!* His hands were already flying across the transporter console, keying the next cycle. "Mr. Spock! I'll have y' out o' there in a jiffy. Stand by—energizing."

The transporter hummed to life. Scott knew the sounds better than he knew his own heartbeat, and this did *not* sound right. Then the device went through the electronic equivalent of a stumble, tapped more deeply into the starship's power reserves, and restarted the beam-up cycle.

With his teeth gritted, Scott willed the transporter to cut through the still disruptive radiation trapped in the reactor's containment structure. He watched as Spock finally began to materialize in the flickering chamber. Two seconds later, the first officer was whole.

He remained on the platform, his helmet still in place. "Initiate decontamination, Mr. Scott."

"Aye, sir." Scott touched the control pad and the decontamination force field filled the transporter chamber with a strobing greenish glow. The engineer kept his eye on the sensor display reporting on Spock's condition. Several seconds later, the procedure completed, normal illumination resumed. "Biosensors say you're clean, Mr. Spock. Residual radiation within acceptable range. Off t' sickbay with you then."

"That will not be necessary," Spock said as he came down the steps.

He found Scott blocking his way, hands on hips. "Regulations, sir, Vulcan first officer or not."

Spock yielded with a compliant nod. "Understood, Mr. Scott." He moved toward the door and noticed Scotty was following.

"Just makin' sure y' get there, sir."

Chapter Twenty-four

"YOU'RE FINE, MR. SPOCK," Christine Chapel said as she turned off the little bioscanner in her hand. The readouts on the monitor display confirmed that he had suffered no ill effects from his radiation exposure.

"That is what I told Mr. Scott," Spock said as he swung his legs over the side of the diagnostic bed.

"It never hurts to make sure," Scotty said. "I didn't want you t' wake up glowin' in the dark."

"Thanks to Dr. Chapel's thorough medical scrutiny," Spock said with an arched eyebrow, "we may rest assured that will not happen."

The door to the examining room slid open and Ramon Ortega entered with a self-effacing nod. "Gentlemen."

Scott's eyebrows rose. "Dr. Ortega! You're the last person I'd expect to see on the *Enterprise*."

"I, uhh, I was concerned about Commander Spock's condition."

"His condition is excellent," Chapel said. "Now, if you'll all excuse me, I've got some other work to do."

"Thank you for your assistance, Doctor," Spock said.

Chapel smiled as she left. "You're welcome, Mr. Spock."

The door shut behind her, leaving Ortega alone with Scott and Spock. The Empyrean was noticeably subdued, without so much as a residual hint of the haughty arrogance with which he had initially treated them just a few short days ago. In fact, he seemed positively humble. "I'm glad to hear you're uninjured, Commander."

"Your concern is appreciated, Dr. Ortega," Spock said. "In what condition is the observatory?"

"We've begun decontamination procedures, cleaning things up."

Scotty looked sharply at him. "You have? With Empyrean staff? I thought this was—"

"I know what I said at our first meeting, Mr. Scott. Obviously, a lot has changed since then. We Empyreans do see to our responsibilities."

"Did I ever say you didn't?"

"As a matter of fact, Mr. Scott," Spock said, "you did imply—"

To avoid any incipient embarrassment of Scott, Ortega intervened with a hasty touch of diplomacy. "Who hasn't occasionally said things we might prefer we hadn't." Then he took a deep breath, as if preparing for a plunge into terra incognita. "Forgetting about the politics and the philosophical debates, our colony owes you both a huge debt of gratitude. Once we all realized the magnitude of the problems at that reactor—and the apparent cause—you could have decided it was *our* problem and just walked away."

"We *could've*," said Scotty, "but we *couldn't* have. That's just not the way we do things, Doctor."

"I know that now. You put your lives on the line for us, for people who didn't exactly welcome you with open arms. I just wanted you to know that your acts of courage did not go unnoticed."

"That didn't sound much like an apology," Scott said with a challenging tone of belligerence.

"Apology?" Ortega asked with a guileless blink of his eyes.

"Mr. Scott—" Spock began, trying to head off any renewed conflict.

But Scotty ignored the interruption, facing Ortega squarely. "Aye, Doctor, an apology. Or don't you think you owe us one?"

"For what?"

Scotty stared in disbelief. "For *what?* For judgin' us as inferior from the moment you decided we didn't fit the Empyrean mold."

"But you *are* inferior, genetically speaking," Ortega said, straight-faced. Then, before Scott could come up with a retort, he added, "Though apparently not as inferior as we thought."

Ortega didn't flinch from Scott's disapproving glare, meeting it with an earnest expression, one that slowly blended into a sly smile. "That was a joke, Mr. Scott."

"I didn't know y' *had* a sense o' humor," Scott replied with his own trace of a smile.

"There's a lot we don't know about each other."

"Maybe it's time t' change all that."

Ortega nodded. "Maybe it is."

Scott made no effort to hide his surprise at Ortega's admission. "Well! Now, *that's* more like it, laddie. Have y' got somethin' in mind?"

Ortega shrugged with genuine uncertainty. "I'm really not sure yet. It's not easy having everything you believe in turned upside down in a matter of a couple of days."

Just then, the door from the corridor opened, and Captain Kirk walked in. "Dr. Ortega, I hope you're pulling the pieces together down there."

"We are, Captain. But we wouldn't have had a chance without your two officers here. I want to make sure you know they really did go far beyond the call of duty."

"I do *now*," Kirk said pointedly with reproachful looks at Spock and Scott.

Ortega took the hint. "Well, I can see you've got things to discuss. And I'd better get back to our cleanup work at the observatory."

"Still plannin' t' get it ready for dismantling?" asked Scott.

"That may not be the Council's choice," Ortega said with mixed feelings. Then he left.

With a quizzical look on his face, Kirk watched Ortega go. "I wonder what he meant by that? That he wants the outpost to stay or that he's *afraid* we'll stay?"

"That is difficult to say, Captain," Spock said, "though it is apparent that our efforts during the crisis have given Dr. Ortega—and other Empyreans—food for thought."

"Speaking of those efforts"—Kirk turned to face his officers and folded his arms across his chest—"you might've destroyed this ship with that transporter stunt."

"But we did not, Captain," Spock said with innocent eyes.

"It might've been . . . *nice* . . . if you'd have consulted your commanding officer before making a decision with such potentially . . . *explosive* . . . repercussions," Kirk said with exaggerated politesse.

"In fairness," Spock said, "Mr. Scott wanted to do just that—"

"I did *not*," Scott blurted with immediate regrets.

He'd simply hoped to bolster Spock. Instead, he sparked the captain's ire.

Kirk flashed him an angry look. "You *didn't?*"

"Well, I—I didn't mean I *didn't,* sir," Scott said, all flustered now and very much aware that he dug a deeper hole with every word. "I meant—I thought—I mean, I *didn't* think . . ." His voice trailed off, and he sighed as he gave up trying to explain.

Appreciating Scott's attempt to support him, Spock mounted a verbal rescue of the floundering engineer. "Captain, what Mr. Scott meant to say—"

"Ahh," Kirk said tartly, "a translation."

"—was this, I believe: We were entrusted with an assignment. We were privy to all the relevant engineering facts, and in our best professional judgment, we ascertained that the time required to brief you—prior to making the only possible decision—would have seriously jeopardized our chances for successfully undertaking the only possible solution."

Kirk turned, adopting a prosecutorial tone. "And *is* that what you meant to say, Mr. Scott?"

"Uhh . . ." Scott swallowed. Then he opted for an oblique plea for the commander's mercy. "It was on the tip of my tongue, sir?"

The captain pursed his lips, glancing from one to the other. "All's well that ends well? Is that the conclusion I'm supposed to draw?"

Scott spread his hands in a deferrential gesture. "If y' wouldn't mind, sir."

"All right, no court-martial this time," Kirk scolded with a wag of his finger. "But *next* time . . ." He shook his head and couldn't help grinning.

Kirk watched them leave sickbay, then turned and went into the treatment ward where he found McCoy just inside the door. Across the dimly lit room, Anna lay motionless on her bed, still on full life support. Her mother sat at her bedside, holding her hand.

"Any change?" Kirk whispered.

McCoy shook his head. "No better, no worse."

"Well, that's something."

McCoy turned with a baleful eye that made it obvious he didn't appreciate Kirk's attempt to comfort him. Kirk hooked McCoy's arm with his own and pulled him into the adjacent dispensary.

"How long're you planning to beat yourself up?" said Kirk after the door shut behind them.

"Isn't that between me and myself?"

"Not as long as I'm your commanding officer—"

McCoy stiffened. "Oh, your wish is my command, Captain, *sir,*" he cut in with a heavy touch of sarcasm.

"You didn't let me finish. I was about to say, not as long as I'm your commanding officer and your friend."

With a grand tip of his hand, McCoy invited Kirk to go on.

"Dammit, Bones, you've done everything you could."

McCoy slumped into a chair. "I know. So why do I feel so damn good about it?"

"Because you're an idiot?" Kirk offered with a gentle smile.

"Bingo." McCoy stretched and rubbed the back of his neck with both hands.

Kirk felt frustrated by his inability to soothe his friend's pain. *McCoy's right, I'm no psychiatrist.* With a shake of his head, he started to leave, then paused in the open doorway and turned back. "Bones."

McCoy looked up. "Hmm?"

"You couldn't be doing more for her if she *were* your own flesh and blood."

"I could be sitting in there, holding her other hand."

"You're right. You could be. So why aren't you?"

"Elizabeth wanted to be alone with her. Mother's prerogative."

Kirk nodded in sympathy, knowing how much it must have hurt McCoy to accede to Elizabeth's request for privacy and, by doing so, to be reminded of the special bond between parent and child. That was a bond McCoy had run away from with his own daughter and a bond he now knew wasn't his to share with Anna.

Kirk was cognizant of the fact that everything Elizabeth had done she'd done for the health and security of her child. He just wished she'd been able to do it without handing McCoy an emotional battering he didn't deserve.

"How come Mark Rousseau's not here with them?"

Lost in his own thoughts and regrets, McCoy glanced up at Kirk. "Hmm? Oh. He went to find young Ethan, the one-man liberation front."

Ethan stood leaning against the cool glass of the observation window in the otherwise empty lounge, looking out past the starship's graceful engine nacelles, looking down at his planet. He'd never been in space before this. He'd seen pictures of Empyrea from orbit. He'd understood intellectually the concept of seeing his world from the all-encompassing perspective of space. But now that he was here, standing on the *Enterprise,* he knew that photographic images and accompanying words of wisdom were simply incapable of preparing anyone for the visceral reality of seeing the globe in its entirety, just hanging there in space.

It looked so fragile. The life-nurturing layer of atmosphere hugging the planet seemed so thin, so insubstantial, like he could blow it away with a puff of breath.

He had read centuries-old accounts of how early astronauts had reacted to their first views of Earth, how their attitudes about coexistence and conflict had been profoundly altered by the startling sight of a world—their own world—without artificial borders and boundaries.

"It makes a big difference," said a rumbling voice behind him.

Caught off guard, Ethan turned so abruptly he almost lost his balance. He hadn't even heard the door hiss open, and here was Mark Rousseau coming toward him. "What does?"

"Seeing the world from the outside looking in."

Ethan nodded, then turned back to the window. "Is it that way for everybody, the first time in space?"

"I think so. It was for me." Rousseau joined him at the window.

"How many different planets have you been to?"

Rousseau frowned for a moment. "I really don't know. I've lost count."

"Guess."

"A hundred, more or less?"

Ethan whistled in amazement. "I can't even imagine that. That world out there, it's the only one I know."

"You seemed pretty determined to leave it behind."

"I guess I was."

"Is that still what you want?"

Ethan hesitated. "I don't know. I don't know what I want."

"Maybe you just wanted the choice."

"Do I deserve a choice after what I did?" he wondered with a penitent shake of his head. "Anna means more to me than anything . . . and she could die because I kept Dr. McCoy from being here when she needed him."

"You didn't do that knowingly and not for long. Besides, we all do things we regret, especially when we're young." An ironic smile came to Rousseau's face. "And some of us, when we're *not* so young. If we're lucky, we get a chance to redeem ourselves later on."

Eventually, exhaustion overcomes stress. Sleep, however restless, overtakes adrenaline or whatever other natural or unnatural stimulant might be pushing the body and mind beyond the limits of endurance. It was late on the *Enterprise,* with dimmed illumination in corridors and common areas.

Mark Rousseau had finally fallen asleep propped up in bed with the PADD displaying the umpteenth draft of his final *final* treaty renewal proposal still held against his chest.

Ethan had accepted McCoy's invitation to remain on board until they knew more about Anna's condition, and he slept fitfully in guest quarters.

In his cabin filled with artifacts from home, Spock rested in the amber glow of an incense lamp, with an eerie Vulcan wind-chime nocturne playing softly.

Scotty slept with a technical journal still glowing on his bedside viewscreen.

Perhaps most surprising of all, considering the weight of responsibility he carried, even Captain Kirk slept—soundly. Years ago, early in his first command, he'd fought an often losing battle with insomnia. It had taken some time, but he'd eventually learned how to put the day's concerns out of his mind at bedtime. It was just one in a long list of survival skills they did *not* teach at Starfleet Academy.

Down in sickbay, McCoy had insisted that Elizabeth March retire to a quiet cabin with a real bed. He knew she'd have to face the Empyrean Council tomorrow for the final debate and vote on what to do about the Federation treaty. But she'd refused to leave Anna, so McCoy had an overstuffed reclining chair placed at Anna's bedside.

That done, he'd managed to talk Beth into accepting a mild sedative. McCoy sat with her for a while and they'd chatted, mostly about how relieved she was that Scotty and Spock had succeeded in averting disaster at the observatory power plant. But, tired as he was, McCoy's grasp of psychology was still keen enough to know what she was *avoiding* talking about: Anna. After a while, Beth had grown drowsy, and she too fell asleep, still holding her daughter's hand.

The only one who wasn't asleep when he should have been was McCoy himself. Not that he hadn't tried. He'd gone so far as getting into pajamas and coaxing a mug of warm milk from the food synthesizer. He'd actually crawled under the covers with the lights out and the hypnotic sounds of rolling surf whispering from his cabin speakers. He *wanted* to sleep. He *needed* to sleep.

But he couldn't. Some demons just wouldn't be banished by warm milk, not even for a catnap. So he threw on a comfortable Starfleet sweatsuit and prowled the deserted corridors for a while. With forced nonchalance, he stopped in the arboretum for a stroll through the greenery, then at the observation lounge for a nightcap. He even visited Engineering in hopes of finding Scotty as wide awake as he was and maybe willing to sit down over a deck of cards for a bit.

But Scotty wasn't there. *He's got the good sense to be fast asleep,* McCoy thought, *which is what I should be . . .*

He left Engineering, stood in the quiet corridor, and resisted the tug pulling him toward one inevitable destination.

Elizabeth March's eyes blinked and she awoke, all her senses and faculties instantly sharp. She wondered what time it was, located the chronometer on the bioscan monitor, and realized it was still the middle of the night.

She'd expected to wake up with a sore neck or back

from sleeping in something other than a bed. Surprisingly, she felt all right. The chair had been much more comfortable than she thought it would be. She smiled when she noticed that someone had draped a light blanket over her during the night. *Probably McCoy.*

And she was pleased to find Anna's hand still clasped in her own. She wondered how that could be possible. *I must've moved sometime. This must be one of those maternal miracles even we mothers don't understand.*

But her fingers did feel cramped. She flexed them slightly, careful not to break contact with Anna's hand. As long as she felt Anna's skin next to hers, and it was warm, she could keep her faith alive.

Then she felt something new, something unexpected. For an instant, Beth wondered if she was still asleep and just dreaming.

Anna's fingers moved, straightening from their comatose curl.

Elizabeth's eyes grew wide, and they welled with hopeful tears. She stood and looked at her daughter's serene face. But she saw no sign of consciousness there.

Maybe it's just a reflex, Elizabeth thought, trying to reign in her hopes before they could soar too high.

Anna's fingers moved again with more strength. Elizabeth squeezed her daughter's hand. Anna squeezed back!

Then her eyes fluttered open, focusing slowly. Her lips parted and her voice came out as a sleepy whisper, like a child waking from a long nap—the answer to Elizabeth's prayers: "Hi, Mother."

Elizabeth leaned close and kissed Anna's forehead. "Hi, baby," she whispered back.

In the open doorway at the far end of the darkened ward, McCoy watched from the shadows, resisting the lump in his throat. He saw no reason to intrude just yet. He would casually stroll in after a few minutes, claiming it had been time for a routine check on Anna. Nobody needed to know he'd been keeping his own vigil for the past few hours. Wiping away a tear before it could roll very far down his cheek, he retreated unseen.

Chapter Twenty-five

Captain's log, Stardate 7598.5.

Dr. McCoy reports that Anna March has recovered completely. More importantly, his risky treatment has apparently produced the desired result: The maternal genetic brand simulated and introduced into Anna's system has infused into all body cells. It remains to be seen whether she'll be able to pass the Empyrean medical tests yet to be administered.

THE HAPPY NEWS about Anna's medical condition enabled President March to devote her full attention to the impending vote on the Federation treaty renewal. When the hundred members of the Empyrean Council arrived at their offices first thing that morning, they each found a copy of Ambassador Rousseau's final draft proposal waiting for them.

They would have the entire morning to huddle with staff assistants, engaged in private review and preparation. That afternoon, the Council would be convening in public session for last comments, brief debate, and the conclusive ballot.

Word of the day's momentous agenda spread via the early vidcom news broadcasts. Barely past sunrise, Empyrean citizens had already begun lining up outside the columned council hall for the few hundred seats available to spectators.

At the window of the president's office, atop the five-story council building, Mark Rousseau watched the queue of people snaking down the marble steps and along the tree-shaded boulevard. "Whichever way this goes, they want to witness history."

McCoy stood alongside him. "Who wouldn't?"

"If you get your way, Empyrea will never be the same." It was Clements, speaking from the open door as he entered the office. He knew March had invited McCoy and the ambassador to be present at the public session, insisting they should be available to answer questions. But he looked distinctly displeased at finding them here beforehand.

"*Either* way, it'll *never* be the same," Elizabeth said as she misted the flowering plants overflowing their hanging baskets in another window alcove. "Sooner or later, people change—whether we want them to or not. And so do societies." She returned to her desk and poured three cups of tea from the Asian-patterned ceramic pot on a simple silver tray.

"I've concluded my investigation on the power plant sabotage," Clements said with a disapproving glance toward McCoy and Rousseau.

"That's what I figured," Elizabeth said, serving steaming cups to McCoy and Rousseau as they sat on a floral sofa near the windows. "Don't mind them, Clements. They're as entitled to hear your report as I am. In fact, *I'll* tell *you* what the results were: inconclusive."

Clements looked mildly surprised. "Are you guessing?"

"Not really," she said, sitting at her desk. "You don't look like a man who's found what he was looking for."

Clements poured himself a cup of tea and sat opposite her. "I think we can rule out involvement by the Federation people."

"Thanks a bunch," McCoy muttered.

"Which means," Elizabeth said with a philosophical shrug, "it was one of us."

And that, she knew, was why life on her world could never go back to the way it was prior to this whole crisis. If the Council chose to renew the Federation treaty, with its stringent limits on actual interaction with Outsiders, that would be a tacit signal to the whole of Empyrean society. She was certain that steps toward greater openness would inevitably follow and accelerate toward unobstructed freedom of interplanetary encounter.

But even if the Council rejected the treaty, ordering the departure of the Federation outpost, the colonists would live with the knowledge that one of their own had intentionally damaged the observatory, putting fellow Empyreans in grave danger and shattering the colonial covenants by which they had lived for more than a century and a half. One unknown individual— or a few—had committed a blatantly criminal act.

Of course, so have I, Elizabeth admitted to herself. But her violations had directly endangered no lives other than Anna's and her own. Whoever had sabotaged the reactor had demonstrated wanton disregard for hundreds of thousands of lives. If one Empyrean was capable of that, then others might be, too. *We'll never be as secure as we were before . . .*

In one way, Elizabeth couldn't help feeling it was for the best that Clements had not been able to track and trap the person or persons responsible for the near disaster at the reactor. The crime committed was so unsettling that any trial would have been a perilous one, with repercussions potentially more divisive—and dangerous—than the original sin.

In other ways, though, she regretted the investigation's failure. In her mind, the biggest unanswered question was not *who* did it, but *why* was it done. Was the sabotage really intended merely to scuttle the treaty renewal?

Or, she wondered, was that too simple a motivation?

Maybe the culprits were actually in favor of the treaty. Maybe they'd been trying to sound the alarm and wake up a generation of complacent Empyreans who'd come to believe so blindly in their ultimate superiority that they not only knew all the answers, but no longer even needed to hear the questions.

Are we really the best of all possible humans? Is that what they wanted us to ask ourselves? How many Empyreans are asking those questions? And is anybody brave enough for honest answers?

Elizabeth honestly didn't know. And that answer was simply not good enough, not if she hoped to find a way to lead her colony through this turbulent passage.

"Yes," Clements sighed, "I'm sure it was one of us." Then he shot a sidelong glance toward Rousseau and McCoy. "Which means it's very unlikely we'll ever discover *who* it was." He couldn't resist this one last taunt, however perverse it might be to trumpet a knack for disruptive criminal behavior.

Clements told President March he'd deliver his full written report the next day, then left. As Elizabeth gathered her notes for the council session, McCoy took out his communicator.

"McCoy to *Enterprise.*"

"*Enterprise,*" Uhura answered.

"Can you find Scotty for me, Uhura?"

"Sure thing, Doctor."

A moment later, he heard that familiar burr. "Aye, McCoy. Scott here. What's up?"

"Scotty, just thought I'd let you know Clements has closed his investigation into the reactor sabotage."

"And what'd he come up with?"

"Nothing much beyond the obvious: that it must've been an Empyrean."

"What a surprise. So, what's the prognosis on that council vote?"

McCoy frowned. "Well, we're not dead ducks yet. But from the scuttlebutt in the so-called corridors of power, it doesn't look too good."

"Sorry t' hear that."

"Yeah. Well, you never know. There're an awful lot of confused people down here."

"Aye. So when're you off t' the big meeting?"

"Now. Tell Jim we'll check in when it's all over."

"We'll be watchin' the news broadcast. Good luck to you, McCoy. Scott out."

Standing in the center of the observatory control room, Ramon Ortega was just signing a work review for a waiting technician when he heard a now-familiar jangling hum behind him. Turning to see the stout form of Engineer Scott materializing, he shooed the technician away and hurried over.

"Engineer! Nobody told me you were cleared to transport down."

Scott shrugged. "That's because I wasn't. But I needed t' talk to you, laddie."

"About what?"

"When you came up to the *Enterprise,* you sounded like you were doin' some soul-searching."

Ortega face revealed his discomfort. "So?"

"Well, I was wonderin' what you found."

"A lot of confusion."

Scott smiled in sympathy. "Well, if it makes you feel any better, lad, I'm sure you're not the only one. What do you *want* to happen?"

"You mean, about the treaty renewal? I really don't

know, Mr. Scott. I'm just glad I don't have to vote on it."

"Aye, but you're goin' to have to *live* with that vote," Scott pointed out. Then he led Ortega toward a computer terminal. "C'mon over here, Doctor."

Ortega followed without resistance. "What for?"

"Y'know, there's a whole *universe* out there you haven't experienced. How does that make you feel?"

"Frustrated, I guess."

"That's what I thought. D'you really want t' ignore it all? Or would you rather know why we stopped usin' that Sternn reactor and how our transporter works?" Then he handed a data cartridge to Ortega.

"What's this?" Ortega asked as he held the cartridge in his palm.

Scotty nodded toward the computer. "Just take a look, that's all."

Ortega inserted the cartridge, and a Starfleet technical journal appeared on the monitor screen. He swiveled toward Scott with a questioning look, but Scott grasped the seat and turned him right back around to face the screen. "*Read,* laddie."

As Scott watched over Ortega's shoulder, the Empyrean skimmed the journal with increasing speed and interest, like a hungry man devouring a menu of delights he's only been able to dream of previously.

After a while, Scotty leaned close to Ortega's ear. "It's all out there," he purred, "just waitin' f'r you."

Ortega's fingers dug into the armrests of his chair. "So what am I supposed to *do?*"

"Make y'r voice heard. Y've got to have *some* clout here."

"I—I guess I do."

"Then *use* it. Y' may never *get* another chance."

For a long moment, Ortega just sat, as if paralyzed by the churning indecision in the pit of his stomach. Then, without warning, he popped up, shoving the chair back so abruptly that he almost took Scott's leg out from under him. "Let's go."

"T' where?"

"The council hall." He was already rushing toward the exit. Scott half-jogged to keep up. "I'm going to make a statement if it's not too late. I want you to be there."

Scott stopped for calculated effect. "Am I allowed? Or is that against y'r rules?"

"Someone I just met a few days ago taught me it's not so terrible to *bend* a rule occasionally."

"It's an *art,* laddie," Scott cautioned. "Not f'r everyone."

"Empyreans are fast learners. I'll take my chances. But we'd better hurry."

Scott flipped open his communicator. "I c'n take care o' that if y' don't mind makin' a grand unscheduled entrance."

"Another new experience, Mr. Scott," Ortega said with a wry grin. "Let's give it a try."

Scott nodded. "Scott t' *Enterprise.* Transporter room—"

Tinted sunlight streamed down into the airy Empyrean council chamber through pastel skylights. With light wood trim, lots of windows, and minimal ceremonial frippery, it wasn't at all like some of the other more ostentatious legislative assemblies McCoy had seen in his travels.

Instead, it was an oddly pleasant setting for what he considered the often excruciating exercise of representative government. He suppressed a shudder at the fleeting recognition of how ill-equipped he would be to serve in such public office. He just didn't have the patience for the seemingly endless verbal jousting and jaw flapping that accompanied so much of governmental business. Though he couldn't recall who'd said it, he'd always found wisdom in the old adage about the untidiness of democracy: There are two things you should never watch being made: sausages and laws.

Good thing I'm a doctor, not a democrat, he thought.

As for their presence at this council session, he and Ambassador Rousseau had turned out to be just so much window dressing. Not a single question had been directed their way, as if the Empyreans had deemed them unworthy of being addressed and unlikely to contribute anything useful to the debate, which the council members seemed content to conduct rather informally among themselves.

From their seats in the spectator gallery above and behind the president's podium, McCoy and Rousseau watched as Elizabeth March hammered the rostrum with her gavel. The murmuring of a hundred voices subsided and the councilors, who were up and about, knotted in sometimes heated discussions with other members, returned to their desks.

"Fellow members," she announced, "if there are no objections and no further comments, I call for a vote on the issue at hand."

As she spoke, McCoy heard a familiar sound behind him. He turned to see Scotty and Ortega nearly materialized, the transporter sparkle fading around them.

"I've got an objection," Ortega called out, his voice echoing down from the gallery. "And I've got a comment or at least a statement."

"As most of you know," March said, "Dr. Ramon Ortega has served ably as liaison to the Federation observatory for the last five years and just worked closely with a team from the *Starship Enterprise* to avert recent disaster. I think his opinion may be relevant to the decision we're facing." The president gestured toward the assembly with outstretched hands. "Does anyone mind if Dr. Ortega makes a statement?"

There were no objections, and March looked up at Ortega. "You can speak from there, or you can come down here, Doctor."

"Here is fine, President March. I don't want to take up a lot of your time. So I'll get right to my point."

On the bridge of the *Enterprise,* Kirk and his officers had already been watching the direct broadcast from the Empyrean council chamber with considerable interest, interest that intensified when Scotty and Ortega appeared rather unexpectedly on the main viewscreen.

With a long-suffering sigh, Kirk made a mental note to have another little chat with Scotty about the preferability of informing the captain prior to taking otherwise unauthorized excursions, then shifted his attention back to the council proceedings.

"I was just a boy when the Federation ship first found us," Ortega said. He spoke softly, as if unaccustomed to addressing large gatherings. Still, the council members listened in respectful silence. "But I was old enough to grasp the importance of the event. My parents were against that treaty. So were my grandparents. And so was I, maybe because *they* were. It's hard for young people not to be influenced by the opinions of their elders.

"As I got older, I kept believing what I'd been taught to believe: that we should distrust Outsiders and that this colony of ours would flourish best in isolation . . . like an exotic flower grown in some hothouse, away from all the other flowers, free from unpredictability and corruption.

"I thought a lot about how human history seemed to be so much of two steps forward and one back . . . how Nova Empyrea would be different, a society that would do away with all the chaos keeping human beings from reaching their full potential, a place where humanity would advance by design instead of by accident.

"To me, that observatory on the hilltop was a threat to everything I believed in." Ortega paused for a breath, licked his lips, and steeled himself for the hard part of what he had to say. "But part of me was curious about the Outsiders who worked there and where they came from. Did they know things I didn't know, things I *should* know? As you all know, that sort of curiosity was *not* encouraged, so I kept it to myself. And by the time I grew up, I'd pretty much forgotten I'd ever wondered about those things.

"When members of this council first considered shutting down the Federation observatory, I was all for it. In five years of dealing with the Outsiders, my opinions hadn't changed at all. I didn't know them, and I didn't really want to."

He took a deep breath, then plunged ahead. "And then the events of the past few days happened. And I've learned that I—and we—*don't* have all the answers. There's a whole universe out there we haven't experienced in four generations. There's a universe of knowledge we should have. We and our human cousins in the Federation share the same roots. We both have strengths and weaknesses, but I *know* we'd both be stronger in combination, because we each have a lot to offer the other.

"We have a chance to make that combination a reality, and I think we should jump at that chance *now* . . . before it's too late. I'm asking you to renew this treaty and *expand* it before we Empyreans have been isolated so long that we become cosmic curiosities—perfect, useless flowers, unable to compete and survive outside our own little hothouse."

He was done and unsure what to do next. He began to blush as he realized how intently the council members had been listening. "Thank you," he mumbled and hastily sat down.

Scotty leaned over with a smile. "That was what I hoped y'd say," he whispered.

Even though the hall remained hushed, President March banged her gavel anyway. "Well, if there are no other comments or statements, I call for a vote on the proposition—yea or nay on renewing the treaty between the Federation and Nova Empyrea. You may enter your votes now."

McCoy and Scotty watched as some council members reached immediately for the ballot buttons on their desks. Others sat back, the expressions on their faces revealing the difficulty of the choice they had to make.

Up at her podium, March checked the electronic tabulation monitor set into the speaker's lectern. There were three columns; until the vote was completed, only the total number cast would be counted. The yea-versus-nay tally would remain secret, even from the president, until all members had committed themselves.

The same numbers that Elizabeth saw were simultaneously displayed on two large screens in the council chamber and in the corner of the broadcast image being viewed in virtually every Empyrean household as well as on the *Enterprise*.

Kirk noticed that the votes registered in irregular bunches, as those council members who were most certain cast their votes quickly, without much additional contemplation. He wondered how these first votes broke down. Were the most decisive council members for or against the treaty?

Even as the number cast rose toward the hundred mark, one or two votes got subtracted from the total rather than added. As Kirk understood the rules, until the process was officially closed, members had the option of withdrawing previous votes and changing their minds.

After twenty minutes, the tally had reached seventy, then seventy-three, then seventy-five, -six, -eight, -nine, eighty. Then, like a meandering stream turning into a waterfall, the remaining twenty votes cascaded in. When the hundredth vote was locked in, President March banged her gavel for attention.

"All votes are in. Is the Council ready for the final tabulation?" She looked around the chamber. No one raised a hand or a voice. "All right. This vote is closed." She brought the gavel down again, and all heads turned toward the display screens, which flashed the totals:

YEA 51   NAY 49

With a satisfied smile, President March banged the gavel one last time and announced for the record: "The proposition carries. The Empyrean Council votes to renew the treaty with the United Federation of Planets."

Epilogue

THINGS SURE HAVE CHANGED around here, Kirk thought as he hurried to the transporter room. Just a few short days ago, upon arrival of the *Enterprise,* Elizabeth March had informed him in no uncertain terms that only extremely limited numbers of additional Starfleet/Federation visitors would be welcome on Nova Empyrea at any one time—and not *very* welcome at that.

And now, scarcely an hour after the treaty renewal's narrow victory in the Empyrean Council, March had personally called the *Enterprise* to invite him, Spock, and Scott to join McCoy and Ambassador Rousseau for the informal initialing of the agreement.

They beamed down to the gardens outside the presidential mansion. A wicker table and a pair of chairs had been set up on the central slate patio along with a serving cart complete with crystal goblets and a bottle of wine. When they arrived, they found McCoy to be the only one there, enjoying the flowers and the comfortably warm afternoon.

Kirk was glad to see his friend looking so relaxed after all he'd endured over the past couple of weeks. "Bones, where are President March and Ambassador Rousseau?"

"Still going over a few details. Maybe patting themselves on the back or, more likely, pinching themselves. I don't know about them, but I still can't believe this all turned out so well."

"How's Anna?"

McCoy flashed a grin. "She's great, Jim. And I'm sure she's gonna pass that genetic scan with flying colors."

"She may not have to." It was Mark Rousseau's booming voice coming from behind them.

Kirk and his officers turned to see the ambassador approaching with Elizabeth and Anna in tow.

"What do you mean?" McCoy asked.

"Well, we've come to some *new* agreements," Rousseau said with a broad smile, bubbling with satisfaction. "I think we're going to see some long-standing restrictions falling by the wayside."

Kirk's eyebrows went up in pleasant surprise. "Oh? Well, that's certainly encouraging."

"Yes, we're witnessing the birth of some real co-operation between us and the Empyreans, and I think we'll see this process culminating with Empyrean membership in the Federation."

"Now, Mark," Elizabeth scolded, "you're getting a little bit ahead of yourself. But we have made a real, solid start. All that's happened and getting the Council to agree to a renewal, well, it was like knocking down a wall and seeing some sunshine from the other side. The first agreement, beyond the old treaty, is all ready to implement."

"And what's that?" asked Kirk.

"An exchange program for technical and scientific professionals and students," Rousseau said.

"And Anna is going to be with the first group," Elizabeth said proudly.

Anna was obviously as excited as her parents. "I'm going to go back to Earth for at least a year of school and travel, and I'll be taking some time to visit my father's family and get to know them a little."

McCoy looked stunned as he forced a feeble smile. "Well . . . that's . . . that's great."

With one glance, Kirk could see the pain of disappointment etched in the lines around McCoy's eyes. Despite his misgivings when Elizabeth first told him that he was Anna's father, McCoy had fully embraced the idea of belated fatherhood—his declarations to the contrary notwithstanding. The fierceness with which he had fought to help Anna had been ample proof of that. Kirk didn't have to be a certified psychiatrist to see how left out McCoy felt now and how determined he was not to rain on anybody else's parade.

"So," McCoy went on, "your first time away from the ol' homeworld. Well, that's gonna be quite a trip."

Anna came up to him and crooked her arm through his. "Yes, it will, but it won't be complete unless I *also* get to spend some time with *you* on the *Enterprise*. I want to get to know my 'other' father, too"—she looked quickly toward Kirk—"if that's all right, Captain."

"I think that could be arranged."

Elizabeth waved two copies of the agreement, printed on bound ceremonial parchment. "Then let's get these signed."

She and Rousseau sat at the table and picked up their pens. As they signed quickly, Elizabeth pointed over at the serving cart. "Somebody take care of that wine. What's an official occasion without a toast?"

"I'll be bartender," McCoy volunteered, filling the goblets for everyone present and passing them around.

President March lifted her glass. "Thomas Jefferson once said, 'One generation cannot bind another.' So"—she looked at her daughter with a glowing smile—"to the future, unbound."

The goblets clinked together, and everybody drank.

Kirk turned to Rousseau. "Congratulations, Mr. Ambassador. I didn't think this was going to be one of your great successes."

"Frankly, Captain, neither did I. And I don't know if it *would* have been without everything you and your officers did, particularly *your* last-minute bit of virtuoso persuasion, Mr. Scott. I don't know how you got Dr. Ortega to make that statement, but you could have quite a future in diplomacy."

McCoy immediately choked on a mouthful of wine. Scotty flashed him a dirty look. Kirk fought back an incredulous smirk, while Spock simply cocked one eyebrow.

Then, conspicuously ignoring his shipmates' reactions, Scotty turned toward Rousseau with a gracious nod. "Thank you, sir. But I think I'll stick with the portfolio I've got."

"Thank goodness," McCoy mumbled.

"Mr. Ambassador," Kirk said, "the *Enterprise* is ready to depart Empyrea whenever you are."

"Actually, Captain, I'm going to be staying here so we can get started on the next stage of talks. I've already exchanged messages with the Federation. They're putting together a complete negotiating team to join me, and another ship'll be here in about two weeks."

"Well, in that case, the best of luck to you. And to you, President March."

Elizabeth shook Kirk's hand. "Thank you for all

your help, Captain, and your patience. The *Enterprise* and her crew will always be welcome here."

"It was our pleasure."

Kirk, Spock, and Scotty moved off to allow McCoy to say his own emotional farewells. First, he clasped Mark Rousseau's hand, then hugged both Elizabeth and Anna. As far as Kirk could tell, no words were spoken. After all that had happened since the *Enterprise* came to Nova Empyrea, there were too many things to say—and yet, no need to actually say them.

McCoy caught up with his comrades and they walked through the garden for a bit. Kirk cast a dubious glance at each of them.

"Something on your mind, Jim?" McCoy asked.

"As a matter of fact, there is. This was not exactly a textbook mission, gentlemen."

Spock responded with an innocent bat of his eyelashes. "How so, Captain?"

"How *so?* McCoy gets kidnapped by a one-man liberation front . . . *you*, Spock, risk the safety of the *Enterprise* without so much as a *hint* to me . . . Scotty beams down, without authorization, to twist an arm and barge into a closed council session . . ." Kirk's voice trailed off and he shook his head in exasperation. "All in all, some of the most *unorthodox* diplomacy I've ever seen."

"Aye, sir," Scott said. Then he paused. "But it *worked.*"

"That's right, Jim," McCoy agreed, "and you can't argue with success."

"Would you care to bet on that?" said Kirk, still shaking his head. "In the future, gentlemen, I'd prefer a little *more* discretion—and a little *less* unbridled valor."

Spock nodded formally. "As you wish, Captain."

"Aye, sir," Scotty added.

"Whatever you say, Jim," McCoy said.

Kirk stopped, turned, and faced them. Heads bowed in contrition, they were the very embodiment of penitence. With a skeptical twinkle in his eye, Kirk suppressed the smile trying to bend the corners of his mouth. *"Riiight,"* he growled. Then he flipped open his communicator. "Kirk to *Enterprise*. Four to beam up . . ."

About the Author

Among his nine books, Howard Weinstein has written five other STAR TREK novels: *The Covenant of the Crown* and *Deep Domain,* featuring the original crew of the *Starship Enterprise;* and three STAR TREK: THE NEXT GENERATION stories: *Power Hungry, Exiles,* and *Perchance to Dream.*

Many fans of "Classic" STAR TREK have also enjoyed Howard's stories in comic book form. He has been the regular writer of DC Comics' monthly illustrated STAR TREK adventures since early 1991, starting with Issue 17.

DC Comics recently published *Tests of Courage,* a trade paperback collection of Howard's special six-part story featuring Captain Kirk, Dr. McCoy, and Captain Sulu's first mission in command of the *U.S.S. Excelsior* (available in bookstores and comic shops everywhere).

Still a cranky New Yorker at heart, Howard now lives in Maryland with his wife, Susan, and their short but faithful canine companion, Mail Order Annie.

AN IN-DEPTH LOOK BEHIND THE SCENES OF THE SMASH-HIT TELEVISION SERIES

THE MAKING OF
STAR TREK
DEEP SPACE NINE®

er 930j by
JUDITH & GARFIELD
REEVES-STEVENS

**Available
from**

POCKET
BOOKS

1020-01

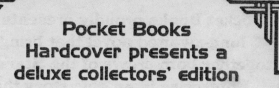

Pocket Books
Hardcover presents a
deluxe collectors' edition

STAR TREK®

"WHERE NO ONE HAS GONE BEFORE"™

A History in Pictures

Text by J. M. Dillard

*With an introduction by
William Shatner*

**Available at
a bookstore
near you**

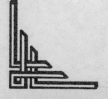

POCKET
BOOKS

1008-02